volume 1, of the series

DETACHED

I HOPE ALL OF YOUR FLOWERS TURN INTO BEAUTIFUL PEOPLE

TANNER LUTHERAN

This is a work of fiction. All of the characters, names, incidents, organizations, and dialogue in this novel are either the products of the author's imagination or are used fictitiously.

ISBN: 978-1-4834-6886-0 (sc)
ISBN: 978-1-4834-6885-3 (e)

Library of Congress Control Number: 2017906804

Because of the dynamic nature of the Internet, any web addresses or links contained in this book may have changed since publication and may no longer be valid. The views expressed in this work are solely those of the author and do not necessarily reflect the views of the publisher, and the publisher hereby disclaims any responsibility for them.

Lulu Publishing Services rev. date: 07/31/2017

Chapter 1

The headlights of my van faded in and out as it vibrated over veins of tar that filled the cracked streets on the outskirts of town.

"Heat, heat, and more heat!" a radio announcer forecasted, his rigid voice rattling through my vintage speakers between gaps of static. "Make sure you—"

I smacked the power button on the dash.

"I can't believe I'm already lost," I said under my breath, spinning the window crank until the warm breeze brushed against my face and the murmur of the city filled my ears.

You're not lost if you don't have anywhere to be.

I muzzled my hand over the stubble growing on my cheeks and rubbed the dark bags packed under my eyes from almost a week without sleep.

Steering between chipped sidewalks, I faced the city that fought to outshine the moon and stars—another case of man playing God. The hoax poured from the spaces between houses that soon became storefronts as I drove toward the lights like a lost ship that had just found shore.

A row of fast food restaurants appeared on my left when I pulled up to the stoplight.

Tacos. My mouth watered.

The light turned green, and I followed my tongue. My old van creaked and rocked from side to side, throwing my suitcase across the mattress that had replaced the back seats while I bumped over the cascading incline to the restaurant and swerved past an enter sign.

Applying a siren of squeaky brakes, I parked with my taillights facing the restaurant and turned off the ignition.

"Three hundred and ninety-one miles." I tapped my fingers on the steering wheel and leaned back in my seat.

Almost four hundred miles away, and it feels like you haven't left yet.

I dropped my gaze to an ashtray beneath the radio, where an orange bottle of pills sat staring back at me.

"Fuck." I shook my head, reaching for them.

I pressed against the cap with my palm and unlocked it, emptying one into my hand.

As I cocked my head back, I threw the little white pill to the back of my tongue and snapped my eyes closed.

Keep moving.

I dug my palm into my forehead and swallowed.

After tossing the bottle back into the cup holder, I stepped out of the van and arched my back, stretching my hands as far as I could above my head. I staggered toward the door, the seven hours of traveling working itself from my bones.

That was a lot of time when used to measure how far I had distanced myself.

I raked my hand through my tawny hair and opened the door.

A young girl took my order, and before I could fill my cup, she called out my number at the counter. I grabbed my tray stacked with two burritos, set my drink beside them, and moseyed around the corner to an empty dining area.

After scarfing down my meal, I pulled my phone from my pocket and brought up the browser.

SAVANNAH, I typed into the search bar.

A map appeared.

One wrong turn without a GPS, and I had ended up four hours from where I wanted to be.

It's just one city from a list of many.

Find yourself. Find yourself. Find yourself.

I'm not lost; I'm in finding.

I pressed my lips into a thin line, my thumb hovering over the glaring touchscreen.

Two young men sat with their tacos and drinks a couple booths away. A tear in the seat across from me caught my eye as I leaned toward them, their conversation blaring over the heightened volume of my thoughts.

"So, what happened to the other band?" the one with his back toward me asked. He shifted the trucker hat on his head and rolled up the sleeves of his plaid shirt.

"I guess they had van trouble," the one facing me said, bobbing his head as he spoke. He took a bite from his burrito, half of his round face visible past the faded styling of dark brown hair on the other guy's head. "They were from Orlando, or somewhere like that."

"I hate that for them." The man with faded hair crossed his arms on the table. "I'm surprised they didn't find a last-minute band to replace them. The mansion generally has a few bands play when they do shows."

"I know." The one with the round face pushed his thick glasses up on his nose and took a sip from his drink. "Maybe Grace will play some of her new stuff from her Grace Christian X project."

They both grew quiet. I glanced up as the man with glasses shifted his gaze in my direction, his hazel eyes locking onto mine.

"How 'bout you?" He rose from his bench, bounded over to me, and held a single sheet of paper out. "You coming?"

"I wish I could!" My voice cracked as I studied the large black and white text that read ANNEX across the top of a flyer, another band and details of the show listed below it. "I've got to get back on the road though." I smirked and waved my phone in the air.

"Where are you headed?" He dropped the flyer onto the table in front of me.

My face tensed as the memory flared of me mopping the floor of a hardware store just a few days prior.

"Uh … " I drummed my fingers on the table.

"Do you go to college out here?" he asked, fixing a piece of hair that had fallen from his suave combover.

"No." I lay my phone on top of the flyer. "I just graduated. I'm traveling is all."

"So why don't you come out then? It doesn't sound like you're in a hurry to get anywhere."

I took a deep breath. "Sure." I sat back in my seat and nodded, sliding my hands to my lap and bouncing my knee. "Where is it?"

"Across the street." He turned and pointed to a faint glow poking through a patch of trees in the distance.

I squirmed and took a sip from my cup. "Sure. Okay."

"The show starts in thirty minutes!" he said, peering back at me. "The gate should be open. You can park there if you need to."

"Harlow, we need to go set up," his friend said from the next booth while crumpling his napkin and standing.

"All right." Harlow grinned. "It was cool meeting you ..."

"Zachary." I nodded.

"Zachary! Zachary. I'll see you there!"

"Sounds good!" I grinned as the two hobbled to the door.

I waited until they had crossed the road and were out of sight before throwing my trash away and heading out to my van. I hopped in and pulled up the page on my phone that still had a map with a blue line giving directions to Savannah.

After starting the route, I plugged my phone in and backed out of my parking spot.

"Head south on Patters Place," a woman's voice instructed as I reached the exit.

On the screen, an arrow pointed left. Broken light filtered through the windshield from the bulb that still shone through the treetops ahead of me.

I flipped on the blinker and veered onto the directed street.

"In a quarter mile, turn left onto Melstein," the voice from my phone relayed.

I glanced over at the brick fence one last time—my mind jerked one way, but my body tugged me the other, steering me through the gate to the mansion.

Chapter 2

Past the vine-ridden metal bars guarding the entrance, trees canopied the roof of a pale brown mansion.

Just turn around. You need to get on the road.

Headlights glared at me through my rearview mirror. There was no way out.

I spun the wheel and parked between an old yellow bus that had been converted into a greenhouse and a black economy-sized car. The vehicle behind me crept past, down the drive and around the side of the house.

I stepped out of the van, squeezing between my door and the bus. The light that had beckoned me from beyond the trees at the taco joint hummed atop a pole thirty feet above my head until a deep, booming voice drowned it out.

"It belonged to a famous artist in the 1800s who denied use of electricity and the change within the city around him." I followed the low tone, rounding the back bumper of my van into the driveway. "The generous artist dedicated the property to art, with strict guidelines that its occupants study their craft away from the distracting indulgences of the world." I strode up to a group of people who silhouetted beneath the lantern light that lit the worn face and full beard of the man speaking.

"Whoever wants a tour, follow me!" He opened the door and gestured inside.

Four of us bunched into the short reach of the oil-fueled lantern while the rest of the group broke off and sauntered around the side of the house. We followed him down the first corridor. Small grains of dust on the banister rolled beneath my fingers, keeping me in line at the back of the group. There wasn't much clutter, but a faint smell of mildew floated off the worn rugs and crown molding. A few heads in front of me, books lined the mantle below a chipped golden frame that pinned a painting of a man in a suit next to his dog against the wall.

"Without phones, televisions—or even music, at times—we are completely self-reliant on entertaining and providing for ourselves." The tour guide beamed with pride.

When we sidled into the kitchen, he showed us the only switch in the house, which gave power to a single naked bulb that hung from the ceiling. An oversized refrigerator stood against the back wall, and a few gas appliances and a rinse sink sat next to it, all of which he considered the unfortunate necessities in the city.

We fell out of the tour through a wooden door with large glass panes that led to the backyard.

Outside stood the maids' house, which had been transformed into more artist dwellings, and a horse stable that served as the main venue. Twenty feet from the two buildings blazed a fire, tamed by a circle of rocks and sand. People danced around the flames, carrying on as if the rest of the world didn't exist. Lost in a shock of culture and vicarious belonging, the group of tourists dispersed around me.

"LET'S GET THIS PARTY STARTED!" a voice blasted through a PA system, its echoes bouncing between the stone walls.

The dancers fled from the fire toward the stables and stampeded to the door. I straggled behind, waiting for the doorway to clear.

"We are Annex!'" the voice amplified again.

People swayed inside to the charged rock music, lights blaring through the open entryway.

Just as I reached the door, I smacked into someone's shoulder.

"I'm sorry," I muttered to a petite girl in her early twenties.

She glanced up, the light from her buzzing phone reflecting off her deep blue eyes.

She tilted her head with a smile and turned away to take the call.

"I can't be there until tomorrow!" she yelled into the phone while stalking off toward the fire, the sleeves of her unbuttoned denim shirt sliding between her wrists and elbows as she flailed her arms. "That's fine. I didn't want to do it anyway." She kicked a broken stick into the flames.

I inched closer to the door, taking one step forward before glancing in her direction once more to eaves drop. Turning away from me, she lifted her arms again — her yellow, high waisted shorts catching my attention. She continued past the fire until the music grew louder than her voice. Finally, I gave up and passed through the opening.

I stepped into the only other room with electricity. Spotlights strapped to bricks lit the wide space. Harlow's voice cracked through the microphone as he kept a beat on the drums behind a girl playing guitar, who cleaned up his raw voice with the sweetest tone I'd ever heard. I swayed, studying the collection of random paintings that lined the walls to avoid eye contact, while the bodies around me moved freely.

The rhythm of the crowd splintered into cheers and applause when the song finished.

"Thank you all for coming out to see us," the bassist said as he and the guitarist strummed an open note, Harlow setting off into a random drum roll.

I stood on my tiptoes to get a better view of the stage but was interrupted by a tug on my shirt.

The girl from the doorway edged up next to me.

"I think we got off on the wrong foot." Her voice strained against the volume of the oversized speakers that blared the band's next song.

My gaze shifted, and I cleared my throat before leaning down, my scratchy voice inches from her ear. "It's okay; you seemed distracted!"

Seconds passed as her stare straightened my posture until she disappeared into a group of girls.

Halfway into the song, I gave in to the beat. My shoes tapped the floor and my shoulders swayed, but my fingers fidgeted and my skin was too tight to jump into the careening crowd. Every so often, the swarm of people shifting would spit the girl out but quickly suck her back in. She saw me too, flashing me short glances and sometimes even a smile.

When the third song ended, it left her standing close by. I felt her presence like an ant under a magnifying glass.

Panting from the heavy dancing, she ambled over to her friends.

I focused on the bass drum, stealing glances out of the corner of my eye. One last look, and I was caught. A couple of the girls next to her laughed, but she grinned. Heat rushed to my face, and I pinched the seams on my collar.

Leave.

I closed my eyes and counted backward from ten to calm myself down.

"Where are you from?" she asked.

I opened my eyes to find her beside me again.

"Not here—this place is amazing!" I shuffled my feet.

The conversation quickly died, and we stood in silence, me with my arms crossed and her with a hand in her pocket while the other rubbed her elbow. It was probably the longest twelve seconds of my life before the guitarist fingerpicked the intro of their fifth song.

"Do you want to dance?" She extended her hand, bowing when the rest of the band joined in.

"Uh, sure!" I said, letting her pull me from my shell into her group of wide-eyed friends. The song thickened but the tempo remained slow, and like that, I was at a middle school dance again. My hands scratched my thighs from inside my pockets as I followed her to the middle of the floor.

"This is a slow dance." She faced me with a smile, tugging on her own fingers.

I nodded and swayed to the echo of the snare drum.

She pulled on my forearm and guided my hand to her waist. "Do you not like to dance?"

My shoulders twisted with my head, and I peered around the room. "No one else is dancing."

"They're boring. Dance with me." She squared herself in front of me with her arms on my shoulders and her fingers hinged behind my neck.

I shuffled to her lead and slid my other hand around her waist, but that wasn't enough. She stepped closer and adjusted my hands to the crook of her back, resting her head against my chest. We rocked from side to side, stepping in a circle. By the time my back was to the stage, we were no longer alone. Almost everyone had a partner and had joined in. Her cheeks bulged against my throbbing heartbeat as my muscles relaxed and my body rested in her grip.

"What are your plans after this?" she asked, her wide eyes peering up at me.

I cocked my head, glancing at the stage. "Don't have any."

She rested her head back on my chest. "Sometimes those are the best plans." Her small voice resonated throughout my ribcage.

She stood next to me for the rest of the show. The band played a few more songs, then Grace Christian X, the female vocalist from Annex played a few of her songs. With only an acoustic guitar and her singing, she was astounding. Her picking mixed with a guttural tone, followed by a softer one, drew out the emotion in each piece. Amazing.

Afterward, they released the crowd like a flock of birds through the door and out to the fire where the party continued, though we dawdled behind.

"I'm surprised we've never met," she said when I stopped to let her pass through the doorway. "What part of town are you from?"

I joined her outside. "I'm not. Just passing through."

"Passing through? Where are you going?" She continued past the fire to the side of the house.

I stopped in my tracks and scratched my neck. "Don't know yet."

"Me either." The words fell beneath her breath like secrets strung to stones.

"What?"

She ignored my question, her rubber soles marking the dirt past the house and toward the parking lot.

"What's your name?" I bargained from the top of my voice,

anchored in place by the fear of pursuit as she neared the parking area.

Her black shoes, finally motionless, kept their direction. She turned her head, silhouetted by a distant streetlight. "It's a little early for that, don't you think?" She took off into the parking lot.

My right cheek raised while the left one fought a smile.

Don't overthink it.

I jogged to catch up, cutting through the air beneath the humming light that shined against the cars.

"Did you drive?" I asked, standing next to the rear of my van.

"I don't have a car. You?"

I gestured to the van with both arms and a cheesy grin, as if it were a prize she had won.

"This is freakin' awesome!" she yelled, cupping her hands around her face and pressing them against the window. "Is that a mattress?!"

"YES!" I laughed, my shoulders bobbing with my halfhearted chuckles.

"Is that for the la-la-ladies?" she teased. "I hope you don't think you'll be getting me back there!" She pointed at me with a serious face.

"No, no! I'm living out of it and traveling around the country." I waved my hands in front of my face. "I just bought it yesterday, actually."

"Well, what are you waiting for? Let's go!" Her tiny hand smacked the red paint that covered the bottom half of the otherwise white van, and she danced to the passenger's side.

"Where are we going?" I asked as we crawled in.

"Have you ever been to Atlanta? And I don't mean clubbing or shows. I mean have you ever *seen* Atlanta?" Her hands floated apart and her eyes crossed after she took her seat, gesturing to the broad spectrum of the unknown within the city.

"No, I can't say that I have." I contemplated whether I had ever taken the time to explore.

Words fumbled through a wide grin as she reminisced about the city—even the alleyways were beautiful with their piss-stained floors and garbage fixtures.

"You just have to think of everything as something you shouldn't touch or see." Her vision grew perplexed, her brows rising.

"What do you mean?" I asked, navigating the van in reverse.

"You know, like when you look at a photo or a painting that is difficult to pull away from … and their subjects had probably been captured a million times before, but somehow what you are seeing is unique." She took a second to breathe, allowing me to catch up.

"Yeah?" I said, stopping at the gated entrance of the mansion, waiting for a gap in traffic.

"Take a right here," she said, interrupting herself. "Where was I?" She tapped her lip with her finger. "Oh yeah! So, when you walk through the city and you see the streets or alleyways, remind yourself that what you're seeing will never be seen the same way again." She crossed her legs and sat on her feet. "I won't even see what you see, because I'm not you." Then she narrowed her eyes and glared at me. "What you're seeing is so rare that it shouldn't be seen or touched by anyone else. Almost like the entire world should be invisible to our senses outside what we are experiencing from moment to moment."

She was convinced the beauty in the world was in the details, and I believed her … though, I'd never completely lived in the moment until I was forced to. We followed the domestic streets until buildings shot out of the pavement like geysers of mortar and glass.

After a few minutes, we pulled into a behemoth parking garage that towered over the city. Inside, we circled the concrete columns from one car-filled floor to the next until, after five minutes of careful maneuvering, we arrived at the deserted top, where we were no longer limited by a ceiling.

I parked, hopped out of my seat, and met her behind the van. On one side of the garage, the sky and earth mirrored each other until they met at the horizon in a sea of black with specks of light. On the other side, there was no horizon at all; buildings blocked the night sky, and we were close enough to feel the magnitude of their stature.

"Look at the streets. Remember it as a snapshot."

I scrunched my forehead and narrowed my eyes, concentrating on the details like she had suggested.

"Now, close your eyes, and tell me what you see."

After a split second of black, the image materialized. "I see people walking through the streets—cars inching in a traffic jam." I tapped my fingers on the brick in front of me.

"Really? That's boring," she said. "I misjudged you."

I tapped harder. "What do you mean?" I chuckled to hide my frustration and opened my eyes.

"I mistook you for a guy with a story to tell," she said with a straight face. "Expectations though, am I right?" She laughed, facing the buildings that barricaded the streets.

Before she crowded me with anymore disappointment, I closed my eyes. For the first time since I was a child, I opened up.

Chapter 3

In my mind, the parking garage mutated into an apartment. The yellow concrete wheel stops behind us morphed into a brown couch that sat across from a four-paned window. The room was unfamiliar, yet pictures of my life adorned the walls and stood on tables. An empty frame hung on the wall between a window and a birdcage that held my childhood trophies over the catty-cornered television. Another frame outlined my mother kneeling at the kitchen sink, tears pouring from her face into the drain while my sister sobbed from a booster seat at the table.

I shook my head and ran my fingers along the edge of the brick partition before moving to the next photo: my last day of college. In it, I held a pen in my hand, furiously filling in dozens of job applications while my roommate, Jim, poked his head through the doorway to remind me of our last outing with the group before graduation. It was hard to believe that had been only a week ago.

Thuds pounded on the pavement beside me, but I kept my eyes closed.

I turned toward the television, where a girl walked in circles in front of it, and though her face was undefined, I sensed that she was beautiful. We sat on the couch, and I spoke to her in a language that only translated into mumbles and laughter. Then the lights buzzed and popped. The fan spun uncontrollably, ripping the wallpaper and pictures from the walls, touching everything but the girl and me while disaster unraveled.

The rough texture of the ceiling melted into raindrops. At last it poured. Still mumbling and laughing, we held newspapers and lampshades over our heads as if they could rescue us from the imminent flood that had already swallowed our legs. The end table lifted with the tide, a family portrait sliding off it into the water. I froze, staring as my father faded from the soggy portrait at my feet.

The only exit was the window, but the disappointment it framed robbed my attention. A bright yellow sun shot flares of light through a pale blue sky. I waded through the water to the other side of the room, the weak burn of late spring warming my fingertips when I pressed against the glass. Thirty stories below me, a parade flooded the dry streets in a famine of regard. Without an audience to perform for, a flock of floats carried waving hands and paper-mâché decorations, marching bands fought for air, people in masks yelled through brass horns, and magicians spun their bodies through space in synchronized motions. Everything centered around an elephant an elephant so large that it had to walk in slow motion to keep the pace of the parade. Bright fabrics of every color imaginable garnished its stone-like body.

My thoughts grew louder as my mind raced.

As humans, we had taken the rights of these beings to make them perform for us, yet we couldn't furnish the attention they deserved. We had whittled their existence, shaving any hope for a normal life, to fit them into a society that we had created.

The resemblance between the life of the elephant in this intransigent way of society and my own existence—ruled by the fear of living outwardly—was uncanny. The panic rose inside me, smothering the words to identify what I was facing. Claustrophobia clouded my thoughts until my vision outlived its welcome. The nameless girl sneaked up behind me and cupped her hands over my ears, kissing my forehead, then let go.

"Can I open my eyes now?" I asked, clawing at the brick in front of me.

"Sure."

Unconcerned with the lump in my throat or the redness in my face, I opened my eyes to find her sitting on the railing—where the window had been in my vision—with her eyes closed and arms crossed.

"I'm trying to see what you saw," she said.

"...Is it working?"

"No. Everything looks like claymation when I close my eyes." She scrunched her nose.

I laughed at her random frustration, and she joined in, opening her eyes to replace clay with flesh.

"Wanna go walk around?"

"You are my tour guide for the night!" I bowed, mimicking her dance invitation at the show.

She snorted. "Shut up."

"What?" I asked, helping her off the ledge. "You are!"

"Cool! No one ever just walks around with me." Her voice faded and she injected a hasty cough at the end of her sentence. I didn't call her out on it though.

We rode an elevator down to the first floor and mixed in with the people on the sidewalks. When the population grew thick, we played Marco Polo, bobbing in and out of slow walkers who shot ugly stares our way as we called out to one another. Anything that stood out to her, she studied. A dirty mail box. Light fixtures full of bugs. A random leaf skidding through the streets, clearly lost.

Together, we contemplated how the objects came to be. I enjoyed her story of the broken bench the most. She personified the planks of wood and metal, insisting it was tired of standing in one place.

"One day, it vowed to make a friend. Moving would not be easy, as it had been stuck there for many years, but the bench was determined." She kneeled and rubbed a long mark on the ground. "It stepped forward, scratching the concrete beneath it, then took another." Her eyes narrowed, and she stood while clenching her fist in front of her chest. "The bench felt confident it could reach the park around the block, where benches could marry in pairs, but with the third step, his wooden bones gave out."

She pushed through the surrounding crowd to a nearby light pole, where a white ribbon hung, looped around the thick metal to raise awareness for lung cancer. The whole city had been decorated with them. Then she broke back through the crowd with the ribbon in hand and fell to the side of the bench.

"It'll be okay!" she cried out, dropping to her knees. "WE CAN SAVE YOU!" Passersby craned their necks in her direction, and those boarding the city bus stumbled up its steps. She wrapped the ends of the ribbon around her hands, put one foot on the bench, and with a small grunt, tugged as hard as she could until the split wood clamped tightly together. She wound the ribbon around its leg a few times, then tied a knot and let the ends drape onto the ground before using a lighter from her pocket to singe them and cauterize the wound.

A man stopped behind her next to a trashcan, shaking his head.

"Well, my work here is done." She stood, wiping her forehead, and trotted off as if nothing had happened.

"Look! Art!" She switched gears like a squirrel and sprinted to a box truck that was parked almost a block away with graffiti painted all over it.

I hitched into a run after her, leaving the crowd of spectators gawking at us.

"What do you think of this piece?" she asked with an arm across her chest and a hand resting on her cheek.

"I don't know." I panted, catching up to her. "Progress?"

"Progress?" she asked.

"Yeah. Graffiti started in the late '60s, early '70s," I started. "Back then, the owner of this truck would have probably painted white over it … but if you look closely, he painted graffiti over the graffiti." I pointed at the center of the box. "See there—the business name and the year it was established."

"I don't think the name of this business is *The Grass Man, established in 2017.*" She giggled. "If so, they need to redo their logo. It looks like a pot leaf."

"Like I said. Progress." I laughed.

Her face went blank. She was no longer amused.

"What?" I asked.

"Nothing." She tugged on her earlobe. "Do you like coffee?" She forged a smile and took a few steps back.

"Yeah," I replied, sliding next to her. "You okay?"

"I'm fine." She tilted her head and knotted a strand of hair around her finger. "I think I just hit a brick wall. I haven't been sleeping well lately."

"That makes two of us." I sighed.

We followed the sidewalk a few blocks past the parking garage to her favorite all-night diner.

"The usual?" a petite young girl with thick-framed glasses called out from behind the counter as we passed the hostess stand inside.

"Please!" the nameless girl from the party answered, leading the way to a booth that had a window overlooking the street.

"How about you? Regular coffee?" the waitress asked me.

"Yeah. That's fine." I nodded, taking my seat.

Seconds later, our coffee was delivered, and we fell into a stare. She covered her smiles with her cup, but her high cheekbones peeked over the rim. I warmed my hands around the steaming mug instead of risking a burn to my mouth and peered down at the table.

She lowered her cup. "My name's Astrid … Mavis." She cleared her throat. Astrid Mavis."

"I like that name; it's pretty." I smiled and ripped the top from a sugar packet.

She smirked before bringing the cup the rest of the way to her mouth.

"What? Was it still too early?" I said, borrowing her sense of humor.

She gently set the mug back on the table and waved at the waitress who strode by.

"Would you like more?" the waitress asked, holding the coffee decanter over Astrid's cup.

"No, just a water please." She lowered her head, patting her hair down.

"Same please." I shot a quick glance at the waitress, then turned my attention back to the strangely serious tension caused by the simple question I had asked. Was it her name she didn't want to share, or herself?

Nothing was said during what seemed like an hour until the waitress returned with our waters.

"Thank you." I relieved the waitress while Astrid reserved her silence, her bangs draped like curtains over her eyes. She hunched over the table.

"My name is Zachary Byrd. I prefer Zachary to Zach. It just sounds better," I said while shrugging.

She lifted her head and smiled at my compulsion, then stabbed the straw into her water. "It's getting late. Where do you plan on staying, Zachary?"

"Um …" I ducked my head, the settling steam from my coffee stinging my droopy eyelids. "I think I'll stay in that parking garage. Should I take you home first?" I spoke out of obligation, my stomach tightening and ramming against the words until they broke free.

She shook her head. "Can I stay with you?" Her eyes grew behind the silky auburn strands covering her brows.

I squirmed in my seat, no longer feeling the drag of fatigue. "No problem. Yeah."

"But promise me one thing: no funny business! We're just friends."

"I promise, I promise." I straightened, surrendering to her request with my hands in the air.

At the parking garage, we moved the van a few floors down as close to the center of the building as we could. She squeezed between the front seats to the back, where she made a space to rest with her feet pointed toward the windshield as I cracked the windows.

After joining her, I peeled the thin quilt from my side of the bed and lapped it over her. "You can have the blanket," I said, wedging myself between the mattress and the plastic trim of the van.

"You sure?" She propped herself up on her elbow.

"Yeah." I scooted toward the edge of the mattress and kicked off my shoes.

She rolled up in the blanket and turned onto her side. "Okay."

I fluffed my pillow and did the same, padding my knees with my hand. Only a few days prior, I had broken away from myself. That night, I had given into fate, and like old routines, it kept me. Like the past, the future wanted me.

You needed to believe that, didn't you?

I eased myself up after her eyes closed and her breathing slowed. The past held me prisoner, taunting me with its reckless sense of abandonment. I reached for the pills in the middle of the dash and threw one to the back of my tongue. The side of her face flushed beneath the dim parking garage lights, her knees curling closer to her chest just before I lay back down.

You want to let the future win, but do you deserve it?

Chapter 4

Persistent rays of sunlight, magnified by the windows of the van, beamed in on us through a sizable opening between columns in the garage. Astrid had moved in her sleep and lay facing me with her hand on my chest and her chin nestled near my shoulder. By then she had shed most of the blanket, leaving herself exposed for me to admire … I was jealous of the drops of sweat that covered her bare legs hidden only by thin cotton shorts, the hair on her head splayed over her pillow.

Against temptation, I coaxed her arm off me and pulled myself into a sitting position. I leaned over my luggage past the front seat and turned the key to the van, blasting the air-conditioning. She continued sleeping—so peacefully.

When I tapped her shoulder, her forehead wrinkled between her long lashes. I called her name while people parking their cars around us slammed their doors, but she simply squirmed in place, twisting the bottoms of her legs out of the blanket.

I climbed into the driver's seat and steered to the exit. Large bumps rocked the carriage with every passing floor until the garage delivered us to the streets, where the buildings laid shadows and reflected the sounds of my engine, fading in and out with each alleyway I passed.

The sun reappeared when I pulled into the open parking spot in front of the diner from the night before. I didn't want to risk leaving the keys in the car for her to have air-conditioning, but I did justice well by leaving the windows cracked.

I stepped out of the van and hobbled toward the diner, sleep still creaking in my body.

"ZACHARY!" Astrid called out from the van.

I hurried to the side door and tore it open. Astrid lay on her back, her ankles crossed, as she picked at her nails.

"Is everything okay?" I stood with one hand resting on the open door and the other on the frame of the van.

"Yeah. I was making sure you hadn't left me." She shrugged.

"I was getting coffee. Would you like some?"

"I would love some." She lifted her legs with a scrunched face and rocked herself into an upright position before scooting to the edge and dropping her bare feet onto the sidewalk.

"Don't you want your shoes?" I asked, worried that the hot pavement might burn her delicate skin.

She straightened her wrinkled clothes and ran her fingers through her frizzy hair. "No, I'm fine." She strode to the door, body odor wafting behind her.

The pitter-patter of her steps transferred onto the cold tiled floors inside and led us to the same booth as the night before. We ordered hot coffees even though sweat still soaked our hair. Afterward, she rested her chin in the palm of her hand and leaned on the table, her heels tucked and propped against the booth.

"I should probably get going sometime today," I said, rolling the salt shaker between my fingers.

"Where are you headed next?"

"I don't know. I didn't plan on coming to Atlanta," I replied as I set the salt shaker down. "I got lost on my way to Savannah traveling without a map." I smirked.

She giggled into the palm of her hand. "Well, I'm glad you did. And that sounds freeing."

Freeing. That was the idea, though I doubt I would have felt that way if I'd gone to Savannah and never met her.

"I've been to Savannah. It's gorgeous." Her eyes widened as she recited the memory with the same excitement she'd had while introducing me to Atlanta.

"Do you go there a lot?"

"No. I went there with friends last summer. Annex played a basement show. A bunch of us rode all the way there in the back of the drummer's truck."

"In the bed of his truck?" I flinched and lifted my mug to my lips. "Isn't that kind of far?"

She flashed a mischievous grin as she wiped the edge of the table with the back of her hand. "Yeah. About four hours. It took forever to get all the knots out of my hair."

"How many of you were back there?"

"Three." She stirred her drink. "Do you plan on going there still? Because if you do, I'd love to ride with you. You can just drop me off on your way back through."

I wasn't sure if traveling an extra eight hours would hurt my plans to drive out west, but I did know that spending another day with Astrid was worth it.

"Four hours each way?" I rubbed the two days of stubble thickening on my chin. "Sure."

After finishing our drinks, Astrid guided us back to her house.

"My mom is probably still asleep," she said before grabbing the handle when I pulled up in front of a squat house, several shingles missing from its bowed roof. "I'll be right back."

"Can I—" I stopped myself as she took off across the yard and reached into the bushes, then yanked out a nicked two-by-four.

I sank in my seat and turned my attention to her neighbors. A few of them peered back through the broken windows of a rusted-out car on bricks with a trash bag where the rear windshield used to be.

She stepped up onto a bucket and propped the window open with the beaten piece of wood before hoisting herself through the opening.

Just as her bare feet cleared the pane, a skinny woman broke through the front door.

"Who the fuck are you?" Cigarette smoke escaped with her shrill voice when she hopped off the front stoop, darting across the yard toward the van.

"I'm just a friend of Astrid's!" I yelled, cranking the window closed.

"What are you? Her pimp?" The lady jumped into the street. "Get out or we'll drag you out!"

"Look," I hollered through the last inch of the cracked window, turning the engine on, "I'll leave! I'm sorry."

She slammed the hood with her ragged, scabby hands, the letters L-O-V-E stitched to her dingy hoodie.

Letters—word—meaning: disconnect.

My coward's ankle shook, teetering on the brake pedal.

"GET OUT!" She screamed one last time.

I threw the transmission into reverse and twisted around in my seat while switching over to the accelerator.

"Fuck!" I yelled, slamming the brakes. A navy-blue '90s Accord had stopped inches from my bumper.

I flipped the van into drive again as the door to the car behind me squealed open. A skinny man gripping a red brick paced closer in my driver's side mirror.

"MOM! What are you doing?" Astrid belted, bolting from the stoop and sprinting across the yard. "Get away from him!"

She leapt past the curb in front of the van.

"Mom, stop!" she screamed again, grabbing the bruised woman by her veiny neck and arms and shoving her into the yard.

I leaned into the pedal.

I peeled away from the curb, and Astrid fled into the street, her arms flailing like string in the wind … but the horn of the junky Honda blared behind her until it filled my mirror.

Blocking his attempts to pass me, we weaved through the cracked suburbia.

His engine wound inches from my bumper.

I whipped my head from side to side—looking past the algae and rot that had painted the neighboring houses. Children stared from their patchy yards like I was in an old television rerun, some of them standing on a cushionless couch as we zipped by. My gaze frantically shifted, and I eased my foot off the gas, afraid that one of them might run into the street.

He tapped my bumper. My van wobbled.

"FUCK!" I yelled, glaring into the rearview mirror.

Through the windshield, a box truck headed toward a *T* that capped the end of the road in my peripherals. I leaned as hard as I could into the accelerator.

Heat and sulfur fumes seeped through the vents as I overworked the engine and closed in on the stop sign.

I grazed the brakes and spun the wheel.

The Accord tapped my bumper again, sending me into a fishtail. The box truck laid on his horn when I swerved in front of it, and my van skipped, threatening to topple over. With a loud *bang,* the crunching metal echoed behind me. My ears rang and my body tensed. My eyes snapped shut as I squeezed the steering wheel until my knuckles popped, and for a split second, the world stopped.

I opened my eyes, and my attention flitted to the mirror; the old car sat motionless in the street, pieces of it scattered across the pavement. The box truck had left a black streak of rubber leading into a nearby yard, where it lay sideways, no more than five feet from a house.

My veins couldn't control my blood. I didn't stop to check on anyone. I didn't even call the police.

I gunned it until street signs for the highway appeared, then I veered onto the exit.

Just keep going. Just keep going.

I repeated the phrase aloud. "Just keep going," I said again, tears fighting past my shock and crowding my eyes. I fell apart when I neared the end of the bridge that exited onto the highway.

You can't keep going.

My vision blurred, forcing me onto the side of the road—my tires buzzed over the rumble strip. I fumbled for the medicine bottle below the dash before the car had completely stopped, then popped the lid off and emptied the pills into my shaking palm.

"I'm sorry!" I screamed at the windshield. "I'm sorry!"

The memory of jumping out of my old truck and people screaming at me to stop crowded my head, a stream of blood overtaking my vision while it creeped out between the tires beneath the driver's side door.

I glared at the pills, waiting for the strength or peace that would allow me to commit and shove them all down my throat.

"Fuck!" I shook my head, catching where Astrid had traced her name into the window from the corner of my eye. Her fingerprints still clung to the glass.

I counted the handful of pills and sorted them back into the medicine bottle. I had twenty-four left of the original thirty … and it had been five days since they were prescribed, having taken two on the first day.

I screwed the lid on. "She didn't take any." I dropped my hands to my lap, the pills rattling in my grip. Her skin had been clean. She had been reserved. Her mind was too fascinating to be strung by the same thread that sustained her mother.

I sat transfixed, absently blinking at the mile marker less than twenty feet ahead of me.

Save someone else's life. The balance will give you purpose.

I let off the brake and veered onto the highway, following it until I came across a stucco motel twenty minutes from the city. Its rooms appeared in the distance, with doors that lined a short breezeway.

I cut over to the exit and rolled into the empty parking lot. Pebbles popped between my tires and the pavement. I shifted into park and left the van running in front of the motel's small lobby.

For forty-three bucks, a young lady with a naked face and black fingernails gave me a room with twin mattresses and cable.

After leaving the lobby, I climbed back into the van and followed the white arrows to my designated room number. A black door in the middle of the breezeway guarded the entrance with aluminum locks.

I parked, then grabbed my backpack by its haul strap and crossed the narrow strip of sunlight illuminating the sidewalk. The room exhaled a fog of stale air when I swung its metal door open.

I forded the space and closed the thick vertical blinds and frayed floral curtains until the only light seeped in from the side of the casement window.

The spring-hinged door closed itself behind me, trapping me in the suffocating room—for a moment, I was convinced it was where I belonged.

You can just exist here. Nothing more, nothing less.

It was calming, but I didn't let myself live in that space for long. I twisted the switch to a bed lamp and kneeled to power on the weak air conditioner that was loud enough to drown out the sound of the highway.

Should I have gone back for her after the wreck? Surely, the neighborhood knew my van and I couldn't just waltz up to her house. The thoughts paralyzed me on the floor.

The air conditioner buzzed, jerking me in and out of concentration. Once its subtle effects had kicked in, I unpacked the contents of my bag into the dresser drawers. I had no intention of staying longer than a night, but I wanted to assess what I had to work with.

Most of my clothes were lighter colors fit for summer. I did have a pair of dark jeans, though, and a hunter-green hooded sweatshirt I had brought in case the nights were ever cold. It wouldn't completely camouflage me, but it carried the advantage of inconspicuousness at least.

I laid the outfit on the nearest bed and sat down at the table between it and the window. I rested my elbows on my knees, clasping my hands in front of my face. If only I could have slept and let tomorrow greet new days without reminding me of her—but that didn't feel likely.

After propping the door open with the swinging lockpin, I trudged outside to my van to retrieve my suitcase that had flung against the back door during the chase.

"You've got to be kidding me." I ran my hand across the wrinkled bumper that was hanging an inch lower on one side than the other. "Shit!" I shook my head and yanked on the rear door handle. My luggage fell out onto the ground as soon as the door opened along with Astrid's shoes and denim button-up.

Proof that she was real.

I threw her things back into the van, grabbed my suitcase by its handle and slammed the door shut. My hand teetered over the bumper's new shape once more.

It's all material.

I sauntered back inside, locking the door behind me before blasting the shower. Steam leaked out from the bathroom around me as I peeled my clothes off and climbed into the tub. I took my time washing the sticky sweat and grime from my body. Having been primitive, soaking in water for the first time in days felt foreign. Shampoo tingled my scalp, and soap stung the scratches and bugbites that covered my body. I twisted the knob until the steam opened my pores and lungs, then I stood with my fingers dangling by my thighs.

Chapter 5

I grabbed the clunky remote off the battered nightstand and turned on the television. After a few seconds of crackling, a spotty picture came in. The news stations were clear though, which was all I really cared about. I spent two hours in my underwear glued to headlines about murders and dispute in Atlanta and surrounding cities.

One story featured a sixteen-year-old boy who had killed his grandparents after they forbade him from attending a party. Following the crime, he had showed up at the party anyway and attended school for almost a week before his grandfather's work reported the couple missing. He'd wrapped their bodies in trash bags and stored them in the upstairs bathtub.

When the realness of hysteria set in, I climbed out of bed and strode over to the television to turn it off. The fixed flow of air killed any silence in the room until my thoughts butted in. A polyphase circuit of memories and plans met at a single terminal, and I projected the combined energy into a visual list of scenarios on the back of my eyelids. The displays were completely unbiased and filtered both good and bad. I, however, honed in on the good, hoping it would ease my churning stomach long enough to talk me into revisiting my glimpse of involuntary ruin.

Involuntary. Involuntary. Involuntary.

Nothing panned out from my pleated ideas. I threw on a T-shirt, shorts, and shoes before slipping outside. I patted my pockets: phone, wallet, keys, keycard. I faced a selfish sun as it took what was left of the day into the horizon, then I broke into a jog.

"Physical. Safety. Love and belonging." I called out the

hierarchy of needs to the rhythm of my stomping feet. "Esteem. Self-actualization."

I chanted a little louder as I picked up my pace. "Physical. Safety. Love and belonging. Esteem. Self-actualization … Physical. Safety. Love and—"

When I glanced up, a dirt parking lot circled around a small convenience store that looked almost identical to one near my childhood home. I hinged my hands behind my head and opened my lungs.

"Why, why, why?" I whispered under my breath, straining to make sense of my undefined thoughts while dust coated the soles of my shoes as I ambled toward the door. I continued past a trash can and rusty air compressor sitting beside the building, then rounded the corner, where a half-full ice machine buzzed next to the entrance.

Slick with sweat, my hand slid against the aluminum handle crossing the glass door, and I stepped inside.

"How are ya?" asked a thick man who sat behind an elevated counter.

"I'm good!" I stunted the truth with an unconvincing tone. "Just wasting time."

"Okay, let me know if you need anything." He peeked up from his crossword and peered past the thin rims of his glasses.

"Thanks," I said, digging into my pocket as my phone vibrated against my thigh.

Mom. The screen embellished my dread.

My thumb hovered over the decline button, but guilt finally took over, and I answered.

"Hello?" I forged a calm tone, distracting myself with an ingredient label on a family-sized bag of summer snaps that had toppled forward, its face lost in a world of candy bars.

"Hey, sweetie, we haven't heard from you lately." She paused for a second. "How have you been?"

I faked a smile to sound convincing. "I'm good. How are you? Is Melaneah out for summer break yet?"

I grabbed the bag of summer snaps.

"She's been out for a couple of days." A faint snicker deadened the line. "Can you believe your little sister will be a senior next year?"

"No. It's crazy." I bit my lip and tilted my head back, staring at a water spot in the ceiling.

She sniffled. "Yeah, it is … Speaking of seniors, when is your graduation ceremony?"

With my head still back, I closed my eyes and cracked my neck, squeezing the bag of chips in my hand.

I exhaled, my chest sinking so much that the pressure radiated down my spine. "I'm not going to walk."

"What? Why not?!" Her sharp voice rattled the earpiece in my phone.

Because I was too busy running. My conscience snapped in the chaotic silence that followed.

I set the bag of chips on the shelf and dug my nails into the back of my arm. "I'm traveling. I needed to get away."

She quieted. "Oh. Is the Bronco safe to drive after the—"

"I traded it in for a van."

"That was—"

"I … I need to go." I stiffened.

"They said he's gonna make it. It wasn't your fault."

"The college is going to mail my degree and whatnot to your house. Tell everyone I said hello and that I love them."

"Zachary!" she said as my thumb grazed the red end button on my screen.

Useless, I thought.

Useless, I felt.

Useless.

"Still finding everything all right?" the man checked with a cocked ear and raised eyebrows. He sat with his forearms resting on the counter's artificial finish.

I took a moment to collect myself before answering, stretching my arm across my chest. “Actually, do you have any air fresheners for cars?”

“Yeah, they’re at the end of this aisle here.” He pointed the tip of his pencil at the back corner. “I personally like the ones that you put under the seat. They look like cans of pomade.”

“Thanks.” I circled around the capped lane of macaroni and various brands of soup to a peg board of auto supplies, grabbed two blue cans of the type he suggested, and headed to the counter.

“Will that be it?” The man set his creased booklet and pencil aside.

My gaze flitted to the assortment of cigarettes that served as his backdrop, wondering if Astrid smoked like her mom. “Yes.” I nodded and dropped my focus back to the counter. “That’s it.”

“I heard you say you’re on a road trip? Where are you going?” he asked as he typed the SKU numbers into his register.

“I don’t know yet. I’m thinking about going home.” I lowered my head, searching for the confirmation of defeat that I was used to.

“How long have you been on the road?” He gripped the support beam at the end of the counter, where a bundle of bags hung from a couple of hooks.

“Uh … “ My hesitation flared. “Two days.” The words burned my cheeks.

“You’ve barely left home!” He chuckled, his goatee slanting with his smirk.

“Yeah. I don’t know if I was ready,” I confessed to the stranger, fidgeting with the seams of my shirt while I waited for my total.

“Life doesn’t care if you’re ready. You have to take more from it than it takes from you and keep going,” he said, fishing below the counter again.

He rolled himself away from it in a wheelchair that I had missed in my derangement.

Then he pulled a frame from a nail on the wooden pole beside the register and turned it where we both could view it.

He and his wife, who barely reached his chest, stood in front of a blue background, her curly brown hair hanging down to her waist. His son, a tall boy with blond hair who looked to be about ten, squatted in front of them while flashing such a broad smile that he squinted. The boy rested his hand on his sister's shoulder, a girl a few years younger with hair that matched her mom's.

"We used to have a restaurant … but I had a stroke, and it took my legs." He lifted his head and smiled. "But that's all it got. I took back much more: I returned to school, became a lawyer, and have since retired with my wife after putting both of my children through college."

I studied the picture, then his wheelchair, before shifting to his adoring eyes as the glossy print was reflected in them. "That's amazing." I spoke above the whispers of dread lifting from my body.

"Anyway"—he shook his head—"your total is $4.83."

I pulled my wallet from my back pocket. Had he told that story to every stranger who was down and out, or was I simply in the right place at the right time?

"Here you go." I slid my card to his side of the counter while he rolled himself to the register. "What's your name?"

"Ken Glover." He lowered his glasses. "Yours?"

"Zachary Byrd," I said with new meaning and broadened shoulders.

"Zachary, it's nice to meet you!" He offered his hand, tan lines of fingerless gloves printed between his wrists and knuckles.

"It's nice to meet you too!" I gripped his meaty palm. "Thank you!"

"No problem." He winked as he released my hand and gave me my card. "Enjoy your trip."

I thanked him once more, retrieved my things, and left.

The walk to the motel proved much darker with my back to the sinking horizon. A contrast of red and white lights glowed before me, brightening the end of the street, and by the time I reached them, I knew … I had to go back for her.

Chapter 6

Bits of outer space poked through the thick clouds, but wind pushed them toward the city, and the dim No Vacancy sign hanging at the entrance of the motel swung steadily back and forth.

Dressed and ready to go, I left my clothes sorted in the drawers and a note on the table specifying where I'd be and who to contact if I didn't make it back before checkout the next day. I hoped for the best and expected the worst. My plan was foolish, but I couldn't separate myself from it.

The drive was short. It felt like I was experiencing a single elongated reflection the entire trip, the variables dictating my angst and excitement, both together and separately.

I approached the city from the south this time. The direct roads led me to a bridge that stabbed into the sky and dove back down into the lights, where there were only a few avenues to choose from at first. With familiarity more awake than expected, I recalled every street, and within fifteen minutes, I had parked at the top of the parking garage with my van centered in plain sight.

It was 11:00 PM by the time I made it downstairs and flagged a taxi to pick me up.

"Johnston Street, please," I requested, opening the rear passenger door and climbing into the cab.

The meter climbed as he took a longer route than necessary, but I wasn't concerned.

The later, the better. Hopefully Astrid's mother would be asleep—or at least distracted—upon my arrival.

My heart raced as the cab neared her house, ramming blood against my clenched fists that bore sweat and last-minute indecision.

"Watch out!" The cabbies voice crackled as he tapped the brakes for a group of teenagers who were crossing the road.

I spotted the car on bricks in the middle of the yard across the street from Astrid's in the near distance. "You can actually pull over here. This shouldn't take long if you can wait for me."

He nodded, and I gave him a generous tip to seal our agreement before quietly exiting the car.

My stomach knotted until a soft yellow light emanated from her blinds. Random people roamed the streets, but none of them were paying me any mind. I covered my head with my hood and strained my ears for any threats, but there was only the distant hum of the cab as I neared her window through the patches of grass and mounds of dirt. I glanced back at my ride, and he turned the motor off, waving with the red cherry of a cigarette glowing in his hand.

My hand floated in front of her window before tapping it twice. The loose wood wobbled once, and then again. Drenched in apprehension, I crouched, hiding against the side of the house while waiting for any indication of life to probe the blinds. Thirty seconds later, and still no response ... so I tapped the panes again, this time louder.

Within seconds, the light that filled her room disappeared and the blinds popped open. I remained in the shadows while Astrid surveyed the street through a swollen eye covered by makeup. I pushed myself into sight, but she flinched.

"Open your window!" I whispered.

She shook her head and balanced on her knees atop a mattress that lay on the floor beneath her window.

"Please!"

After biting her lip, she broke her ties with oscillation. Spanning to the other side of her room, she wedged an old plastic chair between the knob and the floor. Moments later, she shot back to the window.

"What are you doing here?" she petitioned with her fingernails scratching at the chipped paint along the sill.

"How do you feel about going west?" I whispered, running my hands through my hair.

Her face grew serious, studying me with furrowed brows and tight lips. She rolled off her mattress onto a pile of clothes. A dented hardwood floor reflected the streetlights as she scraped garments from it, stuffing them into a nearby suitcase.

"Take this." She squeezed the luggage through the window, followed by a pillow, then she unlocked her bedroom door only to disappear again.

I set the things in a pile on the ground and dialed the cabbie.

"Yellow Cab 413," he answered in a lazy voice.

"Yeah, this is the guy that you just dropped off," I said in a hushed tone, facing the street. "Did you see the house I went to?"

"Yeah."

"Can you park on the street? We're about ready to go."

"Sure thing, boss."

I dropped my phone back into my pocket and checked on Astrid. She was still scavenging the house. When she returned, she wore a short pair of shorts, a tank top, and black shoes like the ones she had left in my van except these ones had a floral print all over them. Sunglasses rested on top of her head, and a backpack hung from her wrist. Wads of one- and five-dollar bills spilled out of a small pocket on the front of it while she crowded it with more balls of cash that she'd pulled out of a box of tissues.

"My mom passed out in the living room." She grunted as she hopped out of the window like it was the side of an old car before plopping to the ground, her backpack smacking the small of her back when she landed.

We grabbed her things and hurried to the taxi.

The driver smiled when we approached.

"Will you take us back to the garage, please?" I requested through the front passenger window while Astrid opened the back door and slid inside with her backpack.

"Sure. You wanna throw that luggage in the trunk?" he asked, pressing the lever.

"Yeah." I ran to the back of the car, dropped the suitcase into the trunk, then hurried into the seat next to Astrid. The driver reset the meter and let off the brakes. Her house disappeared behind us, more slowly this time. No one ran after the cab or yelled from the yard. We weren't chased or threatened by other cars. Even the children who had previously played outside stayed invisible as we passed.

Nobody spoke on the drive back to the garage except for a small radio that barked orders from the dash. It was cleansing, leaving the old and finding the new. A vicarious sense of letting go that I'd never felt before … but hoped I'd find.

She dawdled when we got to the garage. I set her things beside the car and paid the cabbie one last time through his window. He didn't shake my hand but wished us luck.

Luck: it was like some sort of matrix of good and evil, neither disguised nor visible. But it was powerful and couldn't be manipulated; I was a toy in its hands.

I thanked him and threw in an extra few dollars for the sentiment.

"I can get that," I said, reaching down for the handle of Astrid's suitcase that she had dragged to the other side of the sidewalk.

She relented, and I steered it toward the elevator. The lights flashed three times before the doors slid open. Astrid stepped in first and hunched in the corner against her backpack with crossed arms, fixated on the shoe marks and scuffs that painted the floor around her feet.

"I parked on the top floor," I said, pushing the button and taking my place in the opposite corner behind her luggage.

She didn't have much to say, but as soon as the doors closed and the street disappeared, she left her post and pushed her luggage aside with her foot.

"What?" I asked, completely transfixed by her bright blue eyes.

She stepped closer, resting her hands on my shoulders and leaning forward on her tiptoes.

"Thank you." Her words barely pushed enough air to be audible. She hugged me and nestled her head on my shoulder.

We held our silence while the elevator doors opened, then we meandered to the van.

After hopping in and starting the ignition, we circled each floor of the garage and trekked back onto the highway. I let the air clear and the city lights pass before I started asking questions.

"So when we went to get your clothes earlier—what happened?"

"My mom"—she picked at the skin around her fingernails—"wasn't always like this."

"Like what?"

"My dad went to prison when I was young … like nine or ten. We didn't have any money, and then he never came home one day." She swallowed hard as her voice grew weaker. "My mom made me deliver drugs—makes me deliver drugs. I was a little girl with a backpack. Now look at me." She dug her face into her hands and buried them between her knees.

I rubbed her back until she lifted her head.

"I came home almost every day to my mom slumped over her throne of a bucket and a pillow, waiting for her money," she said with her arms crossed and head pressed against the seat, biting into the passive venom in her tongue. "That was her boyfriend who chased you. They needed money, but my phone was dead, and—" She gasped, squeezing her eyes shut to block the tears.

The circumstances were fragile. She had been beaten by her mom's boyfriend because he'd blamed the wreck on her … then dumped her mother, so her mother beat her again.

She dropped her hands to her lap and peered out the window. "You never fight with a drug addict. They have no concept of boundaries. Just take the beating and try to get away as quickly as you can," she mumbled.

"You never got caught? What about your friends—what did they say?" I tugged at the hair on the back of my head.

"I knew it was wrong even when I was little. None of my friends were like me. And I had never introduced my mom to them—I was too ashamed of her. She made me handle the deliveries because no one suspected a young girl. I hated it. I hated it so much." Her voice shook and cracked, and her nails pushed into her forehead while her palms pressed hard against her face.

"Why didn't you leave when you were old enough?" I asked, both knuckles white as I gripped the steering wheel.

"You don't leave unless you have somewhere to go. I've been saving up—I know it's hard to understand, but there is more to leaving than disappearing."

"Did you ever get hurt? I mean, those people you were dealing with ... were they like your mom and her boyfriend?" I took my eyes off the road briefly.

"They were, but I never got seriously injured or anything." She straightened and dried her face with the back of her hand. "By the time people noticed what I was doing, I was old enough to get a taxi or whatever—and then I'd have the driver wait outside when I got to where I was going. I'd tell anyone who threatened to hurt me that 'Savage' was in the car and that he'd come in if I wasn't out within five minutes with the money."

"Savage?" I said, glancing at the mile marker from earlier that day as we zoomed by it. "So he went everywhere with you?"

"No." She sniffled and shook her head. "I made him up. But one time, a guy had tried to take the drugs without paying me—I was maybe 14 at the time—and a random man broke into the house during our argument, then started beating the guy. The money and drugs flew from his hands and landed on the floor in front of me, so I grabbed them and dashed out of the house. When the guy who got beat was found dead a day later, I started the rumor that Savage had done it. Everyone thought he had my back, and no one wanted to fuck with him." She lowered her tone, digging at the skin around her nails again.

"So without him, you could have been—" I stopped while the color drained from my face.

"Raped. Killed. Tortured."

Her chin quivered as moisture formed in her eyes, and she stared out her window.

It was a lot for me to take in but even more for her to let out. She put on her sunglasses and wept, her breath casting a patch of steam onto the window. There was nothing I could do or say to alleviate her pain, so I turned on the radio to offer a sense of privacy.

She reclined the seat and let tears roll down her cheeks past the dark frames of her glasses until sleep overtook her.

When we reached the motel, I set her suitcase upright beside the dresser, replaced the thin pillow on the bed with hers, and pulled the blankets back.

"ZACHARY!" Astrid's muffled yell seeped through the thin walls from outside.

I rushed through the black motel door that I had propped open with my backpack and bounded to the van, where she rested with the seat tilted back and her sunglasses still in place above her smile.

I cracked the door open. "Are you tired?"

"Exhausted. Is this where we're staying?"

"Yeah. I got a room earlier today—figured we may need it to get a clean start on our trip." I rubbed my eyes. "Your things are already inside."

Her gaze met mine as she snatched her backpack from between her feet. "Stop being so damn nice." It was a backhanded compliment, but I took it with pride. Part of me felt like I owed her happiness. For everything she had lost, she deserved that.

I followed her into the room and pointed out her bed, adding that there were toiletries in the bathroom. She thanked me and pulled clothes out of an exterior pocket of her luggage. Still toting her backpack, she locked herself in the bathroom, and seconds later, the shower hissed.

I took advantage of the empty room and changed into shorts and a T-shirt before crawling into bed.

She was taking forever to get ready, but I couldn't figure out why. Her shower had been short. She'd brushed her teeth quickly. Her suitcase clicked open and then latch closed … forty-five minutes later, she approached the foot of the bed, and my body tensed. I imagined her crawling beneath my sheets. My muscles loosened when her footsteps passed and she climbed onto the other mattress. The room felt empty again, as if she and I were disconnected.

I fended off the drought by planning the next morning. She tossed and turned, making my attempt to ignore her impossible. Finally, her bed stopped squeaking and she seemed at peace … then the edge of my bed sank. My eyes widened, and I raised my arm to guide her toward me. Gauze taped to her legs and a bandage on her collar bone scratched my skin as she shifted to get comfortable. But she no longer tossed and turned; after sighing one last time, her long lashes fluttered against my chest, and her eyes closed.

Chapter 7

"Have you ever heard this song?" Astrid asked a couple of days later, dawdling back to our booth at a diner in a place called Muldrow, Oklahoma.

An orchestra of strings swelled as a bass line fell in from the jukebox.

My heel tapped to the slow tempo. "I don't think so."

She closed her eyes and slid into the padded black booth across from me as I snuck a pill to the back of my tongue and chased it with a sip of sweet tea.

"My dad used to play a record that had this song on it during dinner when I was little." Her eyes popped open. "This was the first song, actually."

"When you were little? Was that before—" I stopped myself.

"My life wasn't always so, um …" She looked away.

"Intense?" I had spoken too soon. "Looks like we're both at a loss for words," I said, chuckling.

She smiled. "This was from a good time."

"What happened?"

"We never had money. That's why we lived where we lived. But we were a happy family until my dad lost his job." She frowned and rubbed her nose with the palm of her hand. "I was seven or eight."

I gazed down at the butter knife I'd been twirling in my hand. "So did he find a new job, or …" I set the knife on my napkin and focused on her crinkled brow.

"No. He got involved with the wrong people." She took a long sip from her tea.

"I'm sorry." I slid my hands to the center of the table. "I shouldn't be asking you about it."

"No! No." She set her glass back down. "It feels good to finally say it out loud. It's just a memory now, right?" She rested her hands on top of mine.

"Right!" I smiled.

She retracted her arms and propped herself up with her elbows. "When my dad got locked up, my mom went off the deep end. Within a month, she'd found a new boyfriend. They locked me in my room—some nights, I was lucky if they let me use the bathroom. I remember mornings, sneaking out to go to school. I'd walk through the house, and almost every day, there'd be something missing. First, it was small things, like lamps or the microwave … but as time passed, it was larger things like the couch and the television, until only the kitchen table stood, along with the record player—with the album still in it." She arched her back and stretched. "On the last day of fifth grade, my mom had passed out in the living room, so I snuck into the kitchen and sat at the table one last time." She covered her face with her hands, her reddened cheeks poking through. "Oh my god! I feel stupid admitting this!"

"No!" I reached for her wrists and gently pulled her hands away. "Don't feel stupid."

She dropped her hands to her lap and sighed before continuing. "I actually closed my eyes and imagined that record playing and my family gathered around me." Her chin trembled. "But then I heard someone stirring in the living room, so I grabbed the record, stuffed it into my backpack, and ran out the back door." Her glassy stare drifted toward the ceiling.

I scratched my knees under the table and leaned closer. "That's not stupid at all."

"Yeah." Her finger traced over a deep scratch in the laminate surface. "I came home that night, and the table and record player were both gone. The record is still hidden under the carpet in my closet."

I reclined in the booth as the last few notes of the current song played. "What record is this?" I asked.

She leaned back and lifted her shirt to reveal a round tattoo of the record's label in black and gray on her upper ribs. It read *The Best of the '50s* in a vintage font, followed by the company who had made the mix and even the speed and size of the record.

"That's awesome!" I said. "Was Side A your favorite?" I read the smaller print just before she let her shirt fall back down.

"It was the only side I got to listen to. I imagine Side B would have been just as impressive." She grinned and grabbed a menu to hide behind. "Blah! This would be a good time for a distraction." She dropped the pamphlet to the table.

I pushed my empty plate away from me until it bumped hers in the center.

"Excuse me," I said as our waitress carried a pitcher by our table. "Do you know of anything cheap or free to do around here?"

"Well, a lot of people around here like to go on the trails," she said, setting the pitcher down. She removed her plastic-framed glasses and cleaned them with a cloth inside the pocket of her black apron. "They're about one and a half to two hours from here, but that's about it unless you go to the mall." She placed her glasses back on her face, hiding the arms beneath her curly brown hair.

"Do you think we could make it there before it gets dark?" Astrid slid her elbows onto the table.

"Yeah, shug, it's only 5:00. You have plenty of time to get there. Just stay on Highway 40 until you hit Oklahoma State Highway 10 North and follow that until you see signs for Greenleaf."

"Wait," I reached across the table and grabbed a pen from the front pocket of Astrid's backpack, scribbling the directions on my hand.

"You can use my order pad, hun." The pale waitress reached into her apron and tore off the top sheet before handing it to me. "Once you get there, just look for state signs for hiking and such."

Her directions were thorough, and I'd had no idea we were

already so close to Oklahoma. "You go there often?" I asked, looking up from my hasty scribbles.

"We take the kids out there for picnics all the time!"

I nodded. "So they're short hikes?"

"Some of them." She cleared our plates and balanced them in the crook of her arm. "At the beginning of each trail, there's a sign that tells you about how far it runs and how steep. They make it real easy for ya."

"What do you think?" I hunched over the table and batted my lashes at Astrid.

"We can go anywhere you want." She stirred her tea with a straw.

"Yes!" I clapped my hands together and smiled at the waitress. "Thank you!"

"No problem." She giggled and raised her pitcher. "Would y'all like any more tea?"

"Can we get some to go, please?" Astrid flashed a mischievous grin.

"Sure thing, sweetie." The waitress piled the silverware on the plates and meandered into the kitchen.

"What?!" I straightened the two rolls of unused silverware on the table.

"Can't I just look at you?" Her head pivoted side to side, resting on the palm of her hand.

I turned away to hide my own grin before facing her with a blank expression. "I guess."

We both stared for a minute while my hands worked beneath her line of sight to rip the end from a straw wrapper.

Her shoulders sank. "You are too good to me."

"I'm glad you think so, because—" I raised the straw to my mouth and blew until what was left of the wrapper torpedoed toward her face, landing smack-dab between her eyes.

"You really know how to ruin something, you know that?" She wiped the area of her head where the projectile had made contact. "I have to use the restroom—I'm gonna cry." She laughed and stood from the table, covering her eyes and running toward the back of the building, where a small plaque read Restrooms over the opening to a narrow hall.

"Oh, come on!" I chuckled.

Moments later, the waitress approached our table, this time with a small black book. "You two are such a cute couple. You're very lucky." She laid the book on the table beside Astrid's pen. "My husband and I still want to travel someday. I wish we would have done it before we had kids." She brushed a stray curl behind her ear.

"Thank you!" My smile widened. "We actually just met a couple of days ago."

"Well, it doesn't seem like it. We've all been watching you from the counter; the way you look at each other and carry on, it's like you were made for each other."

I bit my lip to calm my cheeks and slipped a twenty-dollar bill into the sleeve to cover our fifteen-dollar meal. "Keep the change." I handed it back to her.

Her eyes widened. "Thank you!" She dropped the book into her apron.

A lock clanked in the distance, and as I glanced over, Astrid appeared in the entrance to the short hallway. "You ready?" She nodded toward the parking lot.

"That I am." I casually stood and stretched, slipped my wallet into my pocket, then made a dash for the door.

Before it could close behind me, she had squeezed through the narrow opening. "Where do you think you're going?" She diverged from my path and ran for the passenger's side door.

I hopped in the van and slammed the door shut. Just as my fingers grazed the lock, she pulled the handle and threw her forearms onto the seat.

"I almost made it!" I shook my fist in the air and grinned.

She blew the hair from her eyes. "You're not going to get away from me that easily." She chortled a creepy laugh and slunk into the van on her stomach.

I shifted into reverse and waited for her to climb in and close the door. "That wasn't weird." I smirked.

We pulled out of the parking lot and into the thinning traffic of the small town.

As I searched for signs to the highway, Astrid slapped her lap. "Shoot!"

I jumped. "What?"

"We have to turn around! I forgot my tea!"

"I'm not turning around for tea." I chuckled and adjusted my rearview mirror.

"Fine!" She slipped on her sunglasses. "Just pull over here!" She leaned forward and pointed at a white concrete building with a red stripe painted around it. "Wilco," she read off an old porcelain sign.

I slowed and steered into the grassy parking lot.

Astrid grabbed cash from the front pocket of her backpack. "Do you need anything?" she asked, straightening the bills out on the dash.

"No." I leaned back into the seat.

She zipped her bag, threw it behind our seats, then took off across the grass. Her bare feet slapped the slab of pavement that surrounded the pumps as she reached the door.

She was a distraction I couldn't pull myself from as I studied the bent heels of her sneakers on the floorboard and the sand on the dash where her feet had been. If it were anyone else putting their dirty feet on my things, I would have lost it. But with her, there was something calming about how comfortable she felt around me.

Minutes later, she pushed the door open with her back as a cowbell chimed from its handle, and she strode across the parking lot with two paper bags and a pack of cigarettes wedged between her arms. "Do you mind if I smoke in the van?" she asked as she neared the passenger's side.

I rubbed the back of my neck. "I'd rather you not."

"Okay, that's fine." She pulled a few beers from the bags and put them into her backpack. "Let me smoke one before we leave then." She smacked the cigarettes on the palm of her hand. "I haven't had one since we left Atlanta."

I was reluctant but agreed. She stepped away from the van so the smoke wouldn't filter in, and I kept my place in the driver's seat and turned on my phone to check my messages. Nothing. The only person who cared to see or speak to me was smoking her cigarette near a rusted-out dumpster.

"Astrid!" I yelled at the windshield as she often did whenever I left her in the van.

"What?"

"I miss you," I said, a little quieter than before, while staring at my reflection.

The grass rustled beneath her strides to the van, and she rejoined me. "I missed you too."

I saw my family when I stared at her. They were either done worrying about me, or worried sick.

You're too weak to find out.

"What?" She cocked back and blew smoke away from the van.

I shook my head and dropped my gaze, the orange bottle of pills catching my attention in the center of the dash. "Nothing."

"I'll make you a deal." She paused until I gave her my undivided attention, taking my eyes off the alluring bottle. "You quit taking those pills, and I'll stop smoking."

"I haven't taken many since we met!"

She smashed the half-smoked cigarette against the van's tire and rolled it up in the paper bag with the rest of the pack, then ran back to the dumpster before tossing it in. "You ready to go?" she hollered, popping open her door.

I nodded, a grin creeping onto my face. "I'll flush them at the next stop. I don't feel right throwing them out where someone could get ahold of them."

She climbed in and cracked open a beer. "Okay then. Let's go!"

When we finally reached McAlester, a sign directed us down a side road. The sunlight was fleeting, and most of the trails were gated off, but one sat distanced from the others. We parked on a patch of dirt that had been dug into the brush and stepped out of the van.

The beginning of the path glowed in a dull, warm light not much brighter than the stars that poked through a soft blue sky. I walked ahead into the shadows.

"You coming?" I asked.

A few steps later, she hadn't said anything. When I turned, she was standing with one hand out and the other on her hip. "I will not grace this path without a blessing." Her hair draped over her face, perfectly misplaced. The straps of her tank top hid beneath the ones on her backpack filled with beer.

I retreated and kneeled before her, kissing the top of her hand as her royal subject. "You are blessed to walk these grounds, Your Majesty." The smell of cigarettes lingered on her skin, the taste of its methanol poison seeping into my lips.

Poison. End. Don't get too comfortable.

Her Majesty didn't give me any time to reflect as she quickly withdrew her hand, hollering an evil laugh into the unknown hills. She took off through the trail, and I mindlessly followed her up a steady incline toward the top.

The drudgery of the climb was irrelevant. One obstacle after another, the march through fallen leaves and dirt morphed into a perilous caper through land mines and lava.

"What room can you neither leave nor enter?" she shouted with her arms stretched out from her sides, keeping herself centered on the bench's thin metal armrest beneath her.

"I don't know!" My laugh bought me time as I struggled to form an answer. My arms fought the current with invisible oars, rowing on a bench opposite hers.

"You'd better hurry! Your boat is sinking in the lava!" she said, now balancing like a tight rope walker on the back of the bench and coaxing me to row faster.

"Ah, uh. Ugh." Nervous laughter fell from my lips again.

"You're almost out of time!"

"Broom?"

"Not even close!"

"Headroom?"

"Better, but still no dice."

My gaze shot across the gravel floor to the trees behind Astrid. "Could it be … a mushroom?" I asked, hoping for mercy.

"YES," she said with her hands cupped around her mouth to imitate the sound of a loud speaker. "You may now exit the vessel in an orderly fashion."

I fell to the ground and rolled to safety near a water fountain, where leaves stuck to my forearms.

"Now ask me a riddle to deactivate the bombs on the ground beneath me!" she begged.

"But I don't know any riddles …"

"Make one up, or use one from when you were a kid!"

"Okay, um …" My mind scrambled as I flipped onto my stomach. "Someone goes eight days without sleeping; how do they do it?"

"They slept at night!"

Before I could liberate her from certain doom, she leapt off the bench into the chance of death.

"That's not fair! You knew that one!" I said while still lying on the ground, using my elbows to prop myself up.

"Everyone knows that one." She smiled and extended her hand, this time to pick me up.

Slightly defeated, I dropped my head to my chest and pulled myself toward her. She broadened her stance and tucked her elbows until I was back on my feet. As I cleared my clothing of any remaining debris, she moved on to the next thing.

Before I knew it, she had disappeared around a corner, where the shuffling of her feet stopped. Her heavy breathing grew still. I hurried around the bended growth of wood until I saw her standing small like a child, fifty feet from a large tree that clung to the crest of a hill. Its roots dove in and out of the grass, using all its strength to keep steady. A tire swing dangled beneath a canopy of limbs decorated in moss and leaves.

I caught up and stood silently beside her.

"Wow," she whispered.

I reached over until my pinky brushed hers. She turned her wrist, and our fingers intertwined. We moved past the end of the trail, our shoes kicking through full, thick grass, then we wove around the camber of brush onto an open field, past the swamping darkness and into the soft shades of earth. We stopped at the top of the hill and peered down at a modest town that was barely alive beyond the trench in which it existed. No one spoke, not even the burg. The three of us—the tree, Astrid, and I—sat in nature's silence.

As we approached the base of the tree, grasshoppers sang a rhythm while owls carried the melody. Branches dueled as clouds shifted the shape of the sky, hiding patches of fire that burned around the moon. A world sat completely undisturbed by the town below, content with being left alone. Astrid snapped the top of another forty-ounce can and chugged a good portion before she lay down on the grass, enhancing the feeling of being in the wild. The realness was overwhelming yet calming.

How could I turn something so temporary into something permanent?

An hour passed as her drinks disappeared one by one. Our conversations grew shorter while her tongue twisted her words. Effortlessly belonging to the moment, I drifted in and out of sleep, knowing we had nowhere else to be. She uncrossed her legs and fumbled onto her feet. Her ankles teetered and her breath slurred noises that fought for meaning as she moved to the edge of the hill.

"A perfect *home* does not exist!" she yelled as I stood and took a front row seat in the tire swing, her voice shaking into the sleeping streets below. "You have taken something beautiful and have made it ugly for convenience. Now all that's left is for everything to die and fall back to the way it began." Her volume swung in and out as she lifted her drink to her mouth, then dropped it back down to her chest like a microphone.

"Life is a blurred strip of film. You give it your all, and it just takes your will!" She hunched and glanced at me, then at the town. Tears now streamed down her face with sweat glistening on her forehead as she picked the scabs from her heart. She quieted and wiped her face before spinning around. I wasn't sure if she was blushing, drunk, or both.

"The strongest people know when they are weak," I said as I stood.

A smile crept onto her lips behind her frayed hair that partially covered her tear-soaked face. She rushed toward me in long, solid strides, almost like she was working up into a run. I tensed, and she threw her arms around me as if to never let go, knocking me into the swing.

"Zachary?" she said with a soft voice that crackled, her chest still pressed against mine.

The swing bounced against the back of my legs. "Yes?"

"Why'd you leave home?"

Though I knew the answer, I paused. I wasn't trapped inside my own body anymore like I had been when I left home.

"Because of a crazy urge."

Why does the truth feel so uncomfortable?

"Tell me about it," she said, stepping into a bed of clovers that spread like sheets in front of me.

"Uh …" I clutched the swing's rope.

You never fully committed to telling the entire truth; you found comfort in your lies.

She sat down in front of me, so I lowered myself and laid down on the clovers. After she rested her head on my stomach, I slid my hands to my chest.

"I, uh, I guess I was trying to put the worst behind me." I shifted my hand to her shoulder. "I knew it then. But I couldn't shake the heavy feeling that it might all be permanent."

"What was the worst?" Her finger traced circles on my chest.

"Nothing. It doesn't even seem that bad after hearing your story." I laughed.

She pulled her knees into her arms, repositioning her body perpendicular to mine. "Do you think there are any pawnshops nearby?"

"Probably. Why?" Her head bobbed on my stomach as I spoke.

"Because I want to ride bikes." She pouted and turned her head, emptying what was left of her drink into her protruding lips. "Are you ready to go?"

"I suppose."

She shot up from our unmade bed and urged me to close my eyes.

I did as she instructed, the sound of her kicking through the leaves growing distant. But a vision took control of my senses when the air, chilled by the rising moon, withered into the power of the sun.

An image of myself riding an old bicycle down a dusty dirt road rushed in behind my eyelids. A flower stood by itself in the center of the street, as if it wanted to stop me.

I squeezed the brakes, dragging the back tire through the dirt and rocks before dropping the bike on its side. Astrid rustled through bushes next to me, their sound swishing with the vision of switchgrass blowing in the wind around me. The flower grew alone on top of a lanky green body with a dirty orange mane and a scarred yellow face. It stood no more than five inches from the ground with its head hung and posture bent.

I stole inspiration from the dirt. My hands dug into my pockets for anything that might help the flower. Stored in the corner of my pocket like lint or extra string sat a seed. Watering the small pebble of life with my sweaty palm, I used my other hand to frantically dig into the road. A small mound formed around my fingers until my knuckles disappeared into the earth, where I dropped the seed and covered it back up.

Before I could take a full step back, the seed had already pointed a stem at the sky. As the new seed transformed from its broken shell and sprouted leaves, the lonely flower slowly straightened and brightened in color. Once the new life had fully developed, the air grew calm and gray.

I exited the vision as the hops lingering on her breath warmed my face.

"You can open them now." She stood with two fully grown and healthy flowers in her hand, the stems hanging from her grip like crooked teeth.

I didn't want to clutter her gesture with the irony.

She handed them to me and recovered the loose cans from the

grass, then led us back to the van. I kept a short distance between us as her unbalanced head silhouetted against a dark blue sky.

Thousands of people had probably been on that same swing before, but it was like it had been created for us, and the tire swing had grown from the tree itself. Like the moments there had been designed for us. Truthfully, it was the fear of comfort that pushed us away from the hill. The fear of letting too much of a good thing ruin what we had found in each another. Or perhaps it was fear of the place becoming comfortable, more so than the company. But it was out of our control; fear had become our reality.

Chapter 8

"How about we race to that old sign?" Astrid rode past me, each of us straddling bikes we'd found at a pawnshop not far from the trails.

"Do you really want to lose again?" I swerved between the broken yellow lane lines.

"Go!" She sped ahead of me.

I stood and dropped my weight onto the pedal to pick up momentum. "That's not fair!" I hollered. "Cheater!"

"I'm not losing another one!" Her bike wobbled as she threw a middle finger into the air before dropping her hand to the handlebars.

We grunted between eager spurts of laughter. She peeked back to gauge her lead. I was gaining on her but not quickly enough. She worked the pedals hard, sending the frame of her ride dipping left and right. The woven wicker basket on her handlebars crackled, and the rubber of her tires sizzled as they cut across the pavement. I flipped in and out of gears, searching for the best configuration. Before I could catch up, she leaned over her handlebars and passed the sign, throwing her hands into the air.

"Good race—cheater." I scrunched my face, letting off the pedals.

"A win is a win. Don't be sour, you silly boy." She braked in a dusty parking lot, where the old porcelain sign topped a metal pole. "Antique Attic," she read. "Do you want to go in?"

"Are they open?" I asked, squinting at the dirty windows.

"There's a truck here. I'm sure they are."

"I'm not sure if that truck runs, Astrid." I chuckled and swung my leg over the seat of my bike.

The truck was an old mold of rust, glass, and rubber. A Chevrolet logo had been stamped onto the tailgate between flared fender wells.

She glared at me over her shoulder and propped her bike against a column that kept an overhang in place above the front door of the weathered building.

I followed her lead. Abandonment faded as I pushed my bike toward the building. The cement slab beneath the overhang had been recently swept, and what had appeared to be a dark, dirty window proved to be remnants of tint and years of torture from the sun. The door was also peculiar; there wasn't a knob or lever that unlatched it but rather a knotted rope in its place and a single deadbolt.

The hinges ached when I pushed against the weathered wood, and the floorboards moaned while we stepped across its threshold. Inside, immaculately restored artifacts sat categorized on shelves and racks on an open floor. Tall cathedral ceilings hushed our breathing in a dull light. As we neared a counter with an old register and notebook that had the words Sales Log printed on the cover, the clattering of silverware and dishes chimed from the back of the building.

"Hello," I called out. "Is anyone here?"

Muffled voices echoed around the corner.

"Be right there!" a raspy voice answered above the sliding chairs.

Soon after, an older man dressed in a white button-up shirt with suspenders gaited down the aisle in front of an older woman in a light blue dress ending at her ankles.

"We were just sitting down for dinner and didn't hear you come in. Sorry." He nodded and spoke with an unfamiliar dialect.

"Can we help you?" The conservative woman spoke in a frail voice while she turned up the brightness on an electric lantern that hung over the mechanical register.

"We're only passing through. Sorry to disturb your dinner." I shook my head and stepped toward the door.

Astrid kept her place, clasping her hands in front of her. "Do you have any cameras?"

"Cameras? We have a few." The man teetered past a stack of old prints before breaking to the left with Astrid not far behind. "We don't carry anything electric or digital."

She gasped at the collection and then reached for her favorite design. It was a rectangular model that almost looked like a black canteen without the spout. "How does this one work?" She lifted the small box to her narrowed eyes.

"May I see it?" The old man held his hand out.

She passed it to him, and he removed a cover that exposed a lens fixed to an accordion-like mechanism. Then he grabbed a plastic flash from the shelf that slid into a track on the top of the camera.

"Say cheese," he said, pointing the camera at himself, then he snapped a picture with his tongue hanging out of his mouth.

Astrid's eyes widened when the camera clicked. "I need it." Her pitch lifted, along with the corners of her mouth.

The old man wound a crank on the top of it. "I'll sell it for forty-five dollars." He clasped the lens shut, then grabbed a hand-sized yellow rectangular box from the shelf. "You'll have to develop the pictures yourself, but I'll throw in the extra film; it's medium format," he said, handing everything to her.

"That's fine! I'm sure I can learn how!" Astrid slung her back-pack around the front of her chest and dug a wad of cash out. "You can keep the change for the extra film."

The old man nodded and took the money, delivering it to his wife behind the register. "So you two are just passing through?" he asked over the clang of the drawer as his wife processed the transaction. "Where are you headed?" He balanced against the counter.

"We're not quite sure yet ... west, I guess," I said, sharing a smile with Astrid.

"Well, dinner is about ready. Would you two care to join us?"

"We'd hate to impose." She slid beside me. "You've already been so generous!"

"Nonsense. We always cook too much anyway." The old man batted his hand.

"Well ... " She turned to me, fidgeting with the ends of her hair.

"If you insist!" I answered for her.

Astrid blushed and her shoulders fell.

We followed them to the back of the building, where a large cedar table with six chairs was set for two. The tiny kitchen was fully equipped with a gas-powered range and oven in the center of the side wall, and a sink sat to the right beside an old refrigerator. The old man took his place behind his chair, as did I, my mouth watering at the food centered on the table. Once both ladies were seated, the old man and I pulled out our chairs and joined them.

"You want to say grace, Jonas?" His wife clasped her hands on the table.

Astrid's eyes widened.

"Sure." He cleared his throat. "Let us bow our heads."

Everyone dropped their heads and closed their eyes. A few words into the prayer, I peeked at Astrid, keeping my head in place. A second later, she met my gaze. She shook her head and we both grinned. Before Jonas had finished, we closed our eyes again.

"Amen," we all spoke at once.

"Before we start eating," I cut in, "we'd like to introduce ourselves. My name is Zachary, and this is Astrid. Thank you so much for the meal." I extended my hand in the old man's direction.

"It does seem as though we have skipped formalities," he said, putting his palm into mine. "I'm Jonas Schrock, and this is my wife, Mary."

"It's nice to meet you," I said while Astrid and I both nodded.

Jonas let go of my hand and plucked a piece of piping hot bread from the loaf in front of him. "That is fresh!" He dropped the slice to his plate and licked his thumb.

"Just pulled it out of the oven." Mary grinned.

Astrid tucked her hair behind her ears and rubbed the edge of the table while the rest of us filled our plates.

"This is a really nice table," she said after a moment.

Jonas covered his smile with a napkin as he finished chewing his food. "Thank you!"

"He made it himself," Mary added while Jonas propped his head on the back of his hands.

"It's bur oak." Jonas knocked twice beside his plate. "It was struck by lightning years ago, so we had to clear it from the farm."

"Schrock? Isn't that Amish?" I asked, recalling a documentary I had seen. "Would this be considered an Amish-style table?"

"I was, and I guess it could be," he said before giving into a strong pause. "My family left the community." He wiped his mouth, then clenched the napkin in his fist and placed it back in his lap.

I shifted in my seat.

"I made a couple of steaks," Mary said, stabbing the smaller slab of meat with a large fork. "We can split them between the four of us if you'd like." She dug the sharp edge of a blade into the center of the steak.

I reached to the middle of the table for a glass pitcher filled with water and coated with condensation. "Oh, we're fine. This is more than enough!" I said, filling my glass.

Mary nodded.

"Have you always owned this place?" I passed the carrots to Jonas.

"No, no." He scooped a small heap onto his plate. "I was a pilot in the Air Force. Did you know the first bomb fell from a plane in mass warfare in 1911?" He pulled the second steak onto his plate. "Planes had a soft introduction in 1909, but the first big bomb was in 1911."

"Actually"—I cleared my throat—"I did know that."

"Ah." Jonas raised his brows. "Well then, maybe you have already made this connection. Now, I'm no conspiracy theorist, but don't you think it's odd that the first big bomb was dropped in 1911, only for planes to cause such destruction on 9/11, ninety years later?" He froze for a second. "The numbers are just too much alike!"

"Oh my." Mary shook her head and blushed. "Not at the table, Jonas."

I smiled at her. "It doesn't bother me. I was a history major in college. And that's definitely interesting, Jonas." I sliced my carrot with my fork. "But that was Italy in 1911. And wasn't it an aerial bomb over Libya during World War I?"

"Yeah." He reclined in his chair. "The numbers are similar is all. I don't really have any basis to connect the events, otherwise."

"So"—Astrid broke a piece of bread off the loaf—"how did you two meet?"

"Jonas was a farmer and my uncle was a distributor," Mary said. "I lived with my aunt and uncle in New York City. Such a fast-paced life." She paused.

"Her uncle brought her here on business," Jonas cut in.

"We kept in touch through letters, then I came to visit a year later. We were married before fall returned." Mary reached across the table and brushed the top of Jonas's hand, smiling at him.

He returned her affection.

"So are you from here, Jonas?" I asked.

"I moved here in the '60s when I got out of the Air Force. I bought all the land from the crossroad that you pass coming out of town to the dairy farms two miles from here and have lived off it since. Inheritance money." He brandished his knife like a wand. "So please, for the love of God, do not park your vehicle on the side of the road within that area!"

"Why not?" Astrid asked, leaning in with her arms hidden beneath the table.

"Oh, don't get him started!" Mary begged.

"Anyone that owns a farm will tell you that nothing bothers them more than when someone parks their vehicle beside their land. Anxiety. In today's day and age, you have to assume the worst, and I cannot afford crop circles—or a lawsuit."

My gaze shot toward Astrid, knowing that we used his land the night before to park the van and sleep.

Jonas cleared his throat. "So, what's your story?"

"Well, we—" I peered down at my knife smeared with butter.

"We're traveling the country. A little sightseeing before we have to grow up." Astrid relieved me with a smile. "I'm from Atlanta. I worked as a courier but want to go to school for photography."

"And I'm from North Carolina." I straightened in my chair. "I just graduated but worked at a hardware store prior to this trip."

She reached for my hands that were folded on the table. "We met at a concert in Atlanta. You could say that he stole me the moment he met me; he just didn't know it yet." She beamed. "We left a day later and haven't looked back."

Both of us chuckled at our half-truths.

"I've never really traveled," Mary interjected with a longing stare.

Jonas laid his napkin over his plate. "I've never had a taste for it."

Mary dropped her gaze to the table. "Astrid, help me with the dishes?"

"Sure." She stood with her plate in her hand, grabbing one of the serving dishes. "Thanks again for dinner."

After helping Mary clean up, Astrid and I headed to the middle of the parking lot and stood beneath a star-filled sky, like a couple of grasshoppers in a mason jar of fireflies.

Mary strode up behind us as Jonas locked the deadbolt to their store.

"Where are you parked?" he hollered from a distance before joining us.

"Over at the pawnshop. We bought our bikes there earlier." Astrid pointed down the dark street that we had ridden in on.

He clapped me on the shoulder. "That's at least four miles from here, and there are no streetlights! Jump in the back of the truck, and we'll drop you off."

I strolled over to it and gripped the edge of its bed, studying the wooden floor out of the corner of my eye while Mary climbed into the passenger's seat. "That would be great!" I pushed my palm against the metal body after I was satisfied with its safety.

We lowered the tailgate and put our bikes in, leaning them against either side of the truck. After nestling ourselves between the wheels with the tailgate down, I knocked on the back window, and the old truck rumbled to life.

Jonas and Mary were in no hurry to get us to our van. Still, the wind and engine bellowed too loudly to speak over, so we held hands and watched the street float away into the darkness. I soaked in those moments: the hum of the tires and engine, the hypnotizing redundancy of everything disappearing before my eyes. The world had lost its color after sunset while distance bled its hue from even the shadows, blending them together until the brakes of the truck whistled and we stopped beside my lone van in the parking lot.

We jumped out and walked around to the driver's side.

"Thank you again!" I said as Jonas worked the window crank.

"Why don't the two of you stay with us for the night? You can shower and get back on the road in the morning." His words spilled through his grin before the window could fully retract.

"Are you sure?" My body tingled at the thought of a good shower. "That would be amazing!" I shook his hand, then followed Astrid to the rear of the truck to pull our bikes out of the bed.

"Are you sure this is a good idea? We don't really know them," she whispered as I pulled her bike out and set it in front of her.

"It'll be fine!" I said, resting my hand on the crook of her back. "If you get uncomfortable for any reason, let me know and we'll leave."

She smiled, squeezing the brake lever on her bike repeatedly. "Okay. I'm just not used to all of this—the generosity, the care—there has to be a catch." She stared at her handlebars as she spoke.

"There's no catch." I calmed her hand with my own.

"Promise?" She lifted her head until the fear in her shining eyes reflected in the moonlight.

"I promise."

Chapter 9

We rounded a bend in a long dirt driveway, a large chandelier glowing from the underside of a second-floor porch in the distance.

"This place is beautiful." Astrid scooted to the edge of her seat. "I can't believe how big it is!"

"It's an old farm house," I said, ducking to get a full view as we bobbed down the drive. "They're always huge."

"It doesn't look old." Astrid leaned back while we followed their truck around the side of the house.

"I meant the style," I added.

Jonas made a U-turn and backed his truck into a barn that had hay spilling from a wide opening over its double-hung doors.

We grabbed our bags and got out of the van while Jonas finished backing in. The truck headlights died with the engine, and darkness took hold.

"This way." Mary hobbled past us toward the house and onto the back porch. "It looks like the bulb went out." She giggled and fit a key into an oak door before pushing it open. "I can never find that switch." She reached inside, groping the wall before flicking the lights on.

Wide-plank hickory floors spread from the entryway to a mud room that led to the kitchen, splitting the granite island from the mahogany dining table beneath evenly spaced recessed lights. The ceilings were far too tall to touch, even by jumping.

Toting our backpacks like misplaced tourists, we passed through the kitchen and dining area to a hall that connected to the foyer, where the bottom of the stairs met with the front door. Flowing white curtains hung above a darkly stained entry door, contrasting with the charcoal shiplap walls.

"Do you mind?" Astrid glanced at Mary, the toes of her shoes wedged between the floor and glass-paned French doors next to the stairs.

Mary curtsied. "Please."

I turned the handle and gave the door a nudge.

"Heaven." Astrid stepped ahead of me into the room, where the oriental carpets masked hardwood beneath a single chair and floor lamp. Filled bookshelves lined each wall from floor to ceiling.

The back door creaked. "Mary?" Jonas called out. Another door groaned and shut.

"In the study!" Mary answered, leaning into the foyer.

Heavy steps rumbled down the hall.

"You finished with the tour?" He met her outside the French doors and kissed her on the head.

"Just about," she answered, resting her hand on the banister.

"I got fresh towels and washcloths from the laundry room." He juggled the folded stack on his arm. "What do you think about the house?"

"There are windows everywhere! I love it!" I said, poking my head out of the study.

Astrid joined me. "Yeah! You really have a beautiful home."

"So glad you like it." Mary smiled. "Astrid, why don't you follow me to the bathroom you'll be using. Jonas will show Zachary to his." She put a hand on Astrid's back, lightly guiding her toward the stairs.

"Do we smell that bad?" I laughed.

"You could use a good wash." Jonas chuckled, arching his brows and gesturing to a door beneath the stairs. "The knob on the left is hot. Right, cold."

Astrid and I finished cleaning up about the same time and met downstairs at the screen door to the back porch. Jonas and Mary were sitting in white wicker rocking chairs that lit up beneath a new lightbulb and several bug-repellent candles. A pitcher of tea with plastic wrap covering its open top sat on a small table in the center, a deck of cards and poker chips stacked next to it.

"Do you two know how to play cards?" Jonas asked as he picked up the deck and shuffled it.

"I DO!" Astrid waved her hand in the air, swinging the door open with her free hand, her backpack slung over her shoulder.

I laughed and nodded before following her outside.

"We like to call this *Christian Poker.* The chips are your fake money." He glared up at us. "Never ever play with real money—too easy to lose yourself and your pants in the process." He gestured at a wicker sofa. "Take a seat."

"We don't have money to play with anyway!" Astrid squeezed between the coffee table and the love seat. "How did I not see this furniture out here earlier?"

Jonas split the cards once more. "It gets dark out here when the bulbs are out."

"Would either of you like some tea?" Mary stood and leaned over the table to refill Jonas's glass as we set our bags by our feet and sat down.

"Please." Astrid and I spoke simultaneously.

"Pinch, poke, you owe me a coke!" She pinched and prodded my tricep.

"Ouch!" I covered my arm and scooted away from her. "You're something else." I smiled while Jonas dealt the cards.

"Are you not playing, Mary?" I asked when Jonas skipped her.

Mary patted the bottom of her hair. "I like to watch. Reminds me of when Jonas would sit out here with the kids."

Astrid propped her head up on the palm of her hand. "How old are they?"

"Forty-seven, forty-six, and forty-three." Mary arched her back and put her hands on her knees. "I'll get the photo albums!" The wicker chair crackled as she stood.

"Poker and pictures?" Astrid clapped when Mary opened the door to walk inside. "You're going to spoil me!"

Mary turned and batted her hand at Astrid with a giggle, then disappeared into the kitchen.

"Place your ante." Jonas leaned over the table and gave Astrid and I both $200 worth of chips.

We picked up our cards.

I stacked a few chips and slid them to the center of the table. "Twenty-five for me."

Mary pushed the screen door open with her back, hugging a family album in her arms. "Zachary, do you mind switching me seats?" She scooted toward the table.

"Not at all!" I piled my cards into a single stack, moving to the chair beside Jonas.

"She's trying to play a game, Mary." Jonas laughed. "You'll distract her."

"No, no." Astrid smirked. "I can multitask! Please, sit!" She patted the cushion beside her.

Jonas sighed and moved thirty dollars' worth of chips to the center of the table.

"Sixty." Astrid added her chips to the pot, then leaned back beside Mary, who had already opened the album, propping it up on her lap.

"This was back when they were happy playing with sticks in the fields." Mary tilted her head. "They were having a paper airplane throwing contest, but the wind was too strong."

"Yeah, those were the good days," Jonas added. "Our children's generation is so worried about what everyone else is doing. If we cared what people thought like they do, we'd be miserable. I think we gave them too much." He set down a card and picked up another.

Astrid peered over her hand of cards. "Are they all happy?"

"They really are. They—" Mary started.

"I'd hope so." Jonas coughed. "They all went to the schools they wanted to, and they're all married, with good jobs and great kids."

"Here's a picture of all of us over the summer." Mary handed the book to Astrid and straightened her dress. "There are seventeen of us, including the grandchildren and spouses."

Astrid's brows tensed. "You didn't do too much," she said, delicately touching the picture.

The chirping crickets sang through a silence of reflection while Jonas's shoulders fell onto the back of his chair. My mind traced its memories to my childhood before we stopped having family reunions. Meanwhile, Astrid lived vicariously through the photo. She counted the cousins, her eyes sweeping across the page. "That's beautiful," she said under her breath.

"Astrid," I said softly. "It's your turn."

She snapped out of her trance. "Sorry." She shook her head and laid out a full hand of cards before raking in all the chips. "Royal flush."

"You've got to be kidding me!" Jonas laughed. "You want in on the next game, Mary?"

"Ladies have the luck tonight. Deal me in!" She scooted forward in her seat.

Three hours flew by, and the fun dwindled into yawns.

"I think it's that time." Jonas covered his mouth. "I'm partied out."

Mary chuckled, grabbed the tea tray, and slipped into the kitchen.

I sipped what was left of my tea and arched my back. "Yeah. I'm getting tired myself."

Jonas pulled out a briefcase from beside his chair and unfolded it on the table. We returned the chips to their designated spots, then he split the deck and stacked it in two separate piles. After grabbing our bags, we followed Mary inside.

Quilts and pillows lay folded on the counter beside two glasses of milk. "Jonas, why don't you put Zachary in Michael's old room. Astrid can stay in Anna-Beth's."

Astrid's eyes bulged. My shoulders sank.

We both picked up our glasses of unexpectedly warm milk and our blankets before following our hosts to our segregated chambers. The rooms were separated by the staircase, our doors standing directly across from one another.

"I'm making breakfast in the morning," Mary said, opening Astrid's door for her.

"The farm animals should wake you up in time." Jonas twisted the polished brass knob to my room.

"All right." I turned to Astrid as Jonas swung the door open. "I guess this is good night."

"Yep." Astrid pushed her pillow down with her chin, twisting enough to see me. "I guess so. Night."

Jonas and Mary met in front of their room at the end of the staircase that separated us.

I dawdled sideways into my room, feeling every step away from Astrid like a sharp rock in my shoe.

"Night!" Mary smiled, Jonas's arm hanging over her shoulders.

"Night," we both said, glancing at them and then at each other one last time.

I nudged my door shut with my foot and stood behind it. Seconds later, hinges squeaked across the hall ... and then again near the staircase.

I sighed and faced the room. White and gray sheets covered the bed, and gray floor-length drapes hung parallel to a cherry-wood bed frame and nightstand. I set the blankets on the bed and crossed the room to the drapes, then opened the window. Filling my lungs with fresh air, the stench of a chicken coop in the distance wafted in as the glass of milk warmed the palm of my hand. I twisted my wrist and emptied it into the boxwood below. An air conditioner pushed cool air against my shins. I bent down, closed the vent, and pushed the window up a little higher.

Without Astrid, the night held nothing for me. I crossed to the center of the room and fell on top of the bed while the wind gently tossed the curtains.

What was Astrid thinking about? Did she miss me?

I wanted to talk to her about Jonas and Mary, the dinner, the card game, and even the house.

A ticking clock hanging near the entrance echoed off the walls, causing my thoughts to grow louder until a hinge squeaked across the hall. I jumped out of bed, ignoring the clock as I pressed my ear against the door. Small thuds crept closer and closer to my room. I cracked it open.

"Astrid? Are you okay?" I whispered while she pulled the tail of her oversized shirt toward her knees, shuffling from side to side.

"Yeah. This house is just so big and creepy. Are you okay?"

"I'm fine." I shot a glance at Jonas and Mary's room. "What are you doing in the hall?"

"I—there was a—" She shuffled her feet and dropped her gaze.

"Do you want to hang out with me for a bit?" I pushed the door open a little further.

"Sure, if you want." She lifted her head, squeezing inside before hurrying to the bed. I gently closed the door and twisted the lock.

As I turned, Astrid stood near the head of the bed spreading the quilt, her panties peeking from beneath her shirt. My stomach flipped, and my pulse raced. She was so beautiful …

"Looks like we're sharing." She smiled, her shirt lifting as she bent forward to fluff the only pillow in the center of the bed. "What side do you want?" She climbed across the mattress.

"I like to be closest to the door." I ran my hand across my chin, the short bristles of my new beard scratching between my fingers.

"Okay." She bit her lip and curled up on her side.

"Should I turn off the lights?"

"Yeah, but can you turn on the lamp? I still want to see you."

"Sure." My voice cracked as I flipped the switch on the wall. I stumbled through the darkness to the nightstand and twisted the knob beneath the lamp shade. She lit up under its soft yellow glow like a Monet.

I crawled onto the bed and lined my nose up with hers on the other side of the pillow.

"How the children all worked on the farm with Jonas and Mary …" she whispered while her breath brushed against my lips. "It must have been a great feeling to be so close to each other."

"I know. Even now. Too bad there isn't a manual for making families like that." I smiled.

Astrid sighed.

"What's wrong?" I touched her elbow with the tip of my finger.

"Is it bad that I couldn't stand knowing you were across the hall and I couldn't see you?"

"Not at all." I cradled the back of her head with my free hand and scratched beneath her hair. "I was seriously about to go to your room myself." I laughed.

"I don't even want to think about not being able to sleep beside you." Her lashes fluttered before she dug her face into the pillow.

"Hopefully you'll never have to," I whispered.

Her irises, a kaleidoscope of blue, slowly reeled me in. Our breathing grew heavier. Our lips grazed, and goosebumps shot up beneath my fingers on the back of her neck. I slid my hand from behind her head and trailed it down her arm until it met her waist. Our lips touched again; she tasted like peppermint. I pulled her hips closer to mine and ran my hand up her spine. She gasped as I kissed her neck. I rolled on top of her, my arms straddling her shoulders with her legs wrapped around my back. I slowly gyrated, her bottom lip tucked between my teeth.

"Stop," she whispered, pushing her hands flat on my chest.

I sat back on my knees. "What? Are you okay?"

"Yeah, I just—let's slow down."

"Okay." My brows furrowed, and I rolled onto my side.

"I love kissing you." She leaned in, pecking my lips. "But I don't want to mess this up."

"It's okay." I shifted onto my back. "We would probably wake up Jonas and Mary anyway."

"Probably." She giggled and nestled on my shoulder near my chin.

Still, every now and again, we would give into quick kisses and then digress. She had substantial self-control, and I couldn't credit anyone but her for such discipline. It drove me wild to want her so badly. I loved and hated it all at once.

I leaned down for another kiss, but she lay still.

"Astrid," I whispered. "You awake?"

She groaned and smacked her lips.

I couldn't bear to wake her up, so I snuck out of the room and ran across the hall to her room, where the quilt sat folded at the foot of the bed. Again, I closed the vent, opened the window, and fell onto the sheets, a bit more complete than when I had woken.

Chapter 10

ASTRID!

My mind panicked, silencing the clamor of grappling leaves and distant livestock that drifted in through the open window. I jolted out of bed and cracked my door. The hall was empty.

"Astrid! Shit, shit, shit!"

I tiptoed as fast as I could around the staircase and opened the door to my room.

"Astrid," I whispered, slipping through the narrow opening.

She was sprawled out on the bed, her chest rising and falling with each deep breath, the blankets pushed off to the side.

I stepped closer as a beam of sunlight streamed through the window and warmed my body.

"Astrid!" I whispered a little louder, lightly shuffling to the window to close it and open the vent up.

I hopped onto the bed and nudged her shoulder. "Astrid!"

"What?" She waved her arm in the air.

"You fell asleep in my room!" I crawled to the head of the bed and sat beside her.

She shot upright and hoicked her knees to her chest. "Do they know I'm over here?"

"No. I slept in your room and snuck over here before they could notice anything. I didn't want to wake you last night." I focused on my hands and knotted my fingers.

She stretched her arms over her head, pulling her shirt up just above her belly button. Her chartreuse panties cut into her tan lines.

"You are too good to me." She stooped onto her knees, her shirt dipping into the arch of her back as she kissed me on the cheek and sat back on her feet.

In an attempt not to breathe too heavily, I stopped breathing altogether.

I kissed the top of her hand, her skin softer having lost its former taste of cigarettes. My fingers loosened around hers while her knuckles fell from sight.

"Astrid." I panned my head to the side. "I, uh …"

The staircase creaked and popped.

"Shh!" She held a finger up and cocked her head.

Light footsteps grew louder. She stiffened, her hands on my knee.

Floorboards cracked until a door in the hallway opened and closed.

I rolled off the bed and glided to the door, Astrid tracing my steps as she wrapped herself with an afghan that she had pulled from the bottom shelf of the nightstand. I freed the lock and cracked the door. "It's clear." I waved her into the hall and closed the door behind her.

Her tiny feet barely made a sound, but she didn't make it to her room.

"Well, good morning, Astrid!"

My stomach sank as Mary's muffled voice echoed through the door.

Astrid cleared her throat. "Good morning, Mary. How are you?" She pushed her voice an octave higher.

"Good, good. Hope you slept well. Is Zachary up?"

"Um, I'm not sure—I just woke up to use the bathroom. Is Jonas already downstairs?"

"He's collecting eggs for breakfast." Jewelry—presumably Mary's rings—clinked against the banister. "I should knock on Zachary's door to check on him. Food will be ready soon."

"I'll wake him up!" Astrid insisted as I slid toward the bed.

"Well … " Mary paused, forcing me to stop short of leaning back on the sheets. "I guess that's okay. Tell him breakfast should be ready in twenty minutes or so."

I remained still.

"Will do!" Astrid agreed.

A few seconds later, creaks descended the staircase.

"Zachary?" Astrid raised her tone and knocked on my door. "Wake up!"

I opened the door and checked the stairs from the corner of my eye. "Such composure." I grinned.

"You threw me to the wolves, you bastard." She laughed and marched around the staircase to her room.

I hurried to the bed, made the sheets, folded the quilt, and straightened the lamp on the nightstand. "I'll brush my teeth after we eat," I shouted into the hall, pulling my shirt down over my hips. "See ya downstairs."

"Okay!"she hollered as I rushed down the steps and into the hallway.

"Good morning!" I said while strolling through the kitchen door. Grease crackled on the stovetop as Mary slid a waffle onto a stack beside the stove. I stopped at the island bar that was topped with grits, tea, and an assortment of syrups.

"Where's Astrid?" Jonas said with raised brows, darkening the doorway to the back porch with a basket of eggs dangling by his side.

I picked up the bowl of grits, starting toward the table. "She's still getting ready."

"No, I'm not!" Astrid yelled, her bare feet padding down the stairs. "Sorry! Sorry!" She hurried down the hall, then took the grits from my hand and set them in the center of the breakfast-nook table.

"Well …" He shook his head. "Eat what you want; the rest will go to the animals."

"Eggs are scrambled." Mary turned with a sizzling pan in her hand, sprinkling shredded cheese over the yellow eggs with the other. "I hope that's okay!" She then scraped them into a bowl with a spatula.

"That's okay with me!" I said.

"And I've got more if we need them." Jonas lifted the basket and set it on the counter. "Sit! Sit!" he said, shooing us to the table.

I grabbed the napkin rack, syrups, and seasonings off the counter, and Astrid took the bowl of scrambled eggs from Mary. We lined everything up in the center of the table and took our seats.

"What are your plans for the day?" Mary turned to Astrid with a plate of tenderloin.

"I'm sure this is amazing"—Astrid took hold of the plate and passed it to me—"but I don't eat meat."

"Don't mind if I do!" I said, using my fork to pick a few pieces from the plate before passing it to Jonas.

"We were going to get back on the road here shortly though," Astrid continued while she poured syrup onto her waffles. "We've done our best to not have a schedule, but we also try to keep moving." She set the syrup back on the table and cut into the soft, yet crisp, cake.

"What are your plans when the trip is over?" Jonas asked, raising a glass of sweet tea to his mouth.

We gawked at each other. "We don't know yet," I said as I reclined in my chair, resting my forearms on the table.

Astrid glanced at Jonas, then at me, then at Jonas again. "But that's why we're taking the trip anyway, isn't it? To figure it all out."

Jonas hid a smile in his cheeks as he cleaned the last bit of cheesy scrambled eggs from his plate. "Well, I'm full!" He pushed his dish away and rubbed his stomach.

Seconds later, he stood and dropped his napkin onto his plate. "Zachary, do you mind meeting me outside when you're done? I need help with something before you go."

"Sure!" I tilted my head.

"Thanks!" He stepped back and scooted his chair under the table. "I'll be in the barn," he said before tottering out the back door. I turned to Mary.

She covered her mouth with her napkin while she finished chewing. "Just leave your plate; Astrid and I can clean up."

"No worries," I said, reaching for Jonas's empty plate. Mary smiled, and Astrid chuckled, dipping her spoon into a bowl of grits.

The barn wavered in the heat as I tracked a line of flattened grass to it, where Jonas stood with a map stretched out on the hood of his truck and an envelope poking out from beneath his coffee cup.

"This is a map from the early '60s," he said when I approached. "I doubt most of these roads still exist." He turned and admired the vintage art. "These lines here trace the routes that Mary and I traveled between here and New York." He grazed the faded pen ink near the Atlantic. "Over here"—he swung his pointer toward the West Coast—"I found where my brother moved to. He and I haven't spoken since our father died when we were young." He gritted his teeth and wiped light sweat from his forehead with the back of his hand.

A blue star covered a space next to the West Coast better known as Eugene, Oregon. Jonas pried at his words but took a few moments to collect his thoughts. "Do you plan to go through there at all?"

"I don't know." I lifted my chin and patted the scruff down where my beard had ended. "I'm not sure if we can afford traveling that far."

"Oh. I see." His lip curled inward. "I'd hate to ask this of you, but could you do me a favor if you ever make it out there?"

I paused for a moment. "Sure. Yeah."

Jonas pulled the envelope from beneath his cup and handed it to me. "It's a letter for my brother, Amos John Schrock."

"Couldn't you send it in the mail?" I asked. "Astrid and I could drop it off on our way out."

"I've tried to contact him over the years, but he hasn't responded, and I didn't want to drag my family into this," he admitted into the palm of his hand. "Everyone has their secrets. I'm just tired of carrying the weight."

I was at a loss for words and hesitant to accept the responsibility. He folded the envelope into thirds.

"Why bring me into this, then?" I asked, balancing against the truck.

"Mary doesn't know that I have a living brother, and it would bother her to no end if she did. My kids don't know either. I decided a long time ago that I'd never bring it up unless I was sure he'd want to meet them. Why bother them with something I can't change?"

He rambled, retreating further into the barn. "Just—look. If you want to, you can read it before you deliver it. I'd rather you didn't though." He stepped forward and held the folded envelope up to my chest. "But if you must, please wait until you're out of Oklahoma. It explains everything."

I dropped my head. His hand shook in front of me.

"I'll deliver it if I end up there." I slipped the letter from his fingers and slid it into the back pocket of my shorts. "But I have a question."

"What's that?" Jonas slowly dropped his hand.

"After all these years, why didn't you ever go out there yourself?"

He folded up the map, then took a heavy breath, interrupting it with a cough. His eyes shifted until he pressed them closed with his thumbs. "I'm not strong enough to be rejected by him again." His voice shook uncontrollably.

"It's okay." I patted his shoulder.

He opened his arms and pulled me into a hug.

"It's okay," I repeated.

His tears bled through my shirt, pasting it to my shoulder. He heaved and sobbed for what was probably the first time in years.

Chapter 11

"It's been so nice having you two around!" Mary said, hugging me on the back porch.

"Thank you for having us!" I straightened when she let go, the sharp corners of the nagging letter pressing into my thigh.

"Mary!" Astrid said, letting go of Jonas and stepping in front of me.

Picking at my elbow, I crossed my ankles and shuffled sideways to Jonas.

"Be safe out there," he said, offering his hand.

I studied it and the redness on his cheeks before placing my hand in his. "Will do."

Jonas and Mary held each other as we weaved around the wicker furniture toward the barn. After starting the engine to the van, I made a three-point turn, and like the house I had grown up in, the farm sunk into the rearview mirror. Similar to my visions, the reality of it all was intangible.

What did the letter say? Would his brother accept it after having denied it so many times before? Maybe the letters had been going to the wrong place. I didn't want to hide anything from Astrid but thought it best not to share the details of their feud until I was surer of the situation … if at all.

You probably won't make it that far anyway.

I realigned the mirror with the top of the seat, then turned my head. "Can you get the map out of the glove box?"

She dropped her feet from the dash and popped the latch open.

"CONTRABAND!" she yelled, pointing at the folded paper still wrapped in plastic. "How could you? Where did you get this?"

"I'M JUST A MAN!" I cried. "Oh, and I got it at a gas station. I thought it would be more authentic than using my phone."

"I'm disappointed," she said, cutting through the plastic wrap with her fingernails. "What do you want me to do with it?"

"Draw a line from here to Oklahoma City," I said, digging inside the center console for a pencil and passing it to her.

She unfolded the map on her lap and traced over it with the pencil's eraser. "Where is here?" She glanced up, spotting a city limit sign in the distance. "Ah!" She dropped her gaze to the map. "It doesn't look like we're too far." She scribbled a short curvy line across the waxy paper, then folded it and set it on the dash before leaning her head against the window.

The van rocked from side to side when I turned, following the signs back to the highway.

"Oh my god!" She gasped, pressing her hands against the glass.

I let off the gas. "What?"

"Did you see that old park?"

I stretched, straining to see past her head. "No."

"Turn around!" She smacked the window. "I need to take pictures!"

I pressed the brake and pulled onto the shoulder of the road for a car to pass, then made a U-turn.

"Pull in right here!" She pointed at a small building layered with a skin of vines. The drive was narrow and deep with ruts of hardened mud.

"I can't pull up much further," I said, stopping before the van bottomed out.

"This is fine," she said, frantically fishing through her bag for her camera.

I scooted forward in my seat. "This is kind of creepy."

"Maybe." She zipped her backpack. "But look at that sun." Her bag dropped to the floor, and she swung the door open and pranced through the weeds to a swing set.

I got out of the van as her silhouette masked her body running into the rising sun.

She crouched until the tall grass met her shoulders. I rustled through the brush toward her, the clicking of her camera snapping over the swishing of my steps.

"Isn't it weird how there is a ton of grass here and then on the other side of the park there is almost no grass at all?" I stopped beside a large rusted spring that stuck out of the ground behind her. A faded yellow ceramic duck lay hidden in the brush beside it.

Her camera clicked.

"Do you think this will show up on film?" She dropped to her knees.

"Why wouldn't it?"

"Too bright?" She wobbled. "I like to take pictures where the sun seems small enough to be active in it." She stood and wiped her knees with the back of her hand. "But I've never used a camera like this, so I don't know how it'll turn out. All I know is that it only works at a certain point in the sunrise or sunset on my old cameras."

"So what did you take a picture of just now?"

"You see the wooden swing seat that's broken in the middle?" She hunched, squinting and pointing to it. "Not the one that's completely broken. The one that's still connected." She walked up to it, wrapping her fingers around the rusted chain that dropped to a splintered plank. "I took a picture as if the sun were sitting on the swing, like the swing was breaking beneath the weight of the sun."

I kneeled next to her. "This is amazing." I lost myself in her vivid world.

She didn't say anything, and I focused on her vision.

"Let's go!" When I didn't move, she nudged my back.

I fumbled in the dirt. "Are you serious? I'm gonna get ya, girl!" I hopped up and chased her to the van, catching up before she could reach her door.

"Help!" She giggled while I wrapped arms around her waist. "HELP!"

"No one can hear you!" I jerked her against me. "You're all mine!"

"Oh yeah?" She twisted in my grip until my hands slid to her hips.

"Yeah." I pulled her in a little closer, the camera dangling from her fingers.

I leaned in. She lifted her chin. Our lips locked, and though the kiss was small at first, it quickly grew. I shoved her against the flat nose of the van as she set the camera down and wrapped her hands around the back of my head. Her legs spread around my waist.

"Zachary," she said under her heaving breath.

I kissed her neck, my fingers digging into the bottom of her thighs.

"Oh my god."

Wind blew, tossing her hair until it caught on my tongue. I backed off to clear my mouth.

"It's a sign." She smiled, patting me on the chest.

"A sign for what?"

"That we should slow down." She dropped her legs to the ground, then kissed me on the chin.

I groaned. "You're killing me!"

She wrapped the camera lanyard around her neck and jumped into the van while I leaned against the grille with my head hung low.

"Let's go!" She beeped the horn.

Chapter 12

"It's such a nice day!" Astrid stuck her hand out the window. "Let's ride bikes!"

"We're so close to the city though!" My eyes flitted to a mile marker on the side of the road. "We've only been on the road for an hour."

"What are you in such a hurry for?" She pouted, pushing her shoulders into the seat.

"Fine!" I laughed, taking the next exit.

Not far ahead of us sat a local drugstore. I slowed and pulled into the middle of the parking lot. Astrid had the side door rolled open before I could hop out and pass the front bumper. She climbed in and lifted her bike out.

"Can you grab that, and I'll get yours?" She nodded at the handlebars, balancing the frame with her hand.

I picked up her bike and leaned it against my thigh until she pulled mine out.

"Which way do you want to go?" I asked, grabbing my bike with one hand and pushing hers to her with the other.

She shut the door to the van and took her bike. "Away from the highway."

"Should I bring my backpack?" I tilted my head.

"We can share mine. I want to take my camera." She tightened the straps beneath her arms. "I'm hiding some of my money in the van though. It's not safe to carry it around like I've been doing."

"Sounds good to me!" I opened the door for her. "I've got my wallet. That's all I need anyway."

She slid the back door open and popped the grille off one of the speakers, then rolled her cash up behind it and hammered the grill into place with her fist. "That should do it," she said before locking the door and slamming it shut.

"Cool!" I swung my leg over the frame of my bike and took off ahead of her.

Most of the roads shouldered dead-end signs, while others proved to be nothing more than long driveways, much like Jonas and Mary's. We followed our shadows until we found a synthetic pond dug around the bulky roots of a large live oak not far from the main road. We parted from the pavement, dropped our bikes near a shallow ditch, and raced to the small body of water.

"Are there alligators in Oklahoma?" Astrid said in a loud whisper, bending over the reflection of a crooked piece of metal that held a naked lightbulb beside her.

"I don't know. Don't get too close!" I tugged on the back of her shirt. "I hate reptiles! They freak me out!"

"But they're still cool to see!" She fought back, stretching the fabric of her shirt to lean further over the water. When she crouched, I let go.

Fifteen feet from Astrid, a plastic bag sunk between short blades of grass. It looked like the same type of unsealed bag we had filled with feed at my uncle's farm when I was little. I crossed over to the bag and stooped. Sure enough, it was full of small brown pellets exactly like the ones we'd used to feed his catfish.

I gripped the bottom of the bag and slung the feed across the water. The ripples didn't even have a chance to settle before larger splashes took over.

Astrid gasped and stumbled backward into a frantic crabwalk. "What *is* that?"

I doubled over in hysterics.

"What's so funny?" She glared at me, then faced the water again. "Oh my god, are those fish?" She stood and spun to face me.

Struggling to catch my breath, much less speak, I nodded.

"They're huge! What did you do?"

"I found fish food and threw it out there."

"You're such a jerk!" She covered her cheeks with her arm, concealing her smile.

"I know!" I winked. "I think this is a catfish pond. There's probably food for sale somewhere around here."

I turned in place until I spotted a bank of coin-operated machines standing next to the main entrance, which we had completely overlooked. Change itched in the corner of my pockets as we sprinted toward the pellet-filled machines.

"Hold your shirt out like this!" I webbed the bottom of mine between my hands. She followed my lead, and we piled in the feed until the fabric lapped back to our stomachs.

We waddled back, and I threw a handful before we neared the shore. Astrid, on the other hand, teased the fish, only throwing a pellet or two at a time. "How do they know that's food? You can't smell under water!" She stood with her mouth partially open, another pellet falling through her fingers.

"I would think they're conditioned at this point since almost everything thrown into the water is food." I chucked a handful into the rippling water at the center of the pond. "But they actually have sensory organs in their skin."

"That is so weird!" She smiled at the open water.

"Let me have some of your food!" I dropped the end of my shirt. "I'm out."

"Go get your own!"

I dug into my pockets. "I only have two quarters left!"

"No!" She twisted away from me when I stepped toward her.

"Fine!"

I climbed the shallow dip from the shore and made it across the field to the street. My breathing hitched slightly as I picked up speed, eagerly rubbing the quarters between my fingers. After reaching the bank, I fit them into the coin slot one at a time, twisted the knob, and filled my palm with feed.

Like a little boy, I charged with a grin through the summer air to where Astrid stood and threw everything I had left. The whiskers of the butting heads tangled one last time before they disappeared. When my fun was over, I faced her with puppy-dog eyes.

"No!" she yelled, cupping the remainder of the pellets in her hand over the water.

"Don't you do it." I laughed.

"Don't take another step, or they're goners! I'll do it! I'm crazy."

"Now, Astrid." I raised my hands, inching closer. "Let's talk ab—"

"Aaaahhh … " She cut me off with a drawn-out cry that was no louder than my own voice and tossed the food into the water. Her throw was strong, shaking her balance, but she stood undefeated with her feet pointed inward and hand still cupped from the pitch. Again, I burst into laughter, but she held in hers until the rippling pond settled.

Soon, our merriment held no meaning: it was effortless and pure. Simple and finally in reach. We lay in the grass between the pond and the street, holding hands. There wasn't much left to do, but we weren't bored with the silence. There was an unmistakable communication when we touched.

"What are you doing?" she asked as my fingers slid beneath the hem of her shirt.

I circled her belly button. "I want to feel the butterflies!"

"You are so cheesy!" She giggled. "That'd better be all you're feeling."

We stayed at the pond for a couple more hours before grabbing our bikes from the ditch and heading back into town. She wore the lanyard of her camera like a necklace for the rest of the day and even later that evening when we stopped for food.

"Let's sit next to the window so we can people watch," she said, walking ahead of me to a red vinyl booth with a white table.

My shoes squelched across the sticky floor. "This place is kind of dirty … "

Astrid tossed her bag into the booth. "Reminds me of home," she said, her thighs skidding as she slid across the worn vinyl.

"Mmm." I pulled out a napkin from the dispenser on the table and wiped the seat before sitting.

She paid me no mind, gazing out the window at the other side of the street.

I shifted closer to it from my side of the booth. "What are you looking at?"

"Do you see that open dumpster in the parking lot over there?" She pressed her finger against the glass.

I craned my neck to see around a light pole in the distance. "Yeah. What about it?"

"It looks like the sun is falling into it." She lifted her camera to her face, then climbed onto her knees, bobbing to line up the shot.

"May I get you two anything to drink?" a bony waitress with a long face asked as she neared the table.

"Oh. Uh … " My cheeks reddened. "Water."

"Yeah, water please." Astrid lowered the camera and twisted to give the waitress a half-cocked smile, then turned back to the window. "I have an idea!" She plucked a dead fly from the window sill.

I sank in my chair.

"All right." The waitress tilted her head, staring at her, then slipped her pen into her hair and walked away.

Astrid sat down and opened her backpack. "I know I have string in here somewhere." She pulled out an old pencil pouch. "Here we go!" She unzipped the sack and wrapped a thin black thread around her finger before snapping it off the spool with her teeth.

"What are you doing?" I asked, losing my sense of care for prying eyes.

"Setting up an illusion photo." She flipped the fly onto its wings and wrapped the string around its torso. "I don't want to slice it in half by pulling the string too tight." She dipped her head until her eyes were level with the fly. Then she tied a loop loose enough to fit around its stomach, nudging it between the wings and back.

"Here are your waters," the waitress said as she clunked two plastic cups onto the table, her lips curling. "Are you ready to order?"

I glanced at Astrid, who paid us no mind.

"No, not yet," I said while she carefully lifted the other end of the string until the fly was level with the window.

"Actually"—Astrid froze and turned toward the waitress—"can I get a loaded baked potato without bacon?"

"We don't serve baked potatoes."

"Grilled cheese and tomato soup?" She smirked.

The waitress nodded and scribbled on her pad. "Sure." Then she turned to me. "And you?"

"Can I do the same, but with chili instead of soup?"

"Yep." The skinny woman gathered our menus and strode back to the kitchen.

Astrid turned back to the window, the fly dangling before her face with its legs pointed at the ceiling. She tied the other end to the window lock, centering the tiny body on the six-inch by eight-inch pane of glass.

"Do you see it?" She snapped the picture and lowered the camera.

I swayed from side to side to line up the scene. "Not from here."

"Lean across the table!"

She scooted back in her seat, and I propped myself up with my palms.

"Line the fly up with the bottom of the sun."

I closed one eye and did as she said. The fly appeared as though it were catching the sun and dragging it in to the dumpster.

"You really have an eye for these things!" I spoke slowly, imagining the rage that fly must have felt to dismantle an entire source of life.

Her camera clicked beside me. "Thanks," she said and spun the film.

Once our dinner had settled, Astrid packed her bag, and we left. The last minutes of daylight shone along the narrow streets just outside of Oklahoma City, the streetlights flickering on as we pedaled to the drugstore. We surrendered to a lull and took our time while the moments painted themselves into our memories.

Darkness void of shadows spilled onto the asphalt of the parking lot three light poles away, concealing its lines. Our vision strobed in and out between bulbs.

"Can you see the van?" I stood on my pedals and hunched over the handlebars.

"We're too far away," she yelled behind me.

I pedaled harder, my tires skipping the pavement when I cleared the small bump to the drug store.

Were my eyes playing tricks on me? Why were the lights off?

I blinked twice, then widened my gaze.

"It's gone!" I bellowed, squeezing my brakes at the lamppost where the van had been parked earlier that day.

"You're joking." She stopped beside me, straddling her frame.

I threw my bike to the ground and clenched my hands, pacing to the other side of the lot and back to be sure.

"Fuck!" I slammed the bottom of my fists against the pole. The light above me finally flickered on, illuminating tiny shards of glass. "FUCK!" My stomach churned. "We should have headed straight to Oklahoma City like I wanted to." I circled my bike, which lay on its side against the pavement.

"Do you think it got towed?" she asked in a spark of optimism.

"I hope so." I dug my eyes into my arm against the pole. "Is the place we ate at open late?"

Astrid hesitated to answer before nodding. "Yeah! I remember a twenty-four–hour sign on the window."

I lifted my head and massaged my eyes. "Let's go over there and see if they have a phone we can use. Mine was in my backpack, which was in the van." I shook my head. "I can't believe you made us stop. We were so close to the city."

I couldn't even look at her. I stepped over the glass, picked up my bike, and took off onto the road. Astrid's chain rattled as she followed, crossing the bump from the parking lot into the street.

I pedaled harder. My skin itched, sweat cascading from my pores. A neon sign lit the front of the restaurant. I coasted into the parking lot and leaned my bike against the building beside the window where we'd eaten earlier. Astrid hadn't caught up yet, so I continued inside without her.

"Booth or table?" A waitress with an old-fashioned apron that made her look like a nurse strode up to me with a menu in hand as Astrid's bike clinked against the window outside.

"Actually," I said over the bell jingling above the door, "can we use your phone to call local tow companies? I left my van parked at the drugstore earlier, and it's not there."

"There's only one wrecker in town. I have their number right here." She pulled her cellphone from her apron and started scrolling through her contacts. "Do you have something to write with in case you need it again later?"

I patted my shorts before my mind slowed, and I shook my head. "No. Do you have anything I can use?"

"I have something." Astrid sighed, bumping my arm as she brushed past, dropping her bag on the closest table. "What's the number?" She yanked out a sketchbook and pencil.

The waitress handed me a cordless headset and read the number aloud, rubbing a faded tattoo of a cherry on the side of her neck.

"Thanks." I dipped my head and met Astrid at the table where she'd set her bag, then dialed the number.

"Joe's Garage," a raspy, low voice answered.

"Hi, I was calling to see if you picked up a van from the drugstore earlier?"

"No, sir, we haven't towed anything all day. Are you sure you have the right place?"

I tapped the back of the phone with my finger. "I'm at Lantern's Late-Night Diner. My van was at the drugstore just up the street, but the waitress here said you were the only tow service in town?" I tucked my bottom lip between my teeth.

His deep voice hesitated. "I'm sorry. It's not here. Do you need the number for the sheriff's office?"

My stomach sank. The van *had* been stolen. I grabbed the pen and pad from Astrid and glared at her. "Yeah. May I please get that from you?"

Chapter 13

Our clothes dried over the shower rod in a motel coursed with stale air a few blocks from the drugstore. Astrid hadn't spoken to me since we'd met the sheriff to report the theft.

You said it was her fault. Why would you say that?

I splashed my face with a handful of cold water, wiped off with a towel, then wrapped it around my waist. My feet stuck to the tile, leaving prints across the floor as I made my way into the main room. Astrid lay with her back to me, her naked body wrapped with the only sheet in the room, leaving me with an itchy comforter and a narrow spot on the bed that tapered at her knees. Though her eyes were closed, her body tensed as I crawled onto the mattress. She definitely wasn't asleep.

I tossed the towel onto the floor beside me and flipped the comforter over so the coarse cotton and nylon couldn't irritate my skin before situating myself as close to the edge of the bed as possible.

Hours passed, and I didn't toss or turn. I didn't shed any more air from my lungs than I had to. As she slept, I obsessed. I had been arrogant, but guilt was tracing a line of chalk around my body. The longer I lay there, the less I felt the need to sleep at all. Instinct urged me to get comfortable in my failure.

Anyone can be a coward.

I stiffened to the relentless shape of the mattress.

You've yet to bring anything good to this world.

Light peeked through the gray morning sky into the open window.

Insurance money! The thought hit me like a shot of adrenaline.

I tossed off the comforter and snuck into the bathroom. Loose wrinkles were still visible as I pulled my shirt from the rod and slipped the damp fabric over my shoulders.

Get her breakfast.

I bounced on the balls of my feet and pulled my shorts up without even bothering to button them before slipping on my shoes.

After scooting out of the bathroom over to the dresser and plucking the police report from it, I glanced at her one last time. A thin white blanket hid the shape of her body, her face covered by a shadow cast by the curtains.

I will fix this.

I crossed the room to the door, which squeaked upon opening it, and I crammed myself through the small gap before softly closing it behind me.

A car zoomed past the crumbling entrance of the motel. I followed the sound of its exhaust to the street.

An All-Mart sign glowed a couple hundred feet away in the dull morning light. I trailed a car that passed to the large white concrete building until it turned and its taillights receded into a range of hills. I sped across the street to the store's almost-empty parking lot. My reflection grew in the tinted windows of the sliding glass doors stamped into an arched facade of brick.

"... needed in electronics," a man's soft voice said through the intercom as the doors gave way and I stepped inside onto a black spongy rug.

What does she like?

I grabbed a handbasket and sauntered toward the produce section.

"Strawberries," I said under my breath, reaching for a container of them and dropping it into my basket. I shuffled further into the store where coolers held the yogurt. "Original, vanilla, peach ... " I said again, browsing through the fogged glass. "Ah. Vanilla with granola." I opened the cooler, its chilled, fan-driven wind spreading goosebumps across the back of my arms and under my damp shirt. I quickly grabbed the yogurt, then let go of the door and rubbed the bumps down with my hand.

A woman walked by with a school-aged boy hanging off the front of her cart while he played with the clothes that dangled from hangers inside it.

She stopped in the middle of the aisle a few feet from me. "Do you want new clothes or not?" She stomped her foot, her sandals clapping against the floor.

"Yes! Sorry, sorry, sorry!" He hopped off the cart and covered his mouth with a plastic pterodactyl.

An orange sales tag covered the price of a pair of shorts in her cart: six bucks.

You can afford that.

Her cart lurched forward again, and I took off in search of the clothing section.

Mid-Summer Sale and Clearance signs dangled from the ceiling, some twirling in the breeze of air-conditioning.

I walked down the first aisle in the women's section. Shorts, shorts, shorts. I passed bikinis and dresses before stopping at the shorts. I picked a pair from a rack like fruit from a tree and held them up, comparing the size to Astrid's shorts from the night before when I'd washed our clothes in the motel room sink.

These are too big.

I hung the shorts up and meandered further into the racks and shelves to the far wall, where the smallest pairs lay folded on a table beneath a pile of larger sizes. I scraped them up, grabbed a pack of undershirts, underwear, and socks … then wandered into the men's section and did the same thing for myself. I even found a backpack for ten dollars to replace my stolen one.

A stocky cashier scanned my items while I packed my clothes into my new bag, his mass of curls bobbing with each movement.

"Do you have a phone I can use?" I asked when the card reader beeped my approval.

"A manager would have one." He ripped my receipt out of the printer and grabbed the microphone off a snake stand beside him. "Cheryl, customer assistance needed at register eight. Cheryl." His monotonous voice amplified as if he were speaking into a tin can through the store's intercom.

"How can I help you?" A blonde woman approached us before I could pick the bag of strawberries and yogurt up from the aluminum counter.

"Yes, ma'am." I spun to greet her, hoisting my bag onto my shoulder. "I just need to use a phone. Mine was stolen yesterday."

"Ah." She bent over and picked up a trampled receipt from the ground. "Follow me, sweetie. You can use the store line."

We strode to the other end of the store down a short hall to her office.

"What's the number?" She picked up the receiver and held it to her ear.

"It's Hurst Insurance." I pulled my wallet out and handed her the insurance card. She then punched in the numbers and handed me the headset.

After retrieving the theft report from my pocket, I unfolded it on her desk.

"Hurst Insurance. How may I help you?" a woman's voice answered.

"Yes, I'd like to make a claim."

I trotted across the street between passing cars into the motel parking lot. The curtains to our room were drawn, and the bed was unmade.

"No, no, no!" I pressed my face against the glass and scoured the room for any signs of her.

I slid the keycard in, jerked it out, and knocked the door in with my shoulder.

The shower hissed from the bathroom, water slapping the tub floor. I slouched and sighed. I set the yogurt and strawberries on the dresser in front of the television, then laid her clothes out on the bed.

The shower knobs squeaked and the pipes knocked as I zipped my backpack. Moments later, the bathroom door burst open. Astrid rushed out in her old white T-shirt and red gym shorts.

"Oh." She stopped mid step, pulling a white towel tight between her hands. "You're back."

"Yeah. I got breakfast." I stepped over to the dresser and tapped the pack of strawberries.

"I'm not hungry." She rubbed her wet hair with the towel. "I want to get on the road before it gets too hot."

"On the road?" I rubbed my forehead. "How is that going to work without the van?"

"There's nothing going on in this town. I'm heading to the city … it'll be easier to figure things out there." She picked up her shoes and sank onto the edge of the bed, glaring at the package of shirts that I had set out for her. "What's this?"

"I grabbed us some clothes too."

"Ah." She pulled the heel of her shoe over the back of her foot with a finger and stood. "I guess you plan on tagging along?"

"You want to eat first? I bought granola yogurt, your favorite."

She shook her head and strolled over to the door. "I'm fine." After grabbing her bike, she opened the door and walked it out onto the breezeway.

"I need to—" The door slammed.

I took the keycard out of my pocket and placed it on the dresser, then stuffed her clothes into my bag and grabbed a strawberry before sticking my head out the door. "Wait up!"

She had already reached the highway.

You're going to need those pills that you swore off to get through this.

I patted my pockets.

They'd been stolen with the van. "Shit!"

"Wait!" I shouted again, pulling my bike out of the room.

By the time we arrived in Oklahoma City, sweat replaced the clean water that had soaked our clothes only a couple hours before.

The thrum of Astrid's tires led the way, tracing the white lines through suburban neighborhoods and historical architecture. Finally, the shadows of bowed power lines jumped from post to post until the wire dove into the ground.

We rode past sporadic parking lots and struggling structures into the thickness of columned stairways and narrow avenues, pedaling along the shoulder of the road near sidewalks so closely that we brushed past pedestrians as they bulged from shops and markets.

"Shouldn't we get off our bikes and come up with a game plan?" I yelled, pushing a little harder to catch up.

She sank into a coast, the crank of her bike clicking when she spotted an empty post outside a coffee shop and slowed. Trailing her, I swung my leg over the seat of my bike and hoisted it onto the sidewalk.

"So, what do you have in mind?" I asked, hoping the long ride had calmed her resentment.

"Let's split up." She removed the spiraled cable we had bought with the bikes from her bag, ran it through the frames, and locked them, together, to a post.

"Okay …" I tightened my grip around the black padded shoulder straps of my backpack. "We just need somewhere to stay, right?" I swayed to stay in her line of sight.

"I guess." She adjusted her hair behind her ears. "Whatever. I'm going this way." She spun on her heel and crossed the street without so much as a glance.

"Meet back here at four o'clock?" I hollered, sliding one foot off the sidewalk. She gave a thumbs-up without facing me and disappeared into the crowd.

People aimlessly shifted around me while I stood in the way of their coordinated chaos. After taking a deep breath, I jumped into the wave of flesh and moved with them, away from Astrid.

I didn't have a plan, and nothing stood out. The thought of home regained its appeal. Even if I had to stay at my mom's for a while until I got on my feet.

I stopped walking.

You dragged her out of her home.

Blame. Shame.

Coward. You owe this world something great.

I resumed my pace, the crowd thinning until the sidewalk fell off into the street. I stopped before crossing the block and stared like a child; a patient line of men and women formed outside a soup kitchen. Despair dressed in tattered clothing and bags was stained with my new reality. At worst, it was a good place to start.

A strong odor of urine and alcohol intensified as I crossed the street toward the soup kitchen.

"Hi, I'm Zachary." I spoke to anyone who would listen at the end of the line. No one cared. They stood transfixed like rotted trees to the cement, their dirty fingers wrapping around a black gate that bordered the corner of the block.

Time cut its second hand down my back. If I waited there until I could get in, I'd still be facing the same group of people who wanted nothing to do with themselves, much less me. A few more minutes passed, and no progress had been made.

This was pointless. This trip was such a bad idea. What kind of fairy tale did you think you were going to live out by leaving everything behind? Did you really think distance would help you forget?

My shoulders fell. We couldn't just sleep in the gutters. But maybe there was a shelter we could stay in while the insurance money came in. Then again, should I even mention it to her?

My stomach sank. My skin tightened. I wrung my hands and shifted my weight onto the other foot.

A car stopped at the light beside me. Only its tires were visible from the corner of my eye; I didn't need to look up to know what they were seeing. A day earlier, I would have been the one staring from the stoplight at the young man at the end of a soup kitchen line.

A day earlier, I would put myself in his place. I would have been thankful for not being him, and would have even felt bad for him, wondering what kind of luck put him there. But the light turned green, and I was still the young man at the end of the line.

I couldn't bear to lift my head. I turned to leave, only to knock into a tall man behind me.

"Sorry." I spoke to the ground, expecting no reply.

"No worries," the man said in a deep voice. I lifted my head, and he smiled with big white teeth that were all intact. His clothing reeked purely of burnt wood. His appearance surprised me, though his skin was patched with cuts, bruises, and ash.

"My name's Zachary," I said, offering my hand.

"Hi, Zachary. I'm Pete." The rough skin of his hand masked mine with a firm grip, and he peered down the line.

"Where do you stay around here?" I asked, forgetting my bedside manner. Again, he disengaged.

"I don't," he said without breaking focus on his surroundings.

"You don't?" I grabbed the gate and swayed into it.

Pete's eyes relaxed and his shoulders eased. "Where do you stay?"

I sensed his empathy. It wasn't something I was after, but it profited his attention. Still, I didn't want to admit that I was homeless, not even to a homeless man.

"Are you from around here?" he added.

I gazed down at my shoes. "No ... just got in today."

The conversation ended there. I sidled back to my place in line, and Pete went back to his surveillance.

Soon enough, the line wobbled through double doors into a cafeteria. An older lady handed me a plastic bowl over a dented aluminum counter. Tiny bits of vegetables and a couple chunks of beef floated in the brown broth that filled the bowl, with a pinch of bread resting on top.

I waited for Pete to get his share, then followed him to a round table in the farthest corner from the door. He sat perfectly straight and close to the table with his napkin draped over his lap. While others clanked silverware and slurped from their shallow spoons, Pete barely made a noise.

I, on the other hand, was not nearly as composed, holding my head inches above the bowl and shoveling the soup into my mouth. After devouring it, I pushed the empty bowl away and glanced at the counter to see if anyone else was getting seconds.

"What brings you to town?" Pete asked, wiping his mouth with a napkin.

I returned my gaze to the table and rubbed my face with the palms of my hands.

"My van was stolen close to here. My friend and I are trying to figure out what to do," I started, folding my hands in my lap.

Occupants of the tables around us murmured as Pete stared, waiting for me to continue.

"We were traveling, but everything we owned was in the van."

"Where is your friend?" He scooted his bowl toward mine.

I looked off to the ceiling and sighed. "We split up to figure things out. She's going to meet me later."

"So this is a love story." He smirked, discounting any austerity that made up the details.

"No! Not love," I spewed, forging a breath from beneath my barely beating heart that sank into my stomach and surrendered to my own awareness. "So what now?" I asked, lightly flicking the side of my bowl.

"First, we need to meet up with this girl." He crossed his arms against his chest. "There are places to stay. You'll be fine."

I ripped the corners from my napkin. "What if she doesn't show up?"

Chapter 14

"The only type of care you'll ever get from a stranger is respect, so take all you can get." Pete spoke as if he were breathing the words themselves while we passed an older couple who eyed us from behind the glare of a cafe window.

I was surprised at the profound nature of his perspective. He had tied everything about the way he lived together with one simple sentence. It appeared as a sense of progression contained by the ability to survive, and maybe even grow, beneath shadows.

"So where do you get your money?" I asked.

Pete stopped to catch his breath and glimpsed at my imploring face. "Savings."

"Really?" I asked, breaking his concentration again. "Where did you work?"

"Have you ever heard of the barter system?" he said, sidestepping in front of a detailed map of the city that was protected by a piece of glass and a black metal frame.

"Yeah … " I shifted beside him and memorized the pattern his fingers traced across buildings from street to street. "That's where goods and services are traded for other goods and services, right?"

Two blocks north, one east, three more north, and two more east.

"Exactly." Pete tapped twice on the glass and closed his eyes as if he were taking a mental picture.

"So how do you make money through that?" My words trailed off when I spotted the coffee shop on the map where Astrid and I had left our bikes.

"I don't, but I don't spend money because of it. I have a savings if I need it, and I hardly ever touch it … if you don't have savings, then you should pick up a trade."

"Wait, what?" I said, caught off guard by his disguised fortune of freedom as a family of three crowded behind us with a baby crying in a stroller, waiting for their turn at the maps.

"I used to be a train engineer. I quit after eighteen years." He stepped out of the way so the young family could gauge their own whereabouts before giving in to a quick pace up the sidewalk.

"Did you retire?" I questioned while I balanced between the back of the map and the side of the street, jogging to catch up with him.

"Nope. That would have taken twenty years."

"You only had two more years, and you quit?"

He grunted.

I wanted to believe him, but why was he dingy? Then he picked his teeth with his thumbnail—they were so white. And his nails were trimmed. Clearly, he had taken care of himself most of his life.

"That's something my roommate in college would have done." I laughed. "At least you kept a job. He always got fired for advertising his beliefs instead of doing the actual work." I ducked under a low flying open-sign flag, following Pete around an iron table.

"Sounds like my kind of guy!" He dug his hand into his pocket, jingling what sounded like loose change. "I haven't always been as convicted though."

"Oh." I took a few breaths while catching up. "Well, you still remind me of him. So confident in yourself, regardless of your …"

"My what?" He chuckled, pulling a handful of coins from his pocket, then leaned over the park bench in front of us and emptied his hand—loose change clinking into an open container seconds later.

"Your—" I stopped myself again.

A skinny girl, maybe twenty or so, lay curled up around a paper cup on the bench. Her bony body quivered beneath her dirty white dress, even though the air was quite warm.

"Do you know her?" I asked when he flew past an empty bulletin board and up the steps to the door of a tall red-brick building.

"Hey!" he yelled, banging the beefy entrance with both fists. "HEY!"

Pete bounded back down the steps and around the front of the bench and kneeled, carefully reaching out to her. She flinched so hard that her head banged the backrest as soon as the tip of his finger slid beneath her neck.

"It's okay," he said, jerking his arms away. "I'm going to untangle your hair, all right?"

Her bloodshot eyes fixated on him as her head trembled.

He gently lifted her greasy locks that swept to the ground between the spaced planks of the bench.

The door to the building cracked open.

"Pete?" a pale man in a suit said from the doorway, craning his neck through the narrow opening.

Pete looked up at the man, then back down at the girl. "I'm going to pick you up now, okay?" he said, speaking in a soft voice.

It was all the girl could do to nod.

Pete stooped down and picked up her change cup, clenching it between his teeth while he slid his arms beneath her body. He rushed back around the bench with her frame bundled against his chest to the man who stood shielding himself with the door.

"Were you just going to leave her here?" he asked, confronting the man at the door as I ran up behind Pete, catching a glimpse of the blood stain on the girl's dress that streamed down her thighs.

"We have a protocol. There aren't any—"

"Move." Pete hunched over the girl's body.

The man continued to block the doorway and shuffled in place before giving in and stepping out of the way.

Pete kicked the door the rest of the way open and cradled her body while he sidled through the opening.

When I stepped inside, the man in the suit leaned again the wall, adjusting his tie.

"I'll be right back, Zachary," Pete said, trotting down a dimly lit hall that was lined with wood paneling. "McCoy, call an ambulance—NOW!" he said, kicking in another door at the end of the hall and slinking into the next room.

McCoy pushed the exit door open with his shoulder and shooed me through it. "We don't have any more rooms. You'll need to wait outside." He took off after Pete, his rubber-soled shoes clogging across the thin carpet.

The door slammed in his wake, and with the silence, my ears rang. I froze in the middle of the scorching heat.

Chapter 15

An hour later, the door reopened, and Pete emerged.

"She's going to be fine. Got mixed up with the wrong crowd is all." His voice rumbled and he cleared his throat. "Why are you sitting on the stairs?"

"Couldn't bring myself to sit on that bench." I wrung my hands. "It felt wrong."

"You're a good guy," he said, hopping down onto the sidewalk. "Where are you supposed to meet this girl?"

"Over at Grounds Lounge Coffee. Do you know where that's at?" I pushed myself off the stoop.

"Yeah." He turned and trekked around the corner, nodding at the other side of the road. "It's right there. What time are you supposed to meet her?"

"What time is—" I was cut short by a taxi cab pulling away from the curb, revealing our bikes. I stepped into the parking lane. "Someone fucked with our bikes!" I yelled before taking off into traffic.

"Watch out!" he hollered as a car slammed on its brakes, its horn blaring.

My body stiffened, but not enough to stop me. I looked both ways and cleared another lane. Our bikes hung outward, away from the post they had been fastened to, by the black wire lock. Both had been stripped of their seats and front tires.

Pete gaited across the street after me. "What's wrong?" He panted, joining me.

I dropped to my knees and pushed the bikes back against the post.

"These were ours." I twisted the frayed brake line from Astrid's bike around my finger; it had been sliced halfway down the frame. It was the first real disconnect, like an omen.

I let the bike fall over, then I stood and turned toward the coffee shop.

"You okay, buddy?" he asked as he stepped out of my way.

"Yeah." I peered through the shop window at an analogue clock that read 4:10 PM. "We're a little late. She should be here shortly." I wiped the sweat from my brow with my forearm and leaned against the brick wall beside the alleyway.

He scooted the rear tires further from the pole and pushed the bikes upright, out of the way of the sidewalk. "You can probably find used tires and seats cheap. Maybe even free at a junk yard," he said, meeting me by the wall.

I gritted my teeth and looked away. "It's only spilled milk," I said while he squared his back against the brick.

"Good. Just let it go." He sighed. "You'll find something new."

His words were a blow to the gut. I would press on, but I wasn't excited about the future either. He'd simply put everything into perspective.

"I really don't want her to see it though." I coughed, sweat stinging my eyes.

He rocked onto his shoulder and peered through the coffee shop window. "She's almost fifteen minutes late." He turned to the bikes. "I don't think she's coming back to see it."

Let go. Let go.

I'm so tired of moving on.

"Do you have family or anyone who can come get you?" He stepped onto the sidewalk while he dug his hands into his pockets. "Maybe you can grab a train home?"

I drew a long breath and closed my eyes. Her smile painted the inside of my eyelids until her teeth grew so large that they distorted her face. "No!" I barked as my eyes jarred open.

"No?" He shook his head. "You don't have family?"

I stared past Pete, focusing on the broken bikes behind him. "I do." I blinked and imagined passing by where the accident had happened … or worse, seeing the boy's family out in town. "I just don't have a home."

Or a purpose, an idea of who you are, or even what you're made of.

Without her, there was no one to save—or serve. Things were worse than they'd been before we had met. The balance I had allowed to distract me had been interrupted.

We both stood quietly for a few moments while strangers filtered between us.

"I quit my job because of the look on someone's face." He stepped closer. "A look very similar to yours."

I crossed my arms and let my head fall.

"It was a Wednesday." He raised his voice and dropped his gaze to meet mine. "We were moving by 8:00 AM. By 9:00 AM, I was basically in autopilot; we had arrived in a city not far outside of Mississippi. The track crossing was clear, and we had at least a half mile before we got to it. But when I was about twenty yards out, an SUV pushed through the crossing gate and parked with its tires straddling the tracks."

I lifted my head. Pete shook his own and pressed his thumb across his brow.

"I pulled the horn lever and did everything I could to at least slow the momentum, knowing there was no way to completely stop. There was nothing I could do. I remember it so well … I could have counted the freckles on his nose. He looked at me with wide, empty eyes, took his hands off the steering wheel"—he raised his hands—"and set them in his lap." He dropped his arms, his fingers dangling by his sides. "I saw that same look plastered to my own face every morning in the mirror leading up to that day." He cleared his throat and backed up again to the wall. "That look on his face. The look on your face now."

"Do you ever blame yourself for what happened?" I asked, turning toward him. "Even though it wasn't your fault, do you feel the guilt?"

"I …" He started and then tilted his head. "I did."

Pete wasn't as complicated anymore. He'd freed himself, and who I was seeing in him was a result of that.

"Pete," I spoke into a deluge of people who funneled off a nearby bus, separating us from the street.

His shoulders slumped. "Yeah, buddy?"

"I need to make a phone call before we leave," I said, facing him. "Is that all right?"

"Sure."

Numb, I marched around him to the door of the coffee shop.

"It doesn't get easier where I'm going," he said when I grabbed the door handle.

I paused. Going back wasn't an option. Nothing else would be easy anyway.

I nodded, then pushed the door open and stepped inside. "Hello, sir," a girl with milky skin who sat behind a register said as she hopped to her feet and pulled her thick red hair into a ponytail. "How can I help you?"

"I need to use your phone. Is that okay?" I asked with a lump in my throat, somewhat expecting her to say no since I wasn't a customer.

"Of course. Is it local?"

"No ma'am"—I dropped my head—"it's not." I lifted my gaze but kept my head in place.

"Oh." She smiled, reaching for the receiver. "Then just make sure you dial one and the area code."

Her short arm gapped the distance of the bar, and the white coiled cord connecting the receiver to the base sagged on the countertop, tapping it like a short roll on a snare drum.

I lifted my head and grabbed the bottom part of the phone. "Thanks!" I offered a meek smile, holding the cold plastic to my sunbaked face. The phone must have rung at least twelve times before the answering machine picked up with a deliberate speech from Jonas followed by a long beep.

"Jonas! Mary! I hope all is well!" I said with a forced enthusiasm. "Astrid and I are doing great, but the van has been stolen." I spun my finger around the phone cord and glanced up at the ceiling. "The insurance check is being sent to your house. I hope you don't mind mailing it to us once you get it. I'll call you again with an address." I took a short breath to keep my voice from shaking and forged a grin to hide my dismay. "We really appreciate everything you've done for us. Thank you so much! Have a good night!"

I pressed the receiver button with my thumb as my other hand dropped to my back pocket, where Jonas's letter covertly occupied a green cotton patch of fabric. My fingers pressed against the hard corners of the unopened envelope. He trusted me, so I trusted him.

After clearing the line, I pulled my wallet from my other pocket and took out my debit card. There was a 1-800 number posted on the back with a short line that read Check Your Balance above it. I dialed the number and entered my information. There was a short break, followed by several quick beeps, then it stated my balance: just under $2,100.

It was enough to buy another cheap van or to keep traveling by public transportation—but surely not both. At least not until the insurance money came in, and there was no telling how little I would get for a van that was older than I was. But I was determined to finish the trip no matter the outcome.

I could either endure a lifetime of questions or mere moments of weakness.

Take the moments. It's all you can handle.

To be honest, it was all that I wanted to handle.

The barista eyed me while I held the phone, my thumb pressed against the receiver. When I broke from my trance and met her gaze, she held out a small cup of iced coffee. There was a note on the cup that said, "I'm only useful upside down," with an arrow pointing toward the lid.

"This one is on the house," she said while trading me a mixture of mocha, espresso, and ice for the phone.

"Oh, I appreciate that." I slid my card to her. "But I'd like to buy another all the same. My friend is waiting for me outside … it's for him."

"Why is he outside?" She leaned over the counter. "It's too hot out there. Tell him to come in!"

"I would love to," I said, barely recognizing myself in the reflection of her glasses. My hair stood up around my head, and my beard hid the shape of my chin. "But we're about to catch a train."

"Catching a train, huh? When does it leave?" she asked, pumping chocolate over the ice.

"In about thirty minutes," I said while she poured milk into the blender and flipped its power switch.

A curious bulge in her cheeks gave her smile away when she finished mixing the drink and poured it into a cup.

She snapped a lid on and shook the drink, then slid it to me.

"Thank you!" I said, wrapping napkins around the drinks to shield my hands from their chill.

"No problem." Her hair hid what I could see of her eyes as she washed her hands in a sink below the counter.

Catching the seconds with nothing left to say, I followed a long green rug to the exit, where a bell chimed on the glass door and warm light streamed in. When I stepped onto the sidewalk, it felt like I was starting over. Like it was an entirely new trip or experience segmented by who I shared it with and what mattered. Really, I felt like a stranger to myself.

Pete and I sipped our drinks on the heated walk to the tracks. We didn't go to the train yard as I had naively expected; we walked to the outskirts of town, where the trains hadn't yet picked up speed and no one could see us. He pulled out a folded map from his shirt pocket. It was a list of trains leaving the station about a mile from us. He knew where each train was going based on the time. He even knew if a train was passenger or cargo. "We'll be on a cargo line," he told me. We continued between an alley of rocks and a row of trees until the tracks and surrounding landscape mirrored itself.

The train whistled in the distance as we tucked ourselves away behind a curtain of foliage and he explained the process of climbing onto a coupling, or, if we were lucky, how to climb into an open box.

"They're not moving fast, but they're also not slowing down. It's a policy of science … don't overthink it," he finished.

He obviously didn't know me very well. I was anything but ready, yet I did all I could to mentally prepare with my eyes closed, balancing myself in a crouched position with my fingers on a floor of pine.

I imagined myself running next to the train with my backpack strapped tight, snapped firmly around my chest, and pulling myself onto a coupling. Lastly, I pictured the balancing act prior to finding my seat.

Soon thunder emerged from beyond the trees, then a blurred dot of steel and steam gained definition until the cars passed us, each one as intimidating as the last. My heartbeat drowned out my senses, filling my head with anxiety that my body frantically worked to bail through my mouth with deep breaths.

Move.

My backpack remained tight enough to stay attached but too loose to control. My ankles teetered on the uneven rocks beneath me. A cold metal rod barely extended far enough for me to grab. My body overpowered my mind, pulling me up before I had fully processed what was happening.

I braced my legs on the shaking ledge, holding my body upright with a tight grip on the corner of the car. Pete crossed the coupling to the other side of the car, where a small platform jutted out beside a ladder. He slid against the car and sat with his body pinned between his knees and the car, using the ladder to keep steady.

Mirroring his platform stood another, where the following car's coupling secured. I mimicked his actions and used my upper body strength to reach the other side of the car. Beside me, I hung my backpack by a hook on the ladder. The exhilaration of it all deadened the discomfort; adrenaline masked the tension of my folded bones, separating my body from my mind.

He beamed at me. I grinned and bobbed my head. Where I was headed, I didn't know, but it didn't matter. All that mattered was that I had found another way to push forward. Wind tousled my hair, and shadows of power lines detached from the earth and jumped again.

Chapter 16

Even with the inevitable cuts and bruises it posed, hopping off the train was much easier than climbing on. Mimicking Pete, I threw my bag, then tucked and rolled across the rocky edge of the tracks. A few yards down, he stood, not taking the time to brush the dirt from his clothing before pulling the list of trains from his pocket. He wiped a small stream of blood from his forearm that dripped off his elbow with the torn paper.

"The pain becomes irrelevant as the scars populate," he shouted over the rumble of the passing cars.

With that, I ignored my throbbing elbow and caught up to Pete, who had already sprinted across the tracks and was trekking the back roads of an unknown town.

We walked for nearly two miles through farms and past houses and fields, where seasonal crops grew fresh and full.

"If you must take something from a field, try to do it in passing," he said, gesturing to the acres upon acres of corn, potatoes, cucumbers, tomatoes, asparagus, and carrots. "No one notices a meal's worth missing." He stopped and leapt a small ditch, then grabbed a husk. "Why don't we take some corn? I'll show you how to roast it over a fire."

"You go ahead. I'm not hungry." I rubbed my forearm, my thoughts drifting to Jonas and Mary.

"You'll be hungry later," Pete mumbled, holding his bag open with his teeth.

I liked the idea of freedom, but not at the cost of someone else's effort. Having nothing made more sense when I wasn't relying on another's hard work to get by; otherwise, what would I have learned from having nothing?

"No. I'm fine." I waved my hand.

"You're going to be hungry, and I'm not sharing … so I'll get you some." He picked off a few more ears and stuffed them into his bag. "Is anyone coming?" He twisted his head and arched an eyebrow while he closed his bag.

I dug my hands into my pockets and poked at my guilt. I quickly glanced down the street in both directions. "No."

Pete jumped across the ditch to my side and let out a long breath. "We aren't too far now."

"Where are *we* going?" My reclaimed doubt wrinkled my forehead.

He swung his bag around his shoulder and crossed the empty street, his posture stiffer than when we had boarded the train. "It's a place where people like us can live."

"People like us?"

Here you are again, trusting a stranger.

He crossed another ditch and followed a narrow path that separated the field from the trees. Whatever I chose to do would define the rest of my life. If I gave up here, I'd always wonder where it might have led.

Take more from life than it takes from you. Are you an extension of your ideas or a prisoner of your boundaries?

By the time I had started moving again, Pete's steps rustled along the leaves and loose dirt. He didn't care if I followed or not; he was leaving regardless. I hotfooted to the other side of the road down a rutted track. Pete had already neared the end of the field; even with his plodded pace, he was making good time. The tall green stalks of sweet corn and the prickly pines of the Mexican pinions grew closer and closer.

Standing where the trail gave itself to roots and stumps, he peered back at me and smiled. "It gets tricky from here. Be sure to keep up!" With that, he disappeared around a bend in the field.

I picked up my pace to a sprint.

Why are you doing this?

Astrid's face flashed to the forefront of my mind.

When I spotted Pete again, he faced me with a hand on his hip. He smirked, then navigated into a row of stalks, moving against the grain. I ripped through the loose husks like paper. Where the forest swallowed the end of the field, there stood a body-sized cavity between two towering trees. He led me into the woods, and soon, only his whistling and the singing birds filled the silence beneath a vast canopy that hid us from the sun.

The farther we walked, the taller the ceiling of pine and leaves grew. I didn't work to close the gap between us; I was more comfortable seeing everything he faced before I had to cross it.

The sky loomed closer as a patch of eastern redcedars grew smaller and more tightly packed, hiding Pete. Trudging through a floor of fallen lumber and limbs, I stumbled upon the thick brush that had consumed him. The distant sound of a dim crowd filtered through the thicket. I parted the curtain of prickly evergreen to an open parcel of land encircled by a wide tree line. As I neared, I spotted dirty feet peeking out through the opening of a couple of A-framed tarps that hung from ropes and people sitting outside actual tents beside barrels that had been spread sporadically across the patched grass. Pete passed them until he reached a thick green polyester tent that had been zipped closed.

"Zachary!" He waved me over.

Staying in-line with his path, I ignored prying eyes that gawked at me as I made my way past a clothesline draped with torn socks and sweat-stained T-shirts. Pete unzipped his tent.

"This is it," he said with a heavy breath and a light chuckle. "Home."

I had a hard time believing he was proud to call it that. I'd taken everything in with a single glance. It had two cots dressed in blankets, and a trunk sat at the foot of one while a second tarp separated the dirt from the living space.

"Why don't you set your bag down, and I'll introduce you to some people," he suggested, tossing his own bag onto the trunk.

I did as he had asked—against my better judgement—flinging my bag onto the open cot opposite the trunk.

He then opened the flap with his arm, leaving room for me to walk out. "There are three people here you need to know," he said while we strolled side by side through the center of the grounds, counting names off on his hand. "Myself, Lisa, and Jake. Jake is rarely ever here anymore."

"Why are you three more important than everyone else?" I asked.

"I wouldn't say we're more important. We—well, I personally don't have to be here. I chose to because I like to help. Same goes for Lisa—she's about your age. Maybe a little older. Jake is more of a permanent fixture than anything else. That's him over there." He waved at a bearded man sitting with his legs sprawled out in front of him outside a hanging tarp. The man waved back.

"How do you help?" I stopped walking and glimpsed at the broken souls hunched over empty cans of food and various skins of fruits and vegetables.

"We keep these people going until they move on or decide to get help from their families, the government ... or whoever can get them on their feet again."

"Pete?" a soft voice said behind him.

He spun on his heel. "Lisa! We were just talking about you!"

A girl barely shorter than me bounced our way. Her long brown hair trailed down the back of a T-shirt she had cut into a tank top.

"Lisa, Zachary. Zachary, Lisa," he said, gesturing between us.

"It's nice to meet you." Lisa propped her hands on her hips and beamed. "Where did you two meet?"

"The soup kitchen. He's just down on his luck; I don't expect him to be here long," Pete said as if I were his patient.

Heat flushed my face and my shoulders weakened.

"Why don't you show him around?" He stretched and yawned. "I haven't slept."

Lisa nodded. "Sure thing."

There wasn't a lot to see. Not far from the tents flowed a stream, and beyond that lay a forest, where wild berries and other such things grew.

As the night went on, I loosened up. Most of the rusted barrels had been filled with flames. People slumped around them, some cooking things on sticks and others staring into the fire. A few talked. Others grew quiet.

One at a time, they fell out of their small groups and into their tents. Soon Lisa and I were the only two remaining, and she quieted beside me on a large rock. The firelight flashed in her eyes, shadows dancing along the curve of her cheek.

"When flames die down, I imagine them burying themselves," I said, wiping the ash from my shoulder. "Is that weird?"

"Not at all." She poked one of the burning logs with a stick. "They're very self-destructive."

"What made you stay here?" I pressed.

"Because everyone, every day, is different. It's easy to love something when it's always changing. You never need it, and it never needs you."

"How rehearsed," I replied to the subtle offense of conviction.

"Rehearsed." Lisa deadened the word with monotone execution. "Rehearsed was Sunday mornings at church with my family. Rehearsed was how I participated within the *community*. It would have been different if I fit in. I do, however, think we are all actors, but here I can be whoever I want based on how I'm feeling on that day." She shrugged. "People never stay long enough for it to matter."

She was sure of herself, and generally, I would say full of shit. But it worked for her; it was a game that kept her satisfied. So I played along.

"If we are all actors, and you have the luxury of changing roles"—I kept my language as precise as hers—"then who are you playing today?"

Lisa lifted her eyes and glanced at me through her bangs. "Today I am the girl who was lucky enough to meet you." She leaned in so close that her breath cooled on my cheek. "I feel like myself."

Goosebumps shot up my arms. Silence lingered. She grabbed the inside of my leg as her lips moved closer to my ear.

"Who are you?" she whispered, digging into my skin with her nails and softly trailing her nose across my cheek.

When our lips met, power coursed through me. My hands clutched her body, turning her into a submissive ruler of my actions. I traced the top of her panty line below her waist while her hands tugged at my hair and clawed at my back. Without warning, she pulled away from me and strutted to her tent. My chest still pounding, I stood and followed.

I thought about Astrid.

Guilt. This is guilt.

My adrenaline settled, and I tracked Lisa, yanking back the unlaced curtain door when I reached it. She peeked up at me from the floor, wearing nothing but the tan lines on her legs and chest while sprawled out on top of a blanket. I kneeled and stared from the opening of the tent for a few moments, collecting my words.

"Are you going to join me?" she asked, propped up on one arm.

"No," I spoke under my breath. "No, no." My voice grew louder, peppered with an apologetic tone. "Lisa, you're gorgeous. But this isn't something I should do."

She crossed her arms over her chest and dropped her gaze.

I dug my face into my hands, rubbed my eyes, then dropped my arms to my sides. "This trip was supposed to be the end. I guess I let my mania get in the way of my misery." I clasped my hands together to keep them from fidgeting. "Never mind. This is a good example of the wrong place at the wrong time." I laughed and ambled toward the tent's opening. "I'm sorry!"

"Don't worry about it." She smiled and sat up, pulling the excess blanket from under her legs and draping it over her chest.

I tilted my head, standing outside the grasp of her dim battery-powered lantern. "No. I should let you rest." I turned to leave.

"Zachary!" she said in a stern voice, stopping me in my tracks. "Whatever's wrong—whatever brought you here—it isn't going to get any better if you keep hiding from it."

My chest tightened.

"Come sit and talk to me." She pointed her light at my back, my shadow stretching outward.

I focused on the trembling hands of my silhouette.

Her voice softened. "Zachary—what happened?"

"I was headed to school a couple of weeks before graduation after spending the weekend at my mom's." My body tensed before I could get another word out, and the light died. "I was staring at a wreck on the other side of the road, and he just ran out in front of me—I didn't even see him until it happened."

I jerked as cold hands crept up the back of my neck. "It's okay." Lisa whispered in my ear, tugging me into the tent and gesturing to the ground where she'd been lying. "Just breathe."

My crumpled face swelled into tears. "I didn't mean to." I gasped. "He was just a little boy."

"Shh … shh." She held me close, the blanket wrapped around her while she held it closed. "Let it out."

I heaved, my knees weak, but her tight grip around my ribs didn't loosen until I could stand on my own.

"Are you ready to talk about it?" she asked.

I nodded and she let go. We strode the middle of the tent floor and lay beside one another.

"Tell me what happened." She rolled onto her side and wiped the moisture from my cheeks.

"I got out of my truck, and a couple of guys ran toward me, yelling from a nearby junkyard." I took a long breath. "The skinny one crawled through the trail of blood between the tires and unwrapped the boy's body from my driveshaft." I curled up, choking over my words in agony. "I remember hearing him gargle as his mother ran up to his shoes that had landed side by side in the middle of the road. She just screamed and then they laid him out on the road at my feet."

I sobbed and beat my fist against the side of my head.

"Then his grandpa showed up and crawled on the ground beside him. 'Squeeze my fingers if you can hear me,' he kept saying. 'SQUEEZE!'" I lost control, howling at the top of my lungs.

"Lisa?" Pete's voice cut through my baying and ducked through the tent door. "Is everything okay?"

"He's fine." Lisa reached over and brushed the sweat-drenched hair from my forehead.

Chapter 17

The sun found its way into the windowless tent and assaulted my eyelids the next day—reading noon with its glare hovering directly above my head. I sat up, pulling my damp shirt from my chest as a vacuum of musty air brushed against my skin. Pete's cot was perfectly made, and he was nowhere in sight. Discomfort coaxed me to my feet, and after straightening my sheets, I stepped outside.

Everyone bore a vague familiarity from the day before but paid me no mind. My tongue snapped as my eyes strained to focus. *Water. Water.* The surroundings grew clearer until I spotted two stocky men stacking branches between the tents and the tree line furthest from me.

"Hey, guys." I hitched toward them. "How are you doing today?" I smiled and offered my hand as if it were my first day on the job. They each shook it as their mumbles overlapped, giving the impression that they were well—or as well as could be expected at a homeless camp.

"Awesome!" I blurted. "Do you know where I can get some water?"

The first of the two men dropped his last branch from his copper-brown blistered hand and turned to me. "Yes." He shadowed a smirk through a thick beard. "Just past the tree line, there's a spring." He draped a torn white T-shirt from his arm and pointed over my shoulder past the other side of the tents.

"Is it safe to drink?" I asked, shading my eyes from the blazing ball in the sky.

The second man wiped the dirt from his palms onto a torn pair of jean shorts. "It's what we drink."

"Thanks!" I said, then took off in the direction he had pointed, past the tents and into the trees.

I was in a daze, like I had been misplaced inside of my body. Leaves and pine replaced the grass as the running spring spoke above the rustling of my shoes. Through the trees, the ground split ahead of me. I hurried, falling to my knees at the end of my last few strides and cupping my hands—plopping them into the moving stream. The channel rushed past my skin, and hair danced around my wrists. I brought the clean drink to my lips.

"Zachary!" Pete yelled through the distance, cutting me off during my first sip.

I stopped for a moment, contemplating greeting him first, before I dipped my mouth into my cupped hands.

"Good morning." He climbed the small incline across the stream from me and stopped right at the bank, fish hanging from a wire looped around his shoulder. "I think you kept everyone awake with your snoring last night." He laughed.

"Sorry!" I chuckled, dropping the leftover water back into the stream.

"No worries! I'm just giving you a hard time!" He bit his lip to keep his smile from growing. "Look what I caught!" He slid his thumb slid beneath the wire over his shoulder.

"Is that how you usually eat around here?" I stood and dried my hands on my shorts.

"No. Everyone is good about getting their own food. But I do this from time to time when the catch is thick."

"Nice!" I complimented him with raised brows and cheeks. "How did you get over there?" I said, judging the water's depth.

"There's a fallen tree upstream. I'll show you."

I bent down and filled my mouth with one last big gulp of water before we trailed along opposite edges of the shore.

"There's enough fish for everyone." He beamed across the divide. "I caught a group moving upstream with a net."

Reveling in his energy, I let him gloat. "That's awesome!"

"This is it!" He pushed a low-hanging branch out of his way and pointed to a fallen black walnut tree. He tested one of its roots before hoisting himself onto its trunk, then leaned to counter the extra weight of the fish around his other shoulder while making his way across. I pushed my body against a branch that fanned from the end of the fallen tree to clear an opening for him as he jumped back to land.

"Have you seen Lisa this morning?" I asked, letting go of the branches once he cleared the way.

"She had something to take care of. She should be back by tonight."

"So … what should I do?" I asked.

"Do you know how to gut a fish?"

"Yeah. What is that, striped bass?" I asked, referencing memories of fishing with my grandfather when I was little.

"Impressive!" He held the braided wire sprung of fish out for me to grab.

I relieved him of his haul and slid the loop onto my shoulder. "Are you sure this is enough for everyone?"

"It should be. We don't overeat out here, obviously. Even with all the farms around." He pulled a leaf from a nearby bush and tore everything from its stem.

"Why's that?" I wrinkled my nose at the stench that now soaked my shirt.

He dropped the pieces of leaf and grabbed a new one. "I don't know. I guess it's easier to expect less when the future is so uncertain for people like us."

People like us … where do you stand? Who do you stand with?

How long could I stand the way things were?

"There are metal grates behind a barn a quarter mile from here. We use them when we have something to cook. I'll get them while you prepare the fish." He dropped his second fistful of torn leaves to the side and scratched the back of his neck.

I gritted my teeth. Again, I thought back to those days with my grandpa, and how uncomfortable it had made me to cut up fish on the rare occasion I had caught one big enough to keep. "Actually, I think I'd rather get the grates."

"Are you sure? I figured you'd be against using things without permission," he said with a chuckle.

"I'd rather do that than cut up fish." I scrunched my nose and held the wire out for him to reclaim when we passed the trees. "How many grates are there?"

"Well," he said, reaching for the fish again and slinging it over his shoulder, "they have hundreds of them. But we only need one for each barrel." He paused. "They're heavy though—I'll send someone to help you."

When we made it back to the tents, Pete hung the fish on a hook that clung to the rim of a barrel in front of him. "Jake!" he yelled with his hands cupped around his mouth. "Jake!"

Heavy steps and shuffling came from within a nearby tent, where a blue tarp flapped opened. "What?" Jake poked his dirty, bearded face through the curtain doors.

"Fish!" Pete said, holding the catch up.

Jake grinned, revealing his dirty yellow teeth streaked with brown and black. "Need some grates?" he asked, stooped in the doorway.

I waved.

"Yeah. Zachary is going with you."

I pressed through the thick summer air over to him until a stench of sour milk and ammonia hit me.

Jake turned to Pete, then to me. "Jake." He held his hand out. "When did you get here?"

"He got here last night." Pete spoke up for me as my lungs tightened to suppress my sense of smell.

"I didn't see him." Jake took a step toward Pete.

I held my breath.

"You did." Pete sighed, setting the fish on a two-by-eight-inch board that acted as a tabletop, spanning across a barrel outside his tent. "He was with Lisa all night." He leaned forward with squinted brows.

"We've met, just not formally," I added.

"Oh." Jake relaxed his shoulders, studying me again before straightening and hobbling over to an opening between a couple of tents. He then followed the gap into an open field, where the trail wound parallel to the stream about two hundred yards back.

I shrugged at Pete, but he only smiled and shook his head.

"You coming?" Jake yelled, still heading into the northern tree line.

"Yeah!" I worked myself into a jog to catch up.

I brushed through the tall wheat grass as we padded up to the barn, where the tree line ended behind a stable. As Pete had described, gray metal grates lay stacked higher than my waist by the dozens, contrasting the faded red wooden siding of the barn's backside. Jake pulled the grates from the top of the closest stack and leaned them upright against the pile. He squatted to lift them, doubling my load by carrying two in each hand. Without any hesitation, he led the way back.

My fingers stretched around the dry metal, and within my first few steps, I fell behind, my elbows bent against my sides and tucked under my arms to keep my own grates from dragging along the ground. Jake repeated his stories from our trek to the barn. Most of them were about his time at the camp and the random things that he had done, such as the last time he had to get grates … which sounded oddly familiar to the story of the first time that he'd gone to get the grates and how they had built his tent out of rope and tarp.

"I could have never done it on my own," he repeated before moving onto his next story.

I nodded and tuned him out, letting my mind drift.

Pete hadn't hesitated to fillet fish for everyone or take the vegetables from the field for me so I wouldn't go without.

You've let your conscience get in the way of your survival.

The grates slipped in my grip, though Jake kept his pace, rattling on and widening the gap between us.

"Jake"—I grunted between gasps—"I need a quick break."

He plodded onward without response, his pace as strong as ever.

"Jake!" I called again, shouting at deaf ears.

The grate clattered to the ground, its sharp metal corner bouncing off my ankle.

"Fuck!" I yelled, dropping the second grate onto a bed of pine—glaring up to see Jake disappearing into the woods. I leaned against the bark of a nearby tree, kicked off my shoe, and peeled my sock over my heel. Blood flooded a deep gash over the bone.

The pain will become irrelevant as the scars populate.

I wiped the stream of blood from my foot, pulled up my sock, and put my shoe back on.

I closed my eyes and whispered my thoughts, rocking back and forth. "The pain will become irrelevant as the scars populate."

The thought of the young boy I had hit with my truck flashed through my mind, the image of him wrapped in bandages on a hospital bed, tubes feeding down his throat, searing itself into my brain. His symmetry in my life, along with Astrid and how her bandages had scratched me the night I had picked her up from her house, somehow made her story more real.

I fit my fingers between the slits, heaved upward on the grates, and set out to finish what I had started.

When I limped through the trees, Jake appeared, setting his grates onto barrels. Pete waved me over with a sharp blade in his hand, several others circling around him.

One chore, one day. It wasn't much, but I was providing for myself. I was earning my stay—whatever that meant. I wasn't sure anymore. Stay. Stay. What was it that kept me? My skin clung to my bones. Thoughts ran their course, draining what energy my body had left.

"Careful!" Jake met me where the tents began. "The barrels are lit," he warned, relieving me of half my load.

I limped behind him to the last open barrel and dropped the grate on top of it, careful not to get too close to the flames. Pete trailed us, throwing a few slabs of fish onto the fire.

While the crowd grew, I pulled myself from their demanding hands and drifted quietly into Pete's tent. It was empty. I lay down, hoping the effortless act of existing without movement would let me rest.

I retraced the outline of my life, so undefined by the lies that I had tried to shape it with.

What else are you hiding from yourself? Where did it all start?

My dad passing … everything had felt so temporary since then. My family that had subsequently fallen apart. Graduation—why hadn't I walked? Was the wreck an excuse? I'd always been afraid—and still was— of the type of life that certified promise. Just like I'd been afraid of Astrid rejecting me, or worse, forgiving me, leaving me to waste my time contemplating when she was going to leave again. Being a coward was exhausting. I needed to find her. If for no other reason than to give myself closure.

I shot up right, cooling the light sweat around my eyes with the abrupt movement. I swung my feet to the ground, and blood pooled around my heel—a reminder that there would always be something out there keeping me a step behind. I took my shoe and blood-soaked sock off, then fished through my bag for new socks and a piece of cloth that had come with the backpack for cleaning computer screens. I took the sock from the other foot, wiped the wound and placed the cleaning cloth onto it before slipping a clean sock and my shoe over it.

Outside, the swarm of people had already retired to their small groups by their tents. I stumbled through the crowd and strode over to Pete, who stood with his back to the eastern tree line.

"Pete!" I hollered, waving at him. "I need to go back into the city."

He fed inedible scraps of food into a flaming barrel. "What for?"

I bit my lip and shifted my weight off my torn heel. "I need to find Astrid. I should never have left without her." My breathing hitched, tightening my chest as a flow of heat rushed to my cheeks.

"Then go find her," he replied.

I took a step back and grimaced at the foliage that originally delivered me to the camp. I didn't want to ask for his help—he'd already given me so much. But I didn't know how to get to the city, much less where to look for her when I did. "But I—" I turned back to him, but he cut me off.

"Go find her," he said with a solemn face and a wave of his hand.

Coward.

Blood stretched my veins with adrenaline.

"Thanks, Pete," I said with as much sincerity as I could muster and bowed. "I'll try to be back tonight." I glided through the camp on my ankle that had numbed over with determination into the woods.

The sun cast a warm glow onto the forest. Lumber tripped me. Pine pricked me. But then the echo of voices filled the trees, and I stopped in my tracks.

Laughter. Mumbles. Mumbles.

"Lisa?" I yelled into the thick, causing the leaves to stop crunching. "Is that you?"

"Zachary?" a familiar voice answered.

I sprinted after her while she brushed the forest floor with her feet.

"Lisa, I'm leaving to find—" I stood paralyzed as a petite girl wearing a camera around her neck stepped into view.

"Astrid. I was just going to find you."

"I heard." She giggled.

"I'll meet you two back at camp." Lisa smiled and disappeared into the thick of the woods.

Astrid bit her nail, then dropped her hand.

"Astrid, I'm so sorry for getting mad at you. What happened wasn't your fault." I shifted my gaze to my shoes, sprinkled with dirt and bark. "I waited for you though. I swear."

"I know," she said. "Lisa told me everything."

"Everything?" I lifted my head, determined to leave the coward behind.

She grabbed my hand without warning. Her skin—it was so soft and comforting. A touch I'd never forget.

Chapter 18

"This place is amazing!" she said, facing me as I closed the flap to Pete's tent that he'd generously lent us. "I thought Lisa was crazy when she told me about it. The only reason I came was because she knew so much about you." She ran her thumbs under the straps of her backpack hanging from her shoulders.

"I don't know about amazing, but it will do until we figure things out." I smiled, reaching for her bag.

"Zachary." Her words slowed. "We need to talk." She slipped the bag off and held the haul loop by one finger.

I froze, letting the weight of her bag drag her arm down before I grabbed it. I set the bag on my cot, my mind racing.

"Okay, can we talk after dinner?" I asked, squaring my shoulders.

Her eyes shifted, and she glanced in my direction. "Sure."

After leaving the tent and joining the others near the barrels, we buried our troubles for the time being. That night was very much like the previous one, except with more food. The fish was surprisingly good, even seasoned.

"Just take a bite!" Pete held a sliver of meat out for Astrid as he, Lisa, and I crowded around the blazing barrel.

She laughed and pushed it away. "Thanks, but I'll stick to the veggies."

"Good thing you don't have Zachary's moral compass." Pete chuckled, jabbing me in the ribs while stuffing the white meat past his teeth. "He refuses to eat anything we take from the fields," he mumbled through a mouthful.

"It makes me feel bad!" I covered my mouth as I finished chewing and swallowed. "I always think about how disappointed Jonas would be."

"Jonas?" Lisa wiped the corner of her mouth with her pinky.

"Jonas and Mary!" Astrid smiled. "They were the sweetest couple. We met them at their thrift store, and they gave us a place to stay for the night."

"How far have you traveled since you met?" Pete's eyes widened behind the corncob in his mouth.

"Since we met?" I looked over my shoulder at Astrid. "I don't know. A thousand miles or so?"

"Probably more than that! We took a lot of back roads," she said, licking corn from her teeth.

"Well, we're happy to have you here." Pete stuffed the leftover husk through the grate into the flames. "Make sure you open the ceiling vent before you go to sleep; it gets stuffy with two people if you don't." He winked at me from across the barrel. "I'm off to bed."

"I'm right behind you." Lisa brushed her hands together. "See you two in the morning!" She smiled and ran off to her tent.

They were two of the first to go to bed, but the others didn't last much longer.

Astrid and I lay on our backs a foot apart, the thick metal barrel radiating heat by our feet.

"It's getting late," she said, sprinkling a handful of shredded grass onto my chest.

I laughed, letting the weak breeze brush a couple of the blades from my shirt. "At this point in our lives, don't curfews seem a little silly?"

"I guess so." She paused. "Do you think you'd be happier living like this?"

My gaze shifted between the Milky Way and the Big Dipper before skipping to the moon. "What do you mean? Like, in a tent … here?"

"Yeah."

"No." I swallowed, gripping into the turf with my fingers. "There is too much down time. I don't think I could be left to my thoughts like that."

"Mmm."

A few moments passed.

"What?" I said, tilting my head.

"You said you couldn't be left with your thoughts."

"Yeah?"

"But you never talk about what you're thinking."

I paused. "Want to go back to the tent?"

"Sure." She rocked into a sitting position, then stood. I did the same, and we sauntered through the grass, me limping after her.

I unzipped the flap, letting her in first before closing it behind me. Slouched on the edge of Pete's cot, I rubbed my thumbs across my brow. Astrid's shoulders mirrored mine, but she crossed her arms, staring at the pine and dirt on her laces. A battery-powered lantern cast a soft yellow glow that illuminated the off-white tent fabric, contrasting her face and stray hair that braved the space around her head. She straightened and bit the inside of her lip, twiddling her fingers. Seeing someone so beautiful quietly fall apart was punishment enough.

"Why didn't you ever tell me about the wreck?" Astrid asked.

My brows raised beneath my fingers, and I lifted my head.

"I don't know …" It wasn't something I was ready to face—not with her. It proved easier to tell a stranger like Lisa. I didn't want Astrid to think about the wreck every time she saw me.

"I don't want to revisit the last few days. I thought I did, but …" she said, submitting herself to an easement of thought.

"Well, I'm sorry," I said in a hushed voice, hoping it was enough to validate her forgiveness.

"Me too. Neither of us handled it right." She tucked her dark strands behind her ears. "I'm not going to make you talk about it, but I'm here if you ever decide to."

I nodded.

Her simple words made it easy to look past our flaws. Though we were living in the moment, the impact those moments had on our future were growing immensely.

She flicked an ash from her sleeve. "I need to change my shirt."

"Oh." I straightened and squirmed on the cot. "You want me to go outside?"

"No. Just close your eyes," she said, unzipping her bag and fishing out a lesser-used T-shirt.

"I still have the shirts I bought before we left the motel." I hunched over and slid my backpack toward me, grabbing the plastic pack that stretched in my grip as I handed it to her.

"Thanks … " A faint blush filled her cheeks as she poked her finger through the packaging. "Eyes."

"Oh!" I covered my face with my hands, muffling my voice. "Sorry!"

Her back cracked, and her nails scratched the low hanging slope of the tent roof. I opened my eyes a fraction of an inch, barely parting the ends of my fingers. The gold of her skin outshined that of the lantern light. Tan lines illuminated the edges of her bra until she slipped the straps from her shoulders and shed it completely. I squeezed my eyes shut again.

Moments later, a bag zipped. "You're good," she said.

I lowered my hands and opened my eyes, this time completely. She'd already slipped off her shoes and socks, sitting with her feet pointed inward while she gripped the frame of the cot.

I untied my sneakers and kicked them off one at a time, but left my socks on to hide my gash. "Are you ready for bed?" I asked through a yawn.

"Yeah." She picked at a dry scab on her knee.

I killed the lantern and made myself comfortable on the covers of Pete's cot.

After a few minutes, a shuffling sound filled the tent, followed by the squeaky springs of my old bed, then hollow aluminum legs scraped across the tarp, clinking the two trundles together. The darkness hid her face, but I smiled despite myself. I longed for her touch. I shifted my elbow across the threshold of her space. She curled up on her side and scooted toward me until her back brushed against it. Lying there with her so close to me felt like all the effort wasted on starting over had only brought me closer to where I'd begun.

The next morning, the scratching of graphite on paper filled the tent. I rubbed my eyes and turned toward Astrid, who had propped herself up against the stiff cot. A wave of hair, already longer than when we'd started our journey, was draped over her shoulder.

"Morning," I said, propping myself up on my elbows.

"Morning," she echoed.

"What are you doing up so early?"

"I'm writing my mom a letter. She should know why I left and that I'm not coming back."

I leaned over the foot of my bed to search my backpack for my toothbrush. "Do you think she's worried about you?"

"Probably … when she's not high."

I stopped digging through my bag when my hand brushed the letter that Jonas had given to me to deliver. "What if she doesn't reply?"

"I won't give her that power over me. I'm just going to put the return address of a condemned house that is next to hers," she said, clearly having thought it through.

Why had she said *hers*? Had she grown detached from the house since she'd left, or had she always felt that way?

"What are you going to say?" I rubbed the black ink on the envelope still hiding in my bag, debating on whether I should tell Astrid about it.

"I don't know. Do you have any actual paper?" She dropped her hands to her sides, a short receipt in one and a broken pencil in the other.

"No," I said, grabbing my toothbrush from my bag and zipping it. "Pete might though. How much do you need?"

"You don't think he'd care?" She tilted her head.

I glanced at the tent door and listened for anyone outside.

"I won't tell if you don't."

She paused for a second. "Just a few pieces."

I tossed my toothbrush onto the cot and opened his trunk, which emitted a pleasant scent of fresh linens. On the left side, clothes lay pristinely folded, a single dryer sheet centered on top of a blue polo. On the right, a pair of brown ankle-high dress boots sat next to a small basket of underwear and socks. Tucked behind it all was a notebook.

"Here we go," I said, sliding it from the trunk. I ripped the paper from the metal spiral and set the sheets on her cot. She grabbed them before taking the covers off her cot. Then she pulled the surface over her crossed legs in the center of the tent like a desk, facing me.

"Do you have anything I can write on?" she asked, pressing against the cot. "This cot isn't tight enough."

"Here." I held out the notebook, stray papers springing from the metal spiral.

"Thanks. How about a pen or something?" She laughed and held out a crayon-sized pencil. "This thing is worn to a nub."

I opened the trunk again. "Will a mechanical pencil work?" I asked, spotting a couple of white erasers protruding from under his shoes.

"As long as it has lead."

I plucked them from beneath the soles of the boots and rattled them in my hand before nodding and tossing one to her.

"Thanks." She clicked the eraser and hunched over the notebook.

"Do you mind passing me a piece back? I should write my mom too." I fanned the second pencil between my fingers.

"Sure." She handed me the pieces that I had originally ripped out for her and flipped the notebook open to the first empty page.

I blinked, and like that, I was alone again—staring into her life from the outside. She'd done the same, already blocking the rest of the world out.

I stripped my cot and lay on my stomach on top of it. Whenever I'd write a few words, she'd sigh … so I listened in on her silence until I lost track of what I was writing. I'd get a thought out, and she'd stretch her legs beneath her. I cleared my throat and crumpled my letter, which had by then become a rant of what she meant to me.

Eventually, I gave up and left the tent so she could have the time to herself—hoping the space would help her find clarity.

It took three days for her to write that damn letter. She'd leave the tent for an hour at a time if the sun was out, but then she'd return to nap, draw, or, of course, work on her letter. I dreaded the nights because I knew I'd be trapped in that tent and would have to witness her falling apart. Soon her sighs turned into disillusion; her shoulders drooped as she stared at the letter, shaking her head enough to swing her hair that cascaded down the side of her face.

"Are you okay?" I spoke for the first time in almost an hour.

"I'm fine. I just can't believe it's all come to this," she said, rubbing the side of her face.

"Come to what?"

"Nothing. I'm fine," she said, bending the corner of a page.

I knew it was best not to push her.

She didn't say good night that night. She didn't even turn off the light or remake her cot. She shoved everything onto the floor with her forearm and lay down with a thin sheet half covering her body. Crowded by her despair, I was paralyzed.

She closed her eyes and rolled onto her side. "I'm done."

"Done?" I pried, lifting my head.

"Done."

Chapter 19

Lisa dropped our letters in a local post office box the next day. The thought of Astrid's lingered like a dead cow blocking the road.

"You want to go into the city for the day? Maybe eat some real food?" I kneeled beside Astrid at the stream, distracting her with a soft voice.

"No," she said, her barely audible voice giving out. "I need to lie down."

"It'll be okay." I leaned over the water and met her gaze while digging my knuckles into the soft, damp ground.

She didn't say anything at first, water flowing over her still hands. The current thrust a leaf against her thumb, it's stem quivering.

"Thanks." She pushed herself upright, and without so much as shaking her hands dry, she strode back to the camp.

When I returned to the tent to check on her an hour later, her cot had been dragged to its original location—away from mine—and she lay with her back facing me.

"Astrid," I whispered, standing over her. "Are you awake?"

Nothing. Even her breathing had hushed.

"If you're awake and want to talk ... I'm here," I said to the dead air that filled the tent.

Still nothing. I eased myself onto my cot, her absence demanding my attention. Minutes passed like hours, heat cramming the space between the ceiling and my chest. Words pricked at the back of my mind. I wanted to carry her to safety, but the real destruction was festering inside her head. It was an infectious coma; the longer I shared that tent, the more chaos overtook me.

Leaves crunched outside the tent, and a body cast a shadow on the door of our tent. "Astrid? You in there?" Lisa said.

I paused and turned my head toward Astrid, who still had her back to me.

"Yeah," Astrid said after a brief silence, extending her arm into the thick air.

My face tensed, but I bit my tongue.

"What are you doing in there?" Lisa knocked on the tent post. "It's not even dark yet!"

"I was just resting." Astrid sat upright on the edge of her cot as her gaze met mine. "You can come in," she said in a monotonous voice.

Lisa unzipped the flap and let it fall to the side behind her.

"Oh, Zachary!" Lisa stopped at the entrance. "You're here too."

"Yeah, I've only been in here a few minutes." I swung my legs off the cot, blood rushing to my throbbing ankle.

"I was thinking about going on a hike." Lisa shot a glance at Astrid.

Astrid rubbed her eyes with her palms. "Sure, yeah, that would be cool. Let me put on my shoes."

Lisa massaged her elbow.

"You can come too, Zachary." Her gaze shifted between Astrid and me.

Astrid slid the heel of her second shoe on with her finger as my ankle pulsated against my sock.

"No." I adjusted my weight to the ball of my foot. "I think I'll stick around here."

"Okay." Lisa arched her brows. "You ready then, Astrid?" she asked, ducking back outside.

"Yeah." Astrid stood and walked to the tent's opening, then stopped—still facing the lightly flapping door. "We'll be back in a few hours. I'll bring you something to eat if we run across anything."

With that, she disappeared through the opening. I waited a couple of minutes, then slipped off my shoe and sock. I gently tugged at the cloth, but it had adhered itself to my skin.

I grabbed the water bottle from beside Astrid's cot that she'd left behind and poured some onto the fabric. The warm liquid loosened the sock's hold, eliciting a burning sensation. With a grimace, I ripped off the bandage. Where there should have been scabbing, a thin layer of skin oozed. I studied the cloth that I had dressed it with. Soaked in like tea, blood had hardened in the shape of an ameba. I folded the blotted cloth and hitched over to the doorway that Astrid and Lisa had left open.

"Pete!" I cupped my hands around my mouth. "Pete!"

Jake stood from his post beside a barrel a few tents over, dust flying all around him. "That's Pete's tent! Who are you?" He marched toward me, leaning into his stride with clenched fists.

"No! Wait, wait." I waved my hands. "Jake, it's me. Zachary! Pete is letting me use his tent."

He stopped in his tracks and scrunched his face.

"We went and got the grates to cook with the other day. Remember?"

"Oh." His face flushed, his fists loosening. "Where's Pete then?"

I hobbled out of the tent. "I don't know. I think he was going fishing. But I need him. I hurt my ankle—do you mind finding him for me?"

His gaze dropped to the torn patch of skin and dry blood.

"Yeah, yeah!" he said, averting his eyes. "I'll get him." With that, he took off toward the stream.

I bobbed through the flap and limped to my cot. I found my old shirt, stuffed in the corner with the rest of the dirty clothes, and stretched it out at the foot of the cot so I wouldn't get anything on Pete's sheets.

I eased myself onto the cot.

"How did I end up here?" I whispered under my breath.

Stop being so eager to belong.

I turned toward Astrid's side of the tent.

What are you doing to push her away?

What are you doing to hold her close?

I eased my head onto the pillow and swung my legs onto the bed, the metal frame and canvas mattress squeaking like the rusted spigot of my dad's old nursery garden hose.

Sleep it off.

I closed my eyes to calm my racing mind.

You should have been more open to her. What's the harm in being honest?

Rejection. Abandonment.

A memory of the last trip we'd taken as a family before my dad died emerged.

"Zachary," my dad had said, grabbing me by the shoulder with his callused hands and kneeling to my height, "look over there." He pointed to the end of the block, where a Christmas tree bigger than our house stood in the middle of an ice skating rink.

"Is it real?" I had asked, studying the lights that reflected from the tree onto the tinted glass building behind it.

"No, no." He laughed. "If that were a real tree, it'd be much smaller and would be called a fir. We don't grow them at the nursery because, well, we don't have the land yet—but it's my dream to expand so we can grow some for the folks at home." He stood and pulled me into a hug at his side. "I can't wait for you to be big enough to help out. I'd like to hand it all down to you one day."

"Okay," I said, distracted by the flakes that had begun to fall, soaking into the shoulders of my sweater. "Who pours the snow?" I glanced up, but my Dad was still focused on the tree.

"Aida, I'm going to call Benny about setting up a tree sale for next year." He reached into his pocket and fished out cash and a flip phone. "Why don't you take them ice skating, and I'll catch up," he said, holding out a fifty-dollar bill.

"Phil! Please!" She shook her head and shifted my little sister from one hip to the other. "We're on vacation!"

"I won't be long. Just take them skating, and I'll be there in a little while." He stepped toward her and slipped the wad of cash into her shirt pocket.

Bobbing my sister in her arms, she wiped the hair that had blown in front of her face and stared at the big tree, pursing her lips.

"Have fun, Zee!" he said as he punched the buttons on his phone and slipped through the door of the corner bar less than a block away.

You pushed him over the edge. You should have shown interest in his work, and then maybe he would have included you in more of his life.

My dad was absent more than usual that following year. By that winter, he had set up the tree sale using trees from a farm a hundred miles west of his nursery.

"The next step is to grow trees of our own." That was the last thing he'd ever said to me.

My mother had picked my sister and me up early from a church gathering later that week, tears pooling in her eyes when she pulled us aside.

"Your dad is sick." She swallowed her pain, her voice crackling. "We need to be strong for him right now, okay?" She squeezed my knee with a shaky hand.

Between that moment and walking through the hospital doors, everything slowed … as if the clocks were imprinting the memories.

"He's in the ICU," my mom said while rushing us onto the elevator. She clicked the button to the third floor, and the elevator droned over her heavy breathing.

The doors whooshed open after fourteen excruciating seconds.

"Do you know where Phillip Byrd's room is?" she asked a nurse passing by before we could even step into the hall.

"Two doors down." The nurse tilted her head, peering at my sister and me with glassy eyes.

My mom led my sister down the corridor, then swung the door open to his room.

"What happened?" I asked, standing feet from my dad's body, tubes protruding from his mouth.

My mother sobbed, nudging me toward him. "Say goodbye, sweetie. This may be your last chance."

I moved closer, my arms tucked into my chest and pressed against the side of the mattress.

My mom carried my sister to the other side of the room. "Phil," she said in a raspy voice, her blubbering obstructing her words. My sister wailed into her shoulder. "We'll always love you."

My body stiffened, my lips unable to move.

"Zachary, he may not make it. Say something."

I opened my mouth, but nothing came out as the life support machine chirped in my ear.

"God, please … " She rocked my sister, kissing the top of her curly head before she sobbed. "Oh God." She scooted a chair to his bedside and sat, my sister clutching to her tighter than ever.

The chirp screeched in my ear.

"Phil!" My mom set my bawling sister on the floor and jolted from the chair, towering over my dad.

His body convulsed, blood spewing around the tubes and out of his mouth.

"PHIL!" She hollered again, grabbing a nearby rag and wiping the blood from his neck.

Doctors broke through the door and rushed in.

"Back up, son!" A masked man reached around me and grabbed a defibrillator.

A nurse gently guided me to the door. "Honey, you need to step outside."

I was a pawn, unable to move on my own. I stared from the doorway as they ripped my dad's gown open and positioned the paddles over his chest.

"Clear!" the doctor had yelled.

My dad's body jumped after a short beep.

"Clear!" he called again.

A thud sounded in the distance, this time more real. My eyes flew open, and I shot off the cot, darting to the door.

"Pete?" I squinted while a tall figure swung something over his head.

"Yeah?" he said when my eyes focused and he dropped an ax into a log.

"Didn't Jake ever find you?"

"No." He lifted the ax and dropped it again. "What's up?"

"I need something to wrap my ankle with. I hit it with a grate the other day, and it's not healing," I said, gimping into the grass.

"Why didn't you say anything when it happened?" His eyes narrowed, and he set the ax down on a pile of logs. "There's a first-aid kit in Lisa's tent. I'll grab it."

He hustled to her tent while I hobbled inside to the cot.

"How bad is it?" he asked from the entrance before I could get settled.

"Worse than I thought," I said, lifting my ankle onto the end of the cot where the T-shirt had already been dabbed with blood. "It completely scraped the skin off, and the gash over the bone won't close."

"Let me see." He set the white plastic box beside me on the cot and unhooked its latch. "Oh yeah, it gotcha good." He tore open a paper packet and pulled out an alcohol swab. "This is going to burn, okay?"

"Okay," I said, stiffening.

"One, two … " He dabbed the wound.

I scrunched my face, laughing to hide my pain. "You didn't get to three!"

"What's going on in here?" Astrid ducked through the flap.

"I … " Heat rushed to my cheeks.

"Zachary, here, has a little boo-boo." He snickered, squeezing ointment onto a patch of gauze. "But this should fix it," he said, gently pressing it against the wound.

"Oh." She flipped her hair over her shoulder and snatched her backpack. "I just need to grab something. Then I'll get out of your way."

She dug through her bag and dropped it next to her cot, then stepped back outside.

"Trouble in paradise?" Pete asked while wrapping tape around my ankle.

I hunched over. "She's just dealing with a lot. It'll be fine."

"Okay, well"—Pete threw everything he hadn't used back into the box and latched it again—"you're good to go."

"I think I'll let it rest for the night." I sat upright on the cot as he stood. "Thanks for the help though!"

"I was about to make grilled vegetables. I know how you are about eating the farmer's crops, but the better you eat, the quicker you'll heal." He patted his stomach.

"Thanks," I said again. "I'm not hungry right now, but I'll join you if that changes."

"All right, buddy." He set the first-aid kit on his trunk and left the tent.

Once he'd zipped the flap on the door and the space had quieted, Astrid's and Lisa's voices trickled in.

"So, let me get this straight," Astrid said, clearing her throat. "First I rub the chocolate on the bottom of the can. Then I polish it with the candy bar wrapper?"

"That's it!" Lisa said. "I'll do it with you since we found two cans."

"I don't see how this is going to start a fire," Astrid said as the cans crinkled.

"Once we get the bottom of the cans all shined up, you point the polished part at the sun and put a small piece of tinder in front of it."

"I don't know … " Astrid drew out her voice, giggling.

I lay back on the cot and rolled over onto my side, my eyes stuck on her unmade bed.

"You'd better hurry!" Lisa belted. "We're running out of sunlight!"

Astrid giggled again. "Okay, okay! I got it. What should I use for tinder?"

"Just use some pine needles," Lisa said, her words growing short while leaves rustled outside the tent flap. "Here, take these. They should be dry enough."

They both grew quiet. I could hardly stand it, frozen on the cot like a jealous child, not wanting to be heard.

"See the smoke?" Lisa said. "It's starting!"

Astrid gasped. "I can't believe this is actually working! I bet you could survive the wild if you were truly stranded, couldn't you?"

I tilted my head, my white knuckles gripping the edge of the cot.

Lisa's voice dropped an octave. "It'd be difficult, but I'd make it." A moment of silence passed before she spoke again, her tone returning to something more upbeat. "Let's use these to light my barrel!"

Two hours later, my solitude persisted, and I lay on my back, staring at the threads of my ceiling. I listened to the night as the crickets filled in for the voices that muttered outside throughout dinner. I had an incurable restlessness whenever she was away.

A boisterous laugh shot off in the distance. I couldn't take it anymore. I threw the blankets from my body and snuck out of the tent. Lisa's tent flap was unlaced, a faint light glowing beyond the opening.

As I neared her tent, the clearer the heavy breathing became. I crept closer until Lisa came into view.

She was completely naked on her hands and knees, arching into a kiss. Her hair fell over her shoulder, covering the face of the person beneath her … so I moved in closer. Astrid's nails, painted with chipped red polish, clawed at Lisa's ass. Astrid's clothes were on, but that didn't set any limits as Lisa's hand worked hard beneath her elastic waist band. It was like watching a plane crash, Lisa's lips falling from her mouth and down her neck while Astrid turned her head and closed her eyes. When Astrid arched her back enough to slip down her shorts, I turned away. I had seen enough.

I stumbled back to my tent.

Autopilot.

"Food." I eyed Lisa's barrel, where she had left a basket of fruits and vegetables.

"I should leave enough for the bears," I muttered while grabbing squash and radishes from the top of the basket and hurrying off to my tent.

Adrenaline numbed my ankle as I packed my things. The thought of facing the two of them, or worse, enduring their honesty the next day, churned my stomach. I stole the sheet from my cot and took off with my bag in hand.

Alone again, I internally accepted that for the last time, I had passed through the opening of an old home. I blended into the darkness of night without a lantern or flashlight. The air felt very much like it had the night I left home: desperate and undefined. My skin even mimicked that night, like I was chasing it through the forest.

I didn't look left or right. My body didn't register sound or sight. Black leaves falling to the ground around me filled my empty mind like static. The images of her loving someone else stained me while my restlessness *sus*tained me.

I sped up and fumbled over downed trees, scraping my skin on bark and twigs. No amount of speed or force could get me away quickly enough, even though I was without direction. I kept my eyes fixed only a few feet ahead of me so I didn't misjudge any steps. All it would take is a broken ankle, and I'd be left for dead.

Betrayed, broken, worthless.

Misdirected by fate and undirected by circumstance.

I was angry at what had happened but even angrier at myself for letting her mean so much to me. I'd never had success expecting anything from anyone and wasn't sure why I had thought Astrid would be an exception.

Chapter 20

Dirt stained the white cloth when I squirmed out of the sheet I had stolen from Pete's tent the night before. The hissing of trains masked my movements while I packed up and hobbled further from the station through the trees.

I edged up to the tracks and counted four sets of rails, the first two pointing east and the last two facing west.

West. West. West.

I checked my peripherals and emerged from the trees, planting my foot on the rail, then leaped over the coupling of the first set of trains. I did the same with the second track and hid between the cars, leaning against the couplings until I could figure out my next move.

"There are two more trains," I mumbled under my breath, rubbing the vintage steel that connected the cars behind me.

The one nearest to me was carrying machinery, which Pete had once mentioned would likely lead to a large city close by, and the other was freight. The first train blocked off the telling details of the second one, but I assumed it was going farther than the first all the same. With that, my best bet was obvious.

The freight train furthest from me lurched forward as I stepped out from my hiding spot to a clear path that separated me from the last two rows of tracks. I checked my shoelaces when the train gathered momentum, then I tightened the straps of my backpack. Raising my head, I checked the coast again. Astrid split the opening with her back to me, standing clearly between the tracks.

My heart pounded in my chest, and I slammed against the car, taking a deep breath. I had to cross the tracks and make it to that other train without her seeing me. I inhaled and smacked my thigh with my fist, closing my eyes and emptying my lungs.

One. Two. Three.

I opened my eyes and shot across the rocky divide to the first line of tracks.

"ZACHARY!" she yelled.

I hurdled the coupling.

Her feet pounded the dirt behind me as the shifting rocks amplified between the metal carriages.

I fell out of the gap and into another lane that gave way to my escape. Ahead of me, a broken lath jutted out from a cracked door.

"WAIT!" Astrid let out while she caught her balance and sprinted after me.

I clutched the straps of my bag and bolted toward the open car.

The train was barely up to a crawl, but it challenged my strides as I inched closer.

I ripped the splintered plank from the door and swung it to the side before forcing the door open. Out of breath, I stiffened my arms against the stubborn sliding panel until it budged, and I threw my bag in onto a pile of empty crates. Still in a jog, I hoisted myself into the small opening and fell onto the wooden floor one shoulder at a time.

"No, no, no, Zachary, wait!" she yelled again as I tucked my legs inside.

I rolled over on the hard slats and peered around the door to find Astrid less than a car behind. I jumped to my knees and struggled to heave it closed against its bent metal frame. My shoes gripped the floor, putting all my weight against the stuck door. With a loud cracking sound, it let loose just as Astrid's fingers curled around the metal frame.

"Watch out!" I yelled.

Before I could stop the door, it rammed against her delicate bones.

Her shriek pierced the panel.

I clawed at the crack but couldn't break it's hold. I scrambled to the pallets, where my bag had landed. Breaking a board with my heel, I stood and twisted it until it splintered apart. Then I darted back to the door and shoved the skinny piece of wood through the opening above her fingers and shimmied the door open. Her arm smacked the floor, and tears pooled in her eyes as she reached for me with her other hand.

I snatched her by her arm and backpack, then dragged her into the car. She rolled in agony, holding her damaged hand against her chest. After kicking the door closed, I ran back to her and dropped to my knees.

"Let me see it!" I yelled. She uncovered a quivering hand with the other. The skin was torn and swollen. "Can you move them?"

"It h-hurts!" she stammered, slowly flexing her hand in front of her face.

"They aren't broken!" I said with a gruff voice and straight brows. I shed my shirt, ripped off one of its sleeves, and grabbed my water bottle from my bag before pouring water onto her wound and dabbing at them with my sleeve. As the blood washed away and revealed shallow cuts and scraped skin, her anguish subsided. I tossed the sleeve I cleaned the wounds with into the corner, then tore the other sleeve off and tossed it to her.

"Thank you," she said, still sniffling from the shock. She picked up the sleeve and, with shaky hands, wrapped her fingers together.

I had nothing left to say … her presence tied my stomach into knots. I grabbed my bag and walked to the other side of the car.

"What are you doing?" she asked.

"Nothing," I said under my breath, testing the door that we hadn't used.

"You going to jump off and run from me again?" Her knees trembled beneath her.

"You don't deserve that satisfaction," I responded, propping the door open with a scrap from the broken crate before slumping against the nearest wall, fixated on the narrow opening. "Hopefully no one at the train station heard you screaming out there. Luckily, we were running away from it."

"I know what you saw, Zachary." Her voice wavered, but it held conviction.

I didn't break my trance with the passing scenery; it was what it was, and spilling my heart out would never change that.

A steep ditch trailed the ground beside the car like a snake after its prey.

"I was confused, and it's not like you and I are official," she said, tucking a loose strand of her dark hair behind her ears. "She just helped keep my mind off things, which is what I needed."

I scoffed and drummed my legs to a desperate playlist that kept growing in my mind when she shifted toward me.

"Don't you fuckin' move." I glared at her with all my certainty.

She broke into tears again, but this time with wrongfully obtained dignity. Her gasping sounded like lies.

Twenty minutes passed with no sign of civilized life. She sat curled up quietly in a puddle of sweat and tears on the other side of the car, and spite flowed through me like a drunken teenager.

"Are you sure you don't want to cuddle up next to me to make yourself feel better?" I retorted.

She had nothing to say, which aggravated me more.

"Why in the hell were you even out here to begin with? You had no right."

Still, nothing. It drove me crazy, which threw the entire notion that I shouldn't let other people affect me.

Trees gave way to a street outside so I jerked the door shut. Crazy, crazy, crazy. Why do I always repeat things until they lose their meaning?

Three minutes passed.

"I couldn't lose you." Astrid muffled her words into makeshift bandage that covered her torn fingers.

"Well, according to you, we weren't anything anyway." I crossed my arms and glowered at her.

She sat up and locked her gaze on mine. "What? So I felt smothered by you and let someone else show me affection, and that means we don't mean anything to each other?"

"No, it means you didn't respect me enough to tell me how you felt, and then you went and slept with someone else when I obviously lo—" My eyes grew and my cheeks burned as the words sped past my teeth.

"You what?" She straightened and leaned closer.

"Nothing. It doesn't matter. You won't have to worry about me smothering you as soon as I see the next town."

"You know what? You're right." Her voice softened, and she stood and ambled toward me with slow strides, balancing on the teetering floor.

"I guess it's too late now," I said under my breath, focusing on the thread of light that bled in through the closed door. I held my gaze until she sat beside me with her hip touching mine.

"You're stuck in this car until the next town. So how about we sort this out, and then you can do whatever you want. I won't chase you." She dropped the side of her head to her knees, which were pulled into her chest, and gazed at me with those same big blue eyes that had stopped me in my tracks when we'd first met.

I shook my head.

"No more rules," she continued, holding a hand up, "because the two strongest feelings I have ever felt have come from knowing you and losing you … and I can't lose you without a fight." She dropped her hand.

"I think we see each other differently," I admitted, nodding. "Maybe we see everything differently?"

"Who said that we didn't feel the same way?"

I chuckled and dropped my gaze and tugged on my fingers. "Your actions, for one."

"Oh," she said, letting a few seconds pass. "These actions?" She leaned over and kissed me.

"Yeah, those actions," I said, pushing her away.

Through the corner of my eye, I caught her smile. "You know, the difference between last night and right now is this means something."

She leaned in once more, but I turned my head, and she grazed my cheek.

"I never wanted to love you, because until I'd met you, I didn't think it existed. Let me earn the right to keep you," she begged, curling her legs under her and propping herself up with one arm while the other rubbed my thigh.

My heart beat so hard that the abrasions covering my body pulsated, including my wounded ankle. She teasingly bit my lip and trailed my leg beneath my shorts.

"Stop it, Astrid. Seriously." I pushed her hand away, stood, and marched to the stack of pallets.

"Zachary, I'm sorry! What do you want from me?" Her eyes pooled again, her knees pressing into her chest.

"I can't ever have what I want from you, because you already fucked it up. I wanted to finish this trip we're on, find ourselves, and then … I wanted to trust you because you never gave me a reason not to. I wanted to love you."

The confession poured from my chest and flooded the car, making the air heavier than ever. As I spoke, my ears rang, and when I had finished, the ringing faded into her meek sobs.

I sighed and crossed my arm over my chest. "What's wrong?"

"I can't take back what I've done," is all she could say, and she could barely get that out.

While part of me wanted to believe her, my childhood and the life thereafter had taught me that giving second chances meant letting people screw you over twice. So I let her cry, and I took my new post near the pallets.

Chapter 21

Staring at the metal rafters from my back, they scraped against the wooden ceiling, shaking bits of sawdust onto my face. Hours passed, though I no longer cared where we were or where we were going. Astrid slept in the corner near the door that worked. Part of me envied her for not having options; she was forced to figure things out as she went. While I was sure she would've preferred an alternative, I doubt she'd be hopping trains to get by if she had one.

What if we had never met?

My mind raced, attempting to justify the decisions I had made ... my face flushed and my shoulders hunched at how the world might have perceived my choices, and I was ashamed of that shame. But I knew I'd do it all over again, just for the opportunity to meet her.

You're not as mad as you'd like to be. Let it go.

I stood and crossed to the stack of pallets, sorting and rearranging them into primitive pieces of furniture. On the front wall, I stacked two columns high enough to sit on. In the center of the car, I used two more to create a table comfortably accessible from the floor.

I sifted through my bag and counted the various vegetables I had spitefully stolen on my trek to the train station the night before. Astrid lightly snored, slumped in the opposite corner. *She* had done this. I shook my head, my conviction of kissing Lisa myself eating away at me.

Astrid stretched from her dark corner into the sharp ray of light streaming in from the cracked door. Upon waking, her sleep hadn't deadened what had been said. She hoisted herself upright against the wall and pulled her knees into her chest, her posture drenched in regret.

Seeing her like that—so vulnerable.

Don't single out actions you want to hear—the ones that keep you safe.

"Astrid," I said in a low voice with a slight grin, "have a seat in my office." I gestured to the homemade table in front of me and rested against the wall with my eyebrows ruffled and my back straightened.

She smirked and tilted her head before crawling to the pallet table in the center of the car.

I pushed off the wall and met her on the other side of the table, gazing into her eyes as I hunched over its splintered surface. "Let's talk."

"Okay." She nodded, wiping the moisture brimming from her eyes.

"We need to make a plan."

"Okay."

"I want to have you around, and I think it's pretty obvious that you want the same thing." I paused, pulling the hair at my wrist. "But I need to know what we are to each other."

"I know," she said, breaking from her usual script but still leaving passive replies.

I tapped my fingers on the crates. "Okay … so, let's figure out what we are."

Silence.

I dropped my head.

"Do you know why I chased you onto a moving train?" she asked.

I lifted my head to find her eyes focused on a knot in the crate that separated us.

"I hated the feeling of waking up without you beside me. To be honest, I hope I die before you do so I never have to again." She turned to hide her smile until we both chuckled.

"I understand. I feel the same way about you," I said as our laughs faded. "But it's hard to believe you after that stunt with Lisa." I swallowed hard, avoiding her gaze.

She pulled her hair tight against her head. "I didn't need distance," she said, dropping her hands. "I don't really know what I needed … I just felt pressured by you. I don't have a good reason for what I did; I needed a mindless release that I didn't think I could get from you."

"What do you mean, you didn't think you could get it from me?" I blurted, shaking my head.

"I mean, you were already acting really intense, and I knew—well, I had hoped—if we ever did anything, you know, romantically … it wouldn't be because one of us was desperate and the other was filling a fleeting void."

In a really fucked up way, it made sense. I didn't want our first time to be tragic or desperate either.

"Look, you don't have to forgive me right now," she said, clawing at the table, "but make the punishment fit the crime. I can't lose you."

This was one of the few times I was thankful for having nothing more than myself to offer. She could have lived easier at the camp with Pete and Lisa; she knew that there was no glorified destination I was chasing, and I couldn't offer her any more security than she could have given herself.

"So, now what?" she asked with wide eyes.

I stood and moseyed to the door, cracking it open enough to see outside. "I have no idea." I rested my hands on my hips. "I honestly don't know where this train is going or when it's going to end. All I know is we're headed west."

"What's out there?" She hopped up and made her way to my side.

"Not a lot. Trees. Hills."

"You forgot the grass," she said, pointing to few tufts flashing past. "Oh, and dirt."

The car edged a corner, and her body swayed into my arms.

"I think we're safe." She smiled up at me.

I didn't say anything. My hold tightened around her, pulling her hips into mine. I slowly dipped my head as she pushed up from her toes until our lips touched. In that moment, feelings I didn't know I could ever express broke free. I pressed my hands onto every surface of her body, and the adrenaline rushed through me. I coveted her, pinning her against the wall. She teased my waistline with eager fingers, as desire worked past the pain of her injury.

"Don't stop," she whispered, her nails digging into the back of my neck.

I grabbed her by the hair and turned her head enough to bite her lip, but she shoved me back. Her breathing grew steady and heavy. She kicked off her shoes, unzipped her shorts and traipsed past me, easing backwards onto the makeshift sitting area I had pieced together earlier. Then she shed her shirt and shorts and spread her legs, her back arching where her shoulders met the wall. A wet spot on her cotton panties seeped through onto the crate she was sitting on.

My existence was tied to hers as she gyrated, reeling me in as she tracked red marks across her ribs, adding color to the black and white tattoo of her favorite record. I kneeled in front of her, my hands gripping her petite back when it arched, pushing her chest into my face. The smell of cheap perfume covered the faded musk of sweat between her breasts. I grabbed her by her bony hips and straightened while she wrapped her legs tightly around my waist. I fumbled with the clasp of her bra, and she pulled my shorts down. Once her bra was loose, I dropped to my knees, trailing her stomach with kisses until I licked the outside of her boyshorts. I yanked the tight cotton above her ass and tore them down, then slid them past her knees and over her feet. I spread her legs and went back to licking and kissing below her waist, pushing her thighs against her ribs. Her muscles trembled in my grip.

I slid up her body until I was prodding her through my boxer briefs, kicking my shoes off one at a time with my feet. Gasps filled the air as we grinded on top of a pile of clothes, my thumbs massaging her nipples. She slid into a sitting position, forcing me to stand on my knees. After leaning over, she peeled my boxer-briefs off. Then she scooted forward and opened her mouth, gripping me in the palm of her hand until her lips met her fingers. She pulled me out and gasped for air as I locked my fingers in her hair behind her head. She took a large breath and did it again, this time keeping me in her throat for a few seconds before massaging me with her tongue and hands. My muscles tensed as my eyes rolled to the back of my head.

Twisting her hair around my fist, I lifted her to her feet, shaking my underwear from around my knees. I then picked her up off the ground, and controlling her by the crook of her back, I set her down with her legs spread around my waist again. Unable to distinguish where one body ended and the other began, we turned being alive into a drug, a foreign addiction. I straddled her, pinning her to the crate with her dainty ankles over my shoulders. She moaned while I pounded harder, moving in to kiss her. My hand dropped to her collar bones from the side of her face, but she slid them around her neck. I couldn't last any longer. Our souls tangled until they were one. I gasped and rolled off her onto my back.

We both lay panting, our lungs working to catch up.

"We should mark this occasion," she said between breaths.

I laughed, rolling on the ridged plank toward her. "How?"

She stood, still naked, and rummaged through her clothes.

"What are you doing?" I asked while propping myself up on my elbows.

Moments later, she dropped everything but the item cupped in her fist and climbed onto the homemade table. "I thought I'd leave an unknown memory behind for others." She grinned, lifting her arms to string her panties through a hole between a rafter and the roof.

"Wait a second!" I urged from the pallet.

"What?" She froze with her arms suspended over her head.

"How have you been keeping your armpits shaved?" I scratched my scraggly beard and tilted my head. "Because I haven't been able to find a good barber anywhere."

"Oh my god. You are so dumb." She laughed, dropping her arms.

"Don't you think someone will notice them and take them down?" I flashed a mischievous grin.

"They probably will," she said as she lifted the undergarments to the ceiling once more and threaded them through a gap between it and a rafter, "and they'll probably wonder how they got there, which is the point." She stepped down from the table, then tiptoed back to where I was lounging. "Why do you have to be so logical all the time?" She laughed while joining me, using my chest as a pillow.

"I was a history major; logic is all I have."

"Whatever. If you were logical, you wouldn't be lying naked on a freight train to who knows where with a homeless girl."

"Oh yeah?" I paused. "Well, homelessness is where my heart is."

"I meant, you would have never taken—" she began but was interrupted by my smile. "Thank you," she finished with her own form of surrender and glee, nestling closer to me. "So, what are we going to do when we get off this train?"

I wasn't quite ready to leave the moment, but we needed a plan. "Well, we're headed west. We'll just have to see where we end up and then make further plans from there. I'd like to get up near Eugene, Oregon."

"What's out there?" she asked as I raked my nails through her hair.

"Nothing special. I have a friend out there and thought I would check it out." My face tensed.

"Okay." Astrid kissed my neck. Her instant faith in what I had said spawned nothing more than intense guilt for her, my body stiffening as I stopped stroking her hair. But I didn't think it was a lie that would matter, so I relaxed and wove my fingers back through her wavy locks.

You probably won't make it far enough to deliver that letter anyway.

The dimly lit box cradled our exposed bodies in a blanket of soft heat. The trip crossed my mind. Had our hysteria blinded us from the insanity of our quest toward the unknown? There wasn't any tangible progress, only the perception that things were getting better.

Or going to get better?

Planning was the only way we'd turn that nothingness into something.

Strategy—use the insurance money.

Before I could connect all the dots, banging and yelling detonated outside the car. We hopped up, gathering the pile of clothes beneath us.

"What do we do?" Astrid blurted while tossing me my T-shirt.

"Shh," I replied, feeling foolish for leaving a door cracked. "It might be the cops."

"Hello? I can see you! Help me!" A raspy voice wafted through the vibrating panel.

Sweat rolled down my body and soaked into my clothes as I threw them on, an intense itch taking over as I honed in on the desperation in the man's voice. "But cops wouldn't ask for help … "

Astrid's eyes grew, and she shook her head. "We don't know that!"

I pulled away from her. "He saw us. What if he turns us in?"

"Zachary!" She reached for my shoulder, but I was already at the door. "No-no-no-no!"

I sunk my fingers into the crack of the door that wasn't stuck and heaved it open. A thin man who was running alongside the car appeared, holding his tan bucket hat on his head with one hand and reaching out to me with the other. He was losing steam, falling behind the car an inch at a time.

"Grab my hand!" he yelled again and pushed his coke bottle glasses up that were sliding down his nose before thrusting his hand out again. "Please!"

Astrid ran up next to me. "Help him!" She nudged my shoulder with a change of heart.

I grabbed the man by his forearm, and he grunted between sprints.

"Pull!" he cried over the scraping of his shoes over track ties and through ballast rocks.

"He's too heavy!" I let out, losing traction in my bare feet.

Astrid grabbed my waist, and with a few more tugs, we all piled into the car.

"Thanks," the skinny man said between gasps as he sat up and brushed dirt from his Hawaiian shirt. He was more fit for a cruise than chasing down a train.

"No problem," I said, studying him with arched brows.

"I, uh—I missed my flight to California," he lowered his tone and tugged on the brim of his bucket hat, then stood and straightened his khaki shorts. He pulled the door closed again until only a half inch of sunlight streamed through. "You two look too young to be homeless—what are you doing here?"

"We're not homeless." My pride spoke out of turn. "We're traveling."

"We are homeless," Astrid admitted before my story grew, taking a step toward the man. "But you're not. Why were you chasing the train?"

The man sighed and rolled his shoulders. "I'm going to Vegas. I need to make back some money." He sniffed the air, then turned to the wall behind him and tapped on its panels.

"What are you looking for?" Astrid asked.

"Cameras and mics," he said quickly beneath his breath.

"Cameras and mics?" I repeated, convinced he was crazy.

"Yeah. I just want to make sure we aren't up for any surprises."

"Let him do what he needs to do," Astrid said under her breath, tugging on my arm and ushering me over to the pallets, where she and I had been lying naked minutes before. We huddled with our backs to the wall, intently studying the man from afar.

"All clear," he proclaimed as if we were waiting for the results of his analysis.

Nothing slowed him down. He'd glanced over Astrid's panties without a second thought as they dangled like a flag in the wind, shuddering above his head. From corner to corner he turned at the hint of any movement on the track, then cautiously lowered himself to the floor against the wall directly across from us.

"What are your names?" he asked with a quick tongue.

My hesitation rebelled his energy. "My name is Zachary, and this is Astrid."

"Where ya headed?"

"We're not sure—wherever this train ends."

"It ends in Vegas," he said, rubbing his teeth with his finger.

"Vegas?" I asked while studying the wrinkles on his shirt. "How close are we to Vegas?"

He adjusted his hat. "About fifteen hours by car. But this train isn't exactly fast, so it'll be a while longer." *Pop, Pop.* His mouth snapped as spit pooled behind his lips.

My blank stare didn't faze him, so Astrid picked up the slack.

"Are you sure this train is going to Vegas?" she asked.

"Positive." He rubbed his teeth again. "I've been waiting for it to pass through for a week now. This car was the only one I saw with a cracked door; they're really chomping down on security."

Astrid and I exchanged glances. We knew distance was nothing more than an obstacle, but it was an obstacle that proved more difficult over time.

"My name is Jeeves. You can call me Jeeves." His eyes wandered to the corners of the cabin again.

"Jeeves, like from Wodehouse's work?" Astrid asked, unknowingly turning me on with her wit.

"Who?" He was clearly not into vintage English humor.

"Never mind."

He worked past the confusion, taking his hat off and pushing a dent out that had dimpled again as soon as he moved his hand. "Yeah. It's a nickname some bigwig gave me at the tables years ago, and it stuck."

I leaned forward, balancing my hands on my knees. "Do you make this trip often, Jeeves?"

"Not on the tracks. At least, not like this. I have once before, but that was a few years ago, when—" He abruptly turned and focused his attention on the door that was still slightly ajar, then eased his line of sight back to us. "How about you?"

"No. It was kind of a last-minute thing. We're trying to get to Eugene," I answered.

"Eugene? You're going the wrong way!"

I rolled my eyes and let him keep talking.

"Your best bet is to catch a bus from Vegas. It would cost you though."

My guard quickly resurrected. "Yeah, we don't have any money. We'll just have to tough out the tracks." I counted the freckles on Astrid's knee, grabbing her hand.

I could trust her.

The past is real.

Let it go.

Don't be naive.

"Well"—Jeeves rested his shoulders against the wall across from us—"you have a long way to go then."

"We've come this far." Astrid squeezed my hand. "We'll make it."

She *was* there for me.

We faced each other, propping our feet up on the stacked crates that separated us. The thrum and clicking of the tracks drowned out our breathing while the two of us caught longing stares. Jeeves rooted himself against the back wall but only gave his attention to the narrow opening that he had left in the door.

"The city that couldn't," he called out in a monotonous voice. His glasses reflected the passing terrain.

I turned to Astrid, who shrugged, and we both stood. Jeeves slid to the side so we could join him.

"It's like the Smurfs' Village," Astrid said, pushing her face against the wood to get a clearer view.

"Weird, right?" I added, speculating about the tiny hut-like buildings that spread across a steep hill.

"What do you think they do for a living?" she asked. "There isn't much out here."

Jeeves chuckled. "Maybe you're right. Maybe it is the Smurf Village, and everyone just trades work … what is that called again?"

"The barter system?" I said.

"Yeah." He laughed again and rested his arm on his knee. "What I wouldn't give to have it that easy."

Astrid stepped away from the door and glared at him. "Yeah," she retorted. "I bet they have it real easy."

He was oblivious to the offense that he had caused. "Hey, do you two mind closing your eyes? I need to take off this sweaty undershirt, and I'm a little self-conscious." He rubbed his arm.

"We aren't going to judge you." I laughed.

"It will only take a second," he pressed, shoving his finger into the heel of his loafer.

"Let's just give him his space, Zachary." Astrid nodded and trudged back to the front of the car.

She kept her back to him and closed her eyes. When I stepped up beside her, she grabbed my hand and held it close to her.

"This won't take long." He grunted. "I think I'll take a nap. It's been a looong day." He exhaled. "Oh my god."

Astrid squeezed my hand tight.

"You're … " he said with a weak voice. "Good."

When I turned, Jeeves lay already curled up on the floor with his shoes off. "He must have been really tired." I squinted at his bony legs. "Looks like his feet took a beating getting onto the train." I pointed at bruises below his ankles and the small stream of blood pooling between two of his toes.

Astrid didn't pay the marks any mind and sat down. "We'd better save our energy; it's going to be a long trip." She pinched the seams of my shorts. "Do you have anything to eat?" she asked. "I can hear your stomach from here."

The cracked door was no longer flooded with light.

"Yeah." I spoke slowly, knowing I barely had enough for two. "You hungry, Jeeves?" I asked reluctantly.

He didn't budge.

"So do I." Astrid reached for her bag. "Let's share this now, and then we can split yours later," she offered with a flushed face as she pulled an apple and radishes from her bag.

I tilted my head and smiled. "Everything will be okay."

"I know," she said, biting her lip.

I stood and opened the door wide enough to let in what little light was left in the sky.

We moved to the center of the car, where I had situated the crate table.

"It looks like Jeeves isn't waking up anytime soon," I said, folding my legs in front of me.

"Yeah, he acted like a lot of people from home—very much on edge." Astrid let out a heavy breath and twisted the stem from her apple.

"Did you notice he didn't even button his shirt?"

"Yeah." She gripped both sides of the apple and twisted until it split in half. "Weird."

I jerked back. "Where did you learn how to do that?"

"We used to do it at lunch when I was in middle school." She giggled and handed me half.

"So, what do you think about Vegas? Do you want to visit there for a while?" I bit into a radish that had softened in the heat as we passed by the blaring bells of a street crossing.

She grimaced in the dull streetlights that sank through small holes around the cabin. "I think we have enough of *Vegas* asleep over there in the corner." She nodded at Jeeves, and we both laughed. "Plus, don't they say 'whatever happens in Vegas stays in Vegas'?" Her voice grew deep to mimic that of many.

"Yeah, so?"

"There is no part of my life with you that I want to leave in Vegas."

My hands fell to my lap and my brows raised. I never knew her to be so poetic. Of course, her photos were always beyond my own imagination … but looking back, perhaps her visions were merely expressions of beautiful longing? I thought I knew her well, but there was an entirely different side to her that I yearned to explore.

There wasn't a response good enough for such a clever and raw confession, so I just gave her the cutest damn grin I could muster. "Whatever happened to your *illusion* photos?"

"I haven't taken very many since the van was stolen," she avowed, swallowing a bite of her apple and dropping her hands to her crossed legs. "I just hope they didn't get too hot to develop."

"I'm sure they're fine. That's an old camera from way before air-conditioning existed."

She chuckled and placed her hand over her chest. "You really know the right things to say to get to a girl's heart."

"Cheers!" I played along, holding a radish in the air.

"Cheers!" She echoed, tapping what was left of her apple against it.

Chapter 22

The next morning, I awoke, reborn into a sour body from sleeping on shaking boards. Astrid was already up. I took a few moments to admire her sitting at the door that we had worked so hard to open and close, dangling her legs over the edge as if she were at the pool.

"Morning! How did you get that door back open?" I said.

"Morning!" she replied over her shoulder with her eyes hidden behind large sunglasses, pumping her arms out to the side to show off her muscles—dirt and blood residue stained her fingers where the cotton bandages had been wrapped.

"Nice!" I chuckled. "Is Jeeves really still asleep?" I asked, nodding at his slumped form on the other side of the car.

"He probably did heroine. It makes you sleep a lot. I doubt he'll be up anytime soon, so I covered his body the best I could so no one would recognize it in passing."

My body stiffened as her words sank in. She'd relocated the broken crate on top of his body, along with the T-shirt I'd torn up to clean her wounds. I shuffled across the floor boards until a rank odor dripping from his body assaulted my nostrils.

"It smells like he shit himself." I hitched back over to the clean air that blew in above Astrid's head.

"Yeah, they do that," she replied again. "You should have smelled it this morning with the doors closed. That's why I opened them." It killed me to see her cavalier reactions. She had been punished by red hands that could never mold her. Red hands that she would never forget.

"Saves us from having to share breakfast, I suppose," I joked, making light of her memories. I held my breath and ducked to the other side of the crate table to grab my backpack. "I have two radishes and squash," I said into my bag, returning to the clean air as quickly as I could.

"Breakfast is my favorite meal," she proclaimed, her voice carrying into the vastness of the desert. "Not because of the food, but because I believe how you enjoy your morning determines how you'll spend the rest of your day." Her tone was monotonous in every sense of the word.

"Then why do I feel like you're going to have a bad day?" I said as I took my place beside her, holding my bag open for her to choose from the buffet.

"There's not much out there." She cupped the radishes in her hand and popped them into her mouth.

"Yeah, I saw. The desert." I followed her gaze to the ground, chipped by the sun. "Save your water," I added. "Who knows how long it will actually be before we get there."

I broke a piece of squash in half and peered off at a distant cactus that was surely tougher than any human. A shiver shot up my spine.

Before we knew it, we were licking the little bit of juice from our two-piece meal that raced to our wrists.

"We'll have to face that smell if we want to conserve our energy," I said, plunging my hand into my bag. "These are dirty, but it's better than the alternative." I laughed, unrolling the two white T-shirts I had pulled from it.

Astrid blinked, then glanced at the coiled body in the corner. "I'm sure we can handle it." After kissing me on the cheek, she grabbed her shirt and stood, striding back to where we'd slept. "It is so bad." She tilted her head, covering her nose with the palm of her hand.

I got up and went after her. "Oh my god." I covered my mouth and nose with my shirt in one hand and my churning stomach with the other. How was it worse now than when I'd woken? "You'd think we'd get used to it."

I scrunched my nose as I held my breath and folded my shirt in half before lying down with my head an inch from the front of the car.

I covered my face from the nose up with the shirt like a masquerade mask. "It's not that bad."

Boards creaked, shifting beneath my arched back as Astrid situated herself on the floor beside me.

I had never known my life with so little before that point, but I'd never call it rock bottom. Nor could I bring myself to worry about the future. I had nothing to lose and grew excited for what was to come, maybe because it was unknown, or maybe because I had something to build to. Build from—was nothingness something that could be built from? A form of metaphysical construct material?

I extended my arm until the back of my hand met hers. Nothingness gave me infinite potential in any direction. Nothingness didn't come from running away and finding a clean slate to mark my new grave with; it came from losing everything in order to learn true value through the efforts of rebuilding.

Thus, you've marked your weakness.

She intertwined her fingers with mine.

After being introduced to true value, be it love, adventure, knowledge, or my bare existence, my life had value no matter what it contained beyond my veins. My cheeks raised as a wide grin overtook my lips, my heart thumping in my chest. My experience was something to be *proud* of. Something no one could take from me—a reference point if I ever had to start over. It had to be the most beautiful epiphany anyone could ever have. Astrid must have understood it long before she'd met me.

Infinite potential in any direction. Infinite potential.

What was left of my dignity? Who was I? Who had I been before? And why had I felt guilty for being better aligned with the person my past would disagree with?

Swoosh-swoosh! She and I both tore the stale shirts from our faces and shot upright. The train passed by a power grid, bells ringing in the distance at a railroad crossing.

"Jeeves!" I yelled, pulling myself up against the wall. "Wake up! We're here!" The train lost momentum. "Jeeves!"

He didn't move. Astrid grabbed her bag propped it against her shins.

I gripped my hair, running toward his body—and a body was all it was. I turned him over, removing the blanket of broken wood planks and random scrap from his body to reveal a puddle of piss and vomit. The top of his head was burnt and flaking from the sun that beamed through the cracked door. One of his pupils rolled to the side while the other stared straight at me.

"Astrid!" I shook, staggering backwards. "He's dead! Jeeves is dead!"

She closed her eyes, sighed, and twisted her hair tightly behind her head. "He was dead before we met him. Let's go." She tossed her bag out of the car and jumped after it.

I vomited, barely missing his face.

"Oh my god." I moaned, wiping my mouth with my arm.

Dizzy, I dragged my bag by a shoulder strap to the opening and jumped.

Dirt puffed around me while I rolled through the sand into a standing position. "What was that?" I yelled over the rumble of the passing train, still shaky and in shock.

"We can't get caught helping a dead man." She marched past a cactus, heading in my direction.

"Where are you going?" I asked, stepping in front of her.

She stopped in the grip of my shuddering hands. "Toward the street," she replied. "I can see cars in the distance. Figured we would hitchhike north." She jerked her shoulders from my grasp and stepped around me.

"Wait," I said, balancing on a mound of sand as the last car passed. "I have money."

"What do you mean, you have money?" She stopped in her tracks and spun on her heel.

"I was going to tell you on the train, but I didn't want Jeeves to hear. I have money—some in savings and probably more from insurance."

Astrid cocked her head. "Okay, so how does that change anything?"

"We don't have to do this anymore." I inched closer. "We don't have to worry about a place to stay—let's just get to the city."

She slogged up to me, the toe of her shoe digging into the sand. "Why didn't you tell me this when the van was stolen?" She glared at the street before turning her attention to me. "All of this shit could have been avoided!"

"I'm sorry!" I said, throwing my hands up. "I didn't know who I could trust, and I couldn't just give up on you. Plus, I didn't know when I'd really need it."

Her lips tightened, and she stared off into the distance. I rushed to her side. "Look, I'm sorry," I groveled while the train's horn blared in the distance. "Let's go rent a room, take showers, and catch a bus out of here in the morning."

I shifted toward her, but she couldn't hold it in anymore. Once I was within touching distance, she fell apart. "Why can't I catch a break?" She gasped through a swollen face of heat, sweat, and tears. I pulled her into my chest as she quivered against my body.

"I'm sorry!" I kissed the top of her fevered head and squeezed her tighter between my arms. "I can make this right."

She wedged her hands between us and pushed me away. "Let's go." She gasped again and pacified her tears, wiping her eyes with her arms. Like that, she was moving again.

She led the way until the grassy horizon solidified on the outskirts of town. We found a cheap motel that greeted us with a neon sign and a clear sense of the '80s. She held the door open for me without making eye contact.

"Need a room?" a pale old man with black circles around his eyes asked from behind the counter.

"We do." I walked by Astrid, who traipsed over to an air-conditioning vent with her arms crossed.

"Is a single queen okay?" He looked down at a chart.

She nodded, and I followed the man's gaze to the paper he was studying. "That's fine."

"That'll be $132.86." He marked the chart with his pencil.

"Do you have anything cheaper?" I asked.

The old man squinted at me. "We don't do hourly rates here."

"Are you serious?" Astrid beat her fist into the palm of her hand and then flung the door open and stormed outside.

I took my wallet out of my bag and handed the man my ID and card. "We'll take it," I said, stepping over to the glass door to check on her before hurrying back to the counter.

The man returned my card and ID, then held up a keycard to our room and a receipt. I stuffed everything except the key into my bag, then zipped it up and walked outside. Astrid stood beside a cigarette bin.

"Our room is this way." I nodded to the side of the building.

"Can you believe him?" She crossed her arms.

"I know!" I threw my arms up. "You haven't showered in days! I'm not that cheap." I laughed.

She tapped her foot. "It's not funny!"

"I'm just saying that I'm offended." I rolled my eyes, hoping she'd at least smile.

When she didn't reply, I cleared my throat, ducked my head, and started toward the walkway.

She followed me along the front of the building and up a set of stairs that ended at an ice machine with an Out of Order sign taped to it. Around the corner, we passed door after door with Do Not Disturb signs on their handles until we found our room.

"This is us," I said, sliding the keycard into the scratched lock that was bolted to a chipped, teal door.

I held it open for Astrid, and she strode directly into the bathroom with her backpack.

"You hungry?" I asked.

She ignored me, locking the door and turning on the shower. The faint sound of her sniffling carried past the water that beat against the tub through the door.

I locked the door to the room and waited outside the bathroom.

Don't pressure her.

I took my bag off and tossed it onto the desk, where a list of restaurants lay sorted in alphabetic order.

After ordering pizza and calling my mom, who didn't pick up, I called the insurance company, who said my money had not been sent out yet but could be wired to my account instead. Then I called the bus station and got the times for buses traveling to Eugene.

Astrid opened the bathroom door with strands of wet hair stuck to the side of her face and a towel draping from her chest.

"I wasn't sure what kind of pizza you wanted, so I got cheese. Is that okay?"

"Sure." She slogged to the air conditioner, opened the window, and hung her bra over it.

"I love you." I snuck up behind her and kissed her neck.

She closed the curtains and dropped her head. "Thanks."

"I paid over the phone." I let go of her hips, dallying to the bathroom as I pulled my shirt off over my head. "Do you mind signing for it when they get here so I can shower?"

"Sure." She paused. "Zachary?"

"Yes?" I spun on my heel and faced her, my shirt wadded in my fist.

"I love you too."

Chapter 23

The bus station took up half a block. Streetlights shined through the dark morning air and against the cocoa-colored ceramic tiles that wrapped around the side of the building as we made our way to the entrance.

"After you," I said, holding a large tinted door open for Astrid before following her in.

"You can sit down while I buy the tickets if you want." I pointed at a long bank of empty orange plastic chairs that were bolted to a cement floor in the center of the room.

Astrid followed my gaze while random people zipped past us to the sluggish line leading up to an aluminum wall of three ticket windows. "Okay." She sighed. "You want me to take your bag?" she asked, holding her hand out.

"Sure." I slipped it off and passed it to her. "Thanks."

She nodded and staggered to the chairs with our belongings.

I waited until she reached her seat before turning to the roped-off line next to me.

"I can't do that." The man directly ahead of me said to himself, wearing stained gray sweats that matched his greasy hair. "I can't do that. I can't do that," he repeated over and over.

A flat voice spoke up from behind a glass window. "I can help whoever is next."

The line inched forward like a stack of pinballs.

"I can't do that. I can't do that. I can't do that," the man ahead of me continued, swaying from side to side until he finally strode up to the center window.

"May I help you sir?" a middle-aged woman with freckles on her cheeks asked.

"I like the one with two dots." He slapped the palms of his hands on the counter and bounced on the balls of his feet. "You're gonna speak with your savior!"

"I'm sorry!" A young woman dressed in a torn green T-shirt with a honey bun in hand walked around the line to the window where the man stood. "I didn't see that he was already at the front of the line." She wrapped up what was left of her snack and set it on the counter before licking her fingers.

"Where are you going?" The clerk behind the window lowered her tone.

The woman in green pulled her finger from her mouth. "We're going to San Jose," she said, scratching the pimples on the back of her arm.

"Next person in line," a woman called from the left window.

I stepped up to it, still engrossed in the odd conversation beside me.

"Sir"—a lady with a dark fawn complexion tapped the desk across the glass from me—"can I help you?"

"Yes." I nodded, jerking my head toward her. "Sorry. May I please get two tickets for Eugene, Oregon?"

She typed in my request. "That bus leaves in twenty minutes."

"Must be my lucky day." I smiled as if I didn't already know the bus times and pressed my palms against the edge of the counter.

"That'll be $339.36. Cash or card?"

"Card please." I pulled my wallet from my pocket, then took out my card and pushed it through the arched opening at the bottom of the window.

She shoved the plastic into the reader. "Here is your card," she said, taking it out and placing it on the counter. "And your tickets." She ripped a receipt from the printer and slid everything back to me in a small pile through the window.

"Thank you," I said, folding the papers into my wallet.

I turned but was greeted by the smell of sandalwood and body odor.

"Let's go to the vending machine before we leave," the nasty woman with the honey bun said while leading the gray-headed man to the exit. When they cleared the way, Astrid appeared, her legs perched beneath her on the first bank of chairs, paying the exhibit no mind as she studied her chipped nails.

"We leave in twenty minutes," I hollered, moseying toward her while waving my wallet in the air with the tickets fanning out from the sides. "Bus number 3521."

She flashed a grin, then uncrossed her legs and slid our bags off a seat beside her.

"You ready?" I settled in next to her.

"Sure." She slid her hands under her thighs and dropped her head.

Murmurs filled the room.

I leaned forward and propped my elbows on my knees. "I'm sorry for not telling you about the money."

"It's not you," she said, blowing a strand of her hair with her weak breath as she spoke. "The Jeeves thing is messing with me. Like my past is following me or something."

My brows arched, and I rested my chin on my hinged fingers.

"I know." I shook my head. "Me too. All I could see when I closed my eyes to sleep last night was Jeeves and that little boy …"

"I guess we both have our demons," she said under her breath.

"Look"—I lifted my head and cleared my throat—"I thought I could give you a better life when I went back to get you."

"I don't even care about—"

"Astrid." I laid a hand on her shoulder and held her gaze. "Please, let me finish." I took a long breath and dropped my hand. "The truth is, I didn't even know you then. I only went off on a crazy whim to play hero because I needed a redemption story, and you were desperate enough to tag along."

She stared at her knees and sighed.

"But I know you now." I lifted her chin with my fingers. "And I know what we are capable of handling. The worst can be behind us if we let it."

"How do we do that?" She huffed and shrugged her shoulders.

"We let go." I dropped my hand and widened my eyes.

A staticky voice rumbled in a speaker above our heads. "Bus 3521 is now boarding."

She stood and looped her arms through the straps of her backpack. "We can figure this out later. Let's just get out of here. Please."

"Okay," I said, my gaze now fixated on a distant cola machine while she walked away.

You're letting her down.

When the exit door swung open and closed, I broke from my trance, gathered my things, and followed the red signs toward the buses. The windows next to the door darkened as the sun hid itself behind distant buildings. Astrid slipped her camera into her bag after I opened the door.

"Wait up!" I yelled, jumping into a trot.

I caught up to her at a long gray and silver bus with black windows that sat idling; a short skinny man stood beside it, checking tickets.

"I'm with him," she told the man, pointing at me.

"Tickets, sir?" He held his hand out.

I opened my wallet and pulled out the two slips of card stock.

"We hope you enjoy your trip." He scanned the barcodes with a handheld machine, then returned them and directed us up the step of the bus.

Astrid climbed the stairs first, stopping at the front of the bus.

"It's better than the train," I whispered in her ear and chuckled.

"Yep." She followed the aisle to the back of the bus and slid into the window seat with her bag on her lap. I sat next to her and did the same.

"You need not worry," a loud voice yelled from the steps, "because you are in the company of Jesus Christ during your travels. I will keep you safe." The man in sweat pants with greasy hair appeared in the center of the aisle.

"Good night." Astrid wedged her bag between her head and the window and closed her eyes.

The man plopped into a seat near the driver.

Shortly after he was seated, two women with orange complexions painted over their shallow wrinkles hopped up the steps. Each wore matching lime-green visors, light pink shorts, and baby blue T-shirts. "I can't believe we're doing this." The first one pulled a disposable camera out of her purse, something I hadn't seen since the early '90s. "Say cheese!"

The second one posed in front of the windshield, covering a mole on the right side of her face with a brochure.

"Got it!" The first woman said after snapping the picture, her peppered gray hair hiding the strap of her visor. "How cool is this camera?"

They made their way down the aisle with nothing but their purses and the camera in tow.

"Isn't it digital too?" the second woman asked.

"Yeah! It doesn't have a screen, but you can upload the picture straight to your computer with a USB." The first one waved the camera in the air. "Ten bucks! We can still use our phones, but I love the novelty."

They slid into the seat in front of us and snapped a selfie.

Astrid was fast asleep next to me with her head propped against the window. I smiled at her peacefulness, then stood and sidled up to the two women in front of us.

"Hey! Sorry to bother you, but would you mind doing me a huge favor?" I snickered. "My girlfriend is asleep behind you; would you mind taking our picture and sending it to me?"

The two women gaped at each other, bursting into laughter.

"Sure thing!" the one with the camera said.

I sat back down and leaned toward Astrid with my finger below her nose and a wide grin.

"Aaaand … " She pressed the button. "Got it!" she said, lowering the camera. "How do you want me to send it to you?"

"Do you have a pen?" I patted my pockets.

"No." She dug through her purse. "Here, just put it in my phone. I'll save you as a contact." She tapped on the screen a few times. "What's your name?"

"Zachary Byrd. Yours?" I leaned forward in the seat.

"I'm Margaret." Her thumbs danced on the screen. "And this is Brenda." The second woman waved.

"We just picked a random bus number, bought tickets, and hopped on." Brenda chuckled. "How exciting is that?"

Margaret held the phone through the gap between their two seats. "Here you go."

"That is super exciting!" I said, entering my e-mail address below an empty space for my phone number. "We are kind of doing the same thing." I pressed save and passed the phone back to her. "Thank you!"

"Sit in the center!" a voice boomed from the front of the bus, startling all of us. "You bounce less, remember?"

"No! No! No yelling." The man with gray hair covered his ears with his hands, rising from his seat and scurrying into the aisle in front of the woman in green.

"God, you're stupid." The woman grabbed him by the shoulder with one hand, holding a muffin with the other, and shoved him into the window seat several rows ahead of us. "They'd better give you the inheritance money, or I'm leaving you there. You don't deserve me anyway." She sat down.

"Unbelievable," I said under my breath. "Did you see—" I stopped myself when I turned to Astrid, whose chest dipped with each breath.

The trip took one day, two hours, and twenty-three minutes; that was seven minutes less than advertised, which was a small feat, but by the end of the trip, every minute counted.

Astrid slept most of the way. Of course, the bus stopped for refreshments, and she'd stay awake for a couple of hours here and there, but for the most part, she dealt with her past with her eyes closed or in silence.

The man with the gray hair hadn't caused any more disruptions along the way; he got off the bus a little less than halfway to Eugene. He was actually a sweet man; I couldn't say the same for the lady who was with him. She had a bag of snacks and a shirt full of crumbs that she'd brush off into the walkway anytime we'd stop.

Before we got to the station, we were relieved by the scenery. It was beautiful, with the charm of a small town and the bravery of individuality like a larger city. We passed train tracks that poked out from the trees on our way in, where people freely hiked along the rails. I wasn't sure what they were doing there, but it reminded me of the homeless camp. Of course, the only thing that resembled every other city we'd passed since Vegas was the bus station: a cavity serving as a building that hadn't been upgraded in decades. It had vintage flare, but it didn't match the allure of Eugene. Still, as we stepped off the bus, the air felt fresh and new.

Astrid grabbed my hand and smiled. I returned her grin. She felt better. I felt refreshed and optimistic. It was good.

"Okay, how do we find your friend?" she asked, squeezing my hand twice.

But you lied.

I sighed and hung my head. "There is no friend …"

She released my hand and jumped back, balling her fists. "What do you mean there's no friend?" She strained to keep her voice down. "Why did you have us take a bus all the way out here if you don't actually know anyone?"

"I made a promise to Jonas. He didn't want me to say anything," I began.

"What kind of promise?" She rubbed her forehead and closed her eyes.

"Look, it's nothing serious. It's just a letter for his brother." I raised my voice, slapping the back of my hand.

"It seems pretty serious since you kept it from me, Zachary." She squared her shoulders and scrunched her brows.

She had me cornered, so I fast-forwarded through the rest. "That was because he made me promise to not say anything to you or Mary. He didn't want anyone to know what had happened, including me."

She took a step back and lowered her shoulders. "I just wish you wouldn't have lied to me … again." She sighed. "And at the same time, you don't always have to be so damn honest. Jonas never would have known if you'd told me."

"I'm sorry!" I spun around in a small circle and straightened against a post. "Look, he just wanted me to find his brother and personally deliver this." I reached into my back pocket, where the corners of the envelope had dulled, and pulled the letter out. "I told him I would. They've been fighting since they were kids, and he wanted to clear the air."

"What did he do to make his brother so mad? Are you sure this is something you want to be part of?" she questioned, pausing for a moment as she bit her lip. "What does the letter say?"

"I don't know. I never read it—he asked me not to," I confessed, rubbing the back of my neck.

She snatched the letter from my hand and spun on her heel before tearing it open.

"Astrid!" I yelled. "Don't—it's none of our business!"

"Dear Amos," she read in an harsh tone.

I chased after her, hovering over her shoulder to grab the letter back, but she jerked away before I could snatch it.

"Do you want to know what you're getting into or not? I can tell you from experience not all deliveries are easy." She turned to me with glassy eyes as a couple obliviously strolled by. She dropped the letter to her side and waited until they were out of earshot. Her demons were never going to leave, and it was obvious she didn't care what the letter said as much as she did about keeping us out of danger.

I stepped back and folded my hands behind my head. "You're right," I said, closing my eyes. "We should read it."

The paper crinkled in her grip as she unfolded it again.

She cleared her throat and read aloud with a stern and even voice. "Dear Amos, it has been many years since we last spoke. I have tried to reach out to you to no avail."

I shifted my weight from one foot to the other.

"I want you to know why I made the choices I did. I love you and have missed having you in my life."

Her hands and voice shook when she continued.

"I was always sickened by the struggle that we faced as a family. With so much land, I knew we'd be much better off if we used the modern tractors and cars that were available." She sidestepped to let people pass while another bus pulled up about ten feet from us. "When Father died, I thought the family would be relieved by such changes. I had imagined what it would be like not to suffer, but everyone was so resistant, and I was too weak to watch the unnecessary day-in and day-out struggles." After pausing for a short breath, her hands steadied. "That was when I enlisted in the Air Force. I spent years overseas. I never received any replies to the letters I had sent to you and the family. When I returned home, I learned that you had relocated. I have a family, and I want you to meet them … as I'm sure you do. Best wishes, my dear brother, and may God Bless you. Jonas."

The bus that had squeaked up behind us amplified through the breezeway as Astrid folded the letter back up with her anxious pride and pressed it into my palm. "You can never be too safe," she muttered under her breath while her cheeks glowed and she lowered her head.

I kissed her on the forehead and nodded.

"So how do you plan to find him?" she asked. "We're not just going to barge into a stranger's house."

"Well, I was thinking about checking city records for his number since he's Amish."

"If he's Amish, how'd he get way out here?" she asked with her palm raised.

"Fair point. I don't know, unless he changed his ways too. Even so, Jonas doesn't have Internet access either, even though he's no longer part of the Amish community."

"True," she conceded, backing away from the parking lot until her heels rested in the grass across from me. "How about we check the phone book?"

"That's a start. Let's go down to City Hall. I'm sure they'd have record of something if the phonebook doesn't."

She shook her head. "No. I'd rather not ask questions at City Hall. What if he's wanted and we make someone suspicious?" She clasped her hands and bounced on her feet. "Besides, they have phone books online now."

"We have time to figure that out, " I said, staring up at a row of clocks hanging from the posts that supported the breezeway. One o'clock in the afternoon. "First, let's find somewhere to call the insurance company about the van and look for a place to stay while we're here."

She laughed. "Before I met you, a place to stay would have been the first thing on my mind. Now you have to remind me that we need somewhere to sleep."

Despite my efforts, I couldn't hide my smile. "I love you." The words floated through my chest as they left my mouth.

"I love you too," she said, reclaiming my hand.

We walked into the bus station to use the bathroom. While I waited for her to finish, I grabbed a map of the city from a shelf of brochures near the water fountain.

The women's room door opened, and she appeared with her hands dripping wet, out by her side. "They're out of paper towels, and the air dryer machine doesn't work."

"Wipe them on your clothes."

She glared and toweled them off on my beard.

"All right." I smirked and rubbed the moisture from my chin. "So here is a map. The library is about a quarter of a mile away." I held the creased paper out for her to see.

"Why do we need to go there?" she asked, bending over at the water fountain.

"They probably have computers. We can look for a place to stay."

The spout lever popped as she let it go. "Ah." She wiped her mouth with the back of her hand. "Let's go, then." She grabbed the map, and we exited the building.

Chapter 24

The prices kept climbing … $600, $750, $595, $1050.

Everything was too expensive. I swung my cursor to the search bar and clicked the refresh button.

"Astrid!" I whispered as loudly as possible through the library's bookshelves.

"What!?" She peered around the shelf nearest to me.

"Sorry. I didn't know you were so close. Come look at this!" I clicked on the listing that appeared at the top of the fourth page. It was for a small boathouse in someone's backyard on the edge of town. "Rent is only $350, plus utilities."

"That is so cute," she said, her scrunched face reflecting off the computer screen over a picture of a toffee-colored building with blue trim as I scribbled the phone number down.

"Let's call and see if it's available."

She smiled, then covered her mouth with her hand. I knew what she was feeling, because I felt it too.

This is what a silver lining looks like from a distance.

"Should we get a taxi to see if it's available?" I asked, shifting my gaze between her and the computer.

"If you think you can afford it," she said while twisting a strand of her hair.

I tapped my hand on the counter and stood. "We should be fine."

We walked to the front of the library, where a handful of phones were held in separate shallow cubicles, their cords trailing down the wall. I sat and picked up the receiver, while Astrid shuffled her feet beside me. "Okay," I said as I dialed the number.

A younger-sounding lady answered the phone after two rings. "Hello?" she asked in a soft yet crackling voice.

"Yes, hi. My name is Zachary Byrd, and I saw the listing for the boathouse online. Is it still available?"

"Available?" she asked in a high-pitched tone. "I literally just listed it. Do you have any pets?"

"Oh, no. I don't have any pets."

"Good!" she interjected. " I mean, not that I don't like animals—I do. But this place is rather cozy. I thought an animal might get restless in it quickly."

"No worries." I twisted the phone cord around my finger.

"I'm Bethel," she said. "As in where the 1969 Woodstock took place—not the biblical reference." Her words quickened with each syllable. "It's where my parents met."

"Bethel," I repeated. "I like it! Do you mind if my girlfriend and I come look at it now?" My eyes flitted up to Astrid, who smiled. I wrapped my fingers around her soft thigh, and I kissed the bottom of her stomach where her white T-shirt ended and her short blue cotton shorts began.

"Oh, yeah! That's no problem ... Zachary, you said it was?" Bethel recited.

"Yes, Zachary," I confirmed as a middle-aged lady shook her head and pointed in our direction from the checkout desk. "And my girlfriend's name is Astrid." I smiled at her again, beaming to be so official in public.

"And Astrid," she repeated one last time. "I love it. How long will it be before you two get here?"

"We're at the city library now," I answered. "I have to call a cab, and then we'll be right over."

"A cab?" Bethel raised her voice. "That's nonsense. I'm going into town anyway; I have to get a few things from the grocery store. I'll pick you up!"

"Are you sure?" I asked in disbelief.

"Of course," she said. "You can help me carry groceries in return."

I let out a snicker. "Well, that would be great! We'll wait outside."

Astrid raised an eyebrow and shrugged.

"See you soon," Bethel rushed, her response followed by an audible click.

Astrid didn't have to say anything for me to know her anticipation was eating her alive, so I took my time hanging up the phone and stood with a smirk.

"So …"

"Her name is Bethel. She's going to pick us up, and we're going to help her carry in groceries."

She crinkled her nose at the peculiarity of my reply. The situation was unconventional, which we should have been used to, but I suppose if every unconventional instance was unlike the one before it, then it was probably not something one can grow accustomed to.

We pushed past the industrial front doors and strolled over to the benches that were hidden behind a breezeway acting as a bike shelter along the front of the building.

"Is that her?" I asked after several minutes, standing by the bench and peering across the parking lot at a silhouetted head of curls craning from side to side inside an old black SUV.

Astrid stood up beside me, tightening the straps to her backpack around her shoulders.

I glanced back at the door of the library and then back to the car. "No one is coming," I said, nearing the curb where the SUV had parked. "Hey!" I waved at the lady who came into focus, fixing her lipstick behind the glared windshield. "Bethel?" I ducked to get her attention below the vanity mirror on the back of her sun visor.

The library door popped open behind us, and the woman smacked the visor shut as the front passenger window rolled down. "Trey!" she hollered when a young boy in a fedora hat briskly passed Astrid and me.

"Retreat, retreat!" I blurted in a low tone, and we both turned around and darted back to the bench.

Finally, a station wagon covered in stickers from different states pulled up. A woman in her late twenties with dark, silky hair opened the door and stood in the passing lane just as we reached the bench again. "Zachary! Astrid!" She waved from the front of her car. "Is that you? I'm Bethel!"

I smiled and waved at the excited lady who fought her way around the bikes in a pair of black flats. "Hello, Bethel!"

We reached the curb before she could pass the steel tube barrier.

"This is so exciting!" she said, stretching to shake our hands. "I wasn't sure if anyone would be interested since the space is small."

"We like small." Astrid grinned, adjusting the straps of her backpack with her thumbs.

"I'd actually guess that it's bigger than anything we've lived in since we met."

"Minimalists!" Bethel clapped. "I like it! Let's get groceries!"

We crawled into the car with our backpacks. I joined Bethel in the front, and Astrid slid into the back.

"So, are you from the area?" Bethel asked while she turned down the already whispering radio.

"No." I smiled and shook my head. "We're from the southeast, actually."

Astrid leaned up between the front seats. "We hopped trains and took a bus to get here."

"Astrid!" I jerked my head as she reclined in her seat worn with frayed fabric and dark spots.

"Are you serious?" Bethel commented.

I tensed when she adjusted her rearview mirror so that it pointed at Astrid.

"That's awesome! I can't wait to hear more about it!" She nodded and squeezed the steering wheel.

I lowered my head until Astrid appeared in the side view mirror. She sat grinning from ear to ear in the back seat.

Bethel veered into the parking lot of a local organic grocery store. A vintage sign hung at the top of the building, advertising that week's fresh produce.

"Do you carry those everywhere?" she asked as Astrid and I got out of the car.

“I guess so,” I said, feeding my arm through the strap of my bookbag.

Astrid adjusted hers on her back and swung her hair over her shoulder. “The habits of the homeless,” she said, balancing across a parking block.

“I really need to hear about this trip!” Bethel pulled the list from her pocket and grabbed a cart. “Tell me everything!”

So we did. Everything from the day we met to the letter in my pocket for Amos, Jonas’s brother, while she scavenged the shelves.

“I love that you’re so well traveled,” Bethel complimented as she dropped a carton of almond milk into her cart. “Most people expose themselves to the wrong things. It’s a huge problem in today’s society.” She stopped between a rack of chocolate syrup and a freezer of ice cream. “Most people would probably say what you two have done was wrong, but I bet you’ll end up happier than most.” She wrung her hands around the cart handle like a motorcycle throttle and continued down the aisle toward the front of the store. “I used to be a flight attendant solely so I could travel. I rented a room from a couple in Arizona. It was basically a storage unit for my things … I’d stay there four or five nights a month at most.” She stopped again, this time in front of a plastic strip that hung from a rack with packets of crazy straws. “These are fun!” She pulled a packet from the strip and put it in her basket.

At checkout, a guy about my age stood behind the counter with a clean-shaven face, pressed slacks, and an ironed shirt.

“How are you doing today, Foils?” Bethel spoke to him on what I assumed to be a nickname basis.

“I’m good, Bethel. How ’bout yourself?” Foils answered without much effort, sliding her groceries across the scanner in a pair of rubber gloves.

“I’m good. This is Zachary and Astrid Byrd. They might be renting out the boathouse.”

“We’re not—” I stopped myself. My shoulders fell when Astrid’s cheeks reddened. “Nice to meet you, Foils.” I offered my hand as a proper introduction but got no response.

"Foils doesn't shake hands," Bethel said. "He doesn't like to be touched."

"I'm sorry. It's very nice to meet you," I said and stepped back.

"It's okay," Foils said without expression. "It happens to me constantly."

Astrid and I meandered near the quarter machines while Bethel finished paying, then we made our way to the car.

The drive to Bethel's wasn't long at all, even though she didn't once exceed the posted speed limit. She showcased her cautious driving habits without apology. "That's why I've had the same car since I was seventeen!" Dimples sank into her cheeks, complementing her high cheek bones. "That's twelve years!"

"That's pretty impressive!" I reflected Bethel's glow. "What kind of car is this?"

"It's an '81 Corolla, hatchback ... obviously." She pressed the clutch and shifted into neutral, closing in on a stop sign. "Instead of painting it, I decorated it in all these cool stickers. They're actually in order from first visited to most recently visited."

I stared at the hood from my seat, lifting myself with my elbows to count all the stickers on the hood alone. I couldn't. They overlapped and hung upside down. "So you visited all these places?" I asked.

"I mean, yeah. It's easy to go to a lot of places when they're all off exits between two main points. Anytime I planned a trip, I'd leave a day or so before I had to be there and then head back a couple of days before I had to be home. Then, when I started working with airlines, I explored every destination we reached. I actually got fired because I was so exhausted during flights that I'd fall asleep." Bethel chuckled. "It's not funny"—laugh lines creased around her chin—"but it kind of is."

I glanced at Astrid, both of us doing our best to not crack up. "So where do you work now?" I asked.

"I'm a seventh grade teacher at the public middle school."

"Most people would disagree, but I actually really liked middle school!" I turned in my seat, stretching the seatbelt out around my shoulder. "What do you teach?"

"English." She eased up at a stop sign and flipped on her signal. "I think those years are where most kids figure out a path—maybe not so much in their careers, but socially, which I think is equally as important for their futures. I enjoy preparing them for high school, where they find their direction." She tilted her head and let off the brake, hiding the smile poking through her cheeks. "So what do you do … or did you do before coming here?"

"Astrid was a courier; she made personal deliveries," I recited from our conversations with Jonas and Mary. "And I just graduated from college. I was working at the hardware store though."

"Oh, neat! What was your major?" Bethel pried.

"History. You don't happen to know of any historian openings around here, do you?" I joked without true intent.

"No, but I'll be sure to document it if I do!" Bethel chuckled at herself. "That reminds me, though, how do you plan on paying rent if you don't have jobs?" Her brows raised.

"We have money saved for rent. You said that this is a month-to-month lease, correct?" I recalled from the ad.

"It is. But please give me a thirty-day notice before you move out so I can get someone else to take over the lease. My parents left this place to me, and it's harder to keep up than I expected."

"What do you mean, they left it to you?" I asked. "Did they move somewhere else?"

"No. They passed away about a year ago. I was living in California at the time; they died in a boating accident." She cleared her throat.

"Oh my god." Astrid shook her head.

"They were great people. I'm the person I am because of them …"

"I can relate," I said, scratching a minor cut that had scabbed over. "My dad died when I was young."

In the mirror, Astrid crossed her arms and turned toward the window.

Something else you never told her.

"We should start a club." Bethel forged a giggle. "Sorry, that was dark."

"Yeah." I smirked and nodded as the peripheral land opened up to a body of water with dirt parking lot shores lining each side of the road, leaving the buildings behind.

"So this is what I call the neighborhood. Really, it's a bunch of random things that I pass on the way home. Sometimes I try to hold my breath over this bridge." She smiled and glanced at Astrid through the rearview mirror, then at me though the corner of her eye as we approached a beam crossing aged with algae, its concrete path pitting into a rough texture. "Wanna try?" She inhaled a huge gust of air and puffed her cheeks out when the front tires left land.

"This is awesome," Astrid said before puffing out her own cheeks while we bounced over the first beam onto the bridge. I joined in. The car rocked back and forth as it galloped to the other side. Houses lined the river between patches of trees.

Bethel released the breath she was holding and gasped for air. "Who else made it? No nose breathers!"

"I won't lie; I was breathing out of my nose halfway over the bridge." Astrid's eyes widened. "I'm not conditioned for it yet!"

I nodded and grinned. "Yeah. I completely forgot what I was doing. Too distracted by the dramatic scenery change."

"That's what I've always loved about living here," Bethel said, taking a sharp right onto a side road. "It has the best of both worlds, city and nature."

"Look at that cute place." Astrid tapped on the window, pointing at a quaint pistachio-colored house with black shutters.

Bethel blushed. "That's my house!" she said, turning into the gravel driveway. Trees shaded a yard that slightly declined from the end of the driveway all the way to the water, where the top half of the boathouse peeked from behind the hill. "You are welcome to my house, but you do have your own kitchen and bathroom out back."

Astrid and I both nodded. "Can we see it?"

"Oh! Of course." Bethel put the car in park and popped her door open. "Just leave the groceries."

We trailed around the side of the house where the yard opened up to the river, and another small structure stood facing the water.

"Are you renting both out?" I asked, passing a long table twenty feet from the back porch of the main house.

"No." She shook her head. "I didn't post a picture of that other building because I was afraid it would scare people off. Sorry. The kitchen and bathroom are in there. My dad built the houseboat, which is the floating one, as an art studio for my mom. The boathouse was for when they would fish back here." She chewed on her thumbnail, then dropped her hand. "I converted the studio myself. Sorry if I was a little misleading."

"Don't be." I stood in the divide between the two structures, wind blowing against the stiff hairs of my beard. "I love the symmetry."

Astrid ignored both of us completely, gallivanting to the houseboat and around the simple deck that outlined it. "There are windows all the way around!" she shouted, circling around to the front door.

"Yeah, my mom would pull back all the curtains so that everywhere she looked was water. She said it made her feel humble," Bethel replied, covering the nape of her neck as I moved toward the boathouse.

I stepped onto the deck that lined the end of the yard above a seawall. A glass door with large, parted teal curtains that hung from ceiling to floor contrasted the gray paint that darkened the walls behind them. I slid the door open and stepped inside. A stainless-steel refrigerator and oven sank into an L-shaped kitchen counter in the corner of the room.

Circling the table that sat in the center of the floor, the tips of my fingers brushed across its white laminate surface, the faint lines of the gray tile backsplash staggered between the countertop and matching shelves that held stacked dishes. I inched to the other side of the room, where I faced a half-open whitewashed wooden door that hung in front of a standing shower and toilet.

"This bed is life!" Astrid's voice drifted in through the open door.

I shifted around the table and out the door.

"I'm glad it's to your liking!" Bethel said, standing in the doorway of the houseboat as I crossed over to her.

She stepped aside to let me in as a strong gust of wind blew against the trees that canopied the end of the yard. I joined Astrid on the bed, and the tin roof rattled beneath the weight of the leftover raindrops from the day before. Beams of light passed through the large glass windows that completely covered every wall except at the sliding glass door.

"It's perfect," Astrid said.

"I think you have yourself some new tenants!" I beamed, leaning back with my arms stretched out on the comforter.

"We must have dinner to celebrate." Bethel clapped her hands together. "It'll be about an hour—is that okay?"

I scooted to the edge of the bed. "Of course. That'd be great, but I have to go into town to get the rent money first."

"Don't worry about it. You can do all that tomorrow. Just get settled in, and I'll come get you when dinner is ready. I'm a vegetarian, so I'll be making a vegetarian dish. I hope that suits your taste."

"So am I!" Astrid smiled and cupped her hand around her mouth, lowering her voice to a whisper. "We'll convert him."

Bethel winked and laughed. "You're going to love it here then! I cook all the time!"

"Do you need any help?" I asked.

"Not at all. Get comfortable." She stepped onto the deck and took off toward her house.

We drifted into awe. The houseboat held a similar charm to the first night we stayed in the tent back in Oklahoma, though I couldn't pinpoint why. Maybe it was because Astrid was there, and we were okay. Maybe I was mistaking the sense of home as a sense of charm. She opened the windows while I closed the door and switched off the air conditioner that crooned above it.

Home. It was definitely a sense of home.

Chapter 25

"Do you know what you want?" Astrid asked as we took our seats at one of the town's outdoor restaurant's patio tables, where Bethel had dropped us off the next morning. She picked up a menu, her eyes racing across the bold text. "Why do I feel greedy for having so many options for a meal?"

"I don't think *greed* is the right word for it, but after living at the camp and the experience on the train, something definitely feels … I don't know. Off." I closed my own menu and slid it to the center of the red table. "I'm honestly not that hungry. I can still feel dinner from last night." I drummed my fingers along the painted aluminum tabletop. "I think I'll get a fruit salad and water."

"You know what?" She clapped her menu shut between her hands. "Me too." She crossed her ankles on top of the empty black-brushed metal chair next to her and unfolded the newspaper she had plucked from Bethel's yard earlier that morning. She pulled a pen out of her bag and circled something on the Events page before setting it on the table.

"Will you pass me the stories?" I said, extending my arm and stretching my legs out on the same chair.

She removed the ads from the bundle and folded them next to her pen. "Sure," she said, combing through the pages one last time.

I snagged her section from the table. "Why is everything on that page circled?"

"Because I'm want to get a feel for the area!" She grabbed the paper painted in her blue scribbles and threw the stories into my lap. "It's like people-watching. I get to see what motivates them."

"Ah!" I picked up the stack from my lap and read the front-page headline: "Local man burns down his own business." I lowered the paper to make eye contact with Astrid. "What do you think motivated him? Insurance money?"

"Uh … " She sat up in her chair, resting her forearms on the table.

"AHEM!" I exaggerated, snapping the paper and shielding my face with it again. "Before you say anything, I was just kidding. I like it here."

She kept quiet, a leg of her chair tapping the uneven brick patio as she leaned back.

A nearby door squeaked, and a sharp voice gasped behind me. "How long have you guys been out here? I didn't see you walk up!"

I dropped my feet from the chair and craned my neck to a chiseled girl in a black athletic polo and khaki shorts.

"You're fine," Astrid answered, her faded black shoes still crossed on the chair.

The girl pulled her order pad from her pocket. "I'm so sorry!" Do you know what you want?"

"It's really no problem." Astrid tucked her russet hair behind her ears. "And yes! I think so. Zachary?"

"Oh. Yeah." A black name tag pinned to her shirt peeked out from beneath her long, thin blonde hair. "I'm ready. We both want the fruit salad and water please, Ally."

"That's simple enough! It'll be right out." She returned her blank pad to her apron and strode back inside.

Astrid picked up her pen and circled more content while I unfolded my sections and blankly stared at the first sentence on the second page. My mind would only recite the first word: *carriages*. By the time the waitress returned, it was reeling and the letters had blurred into a fuzzy line. Their voices jumbled together as the waitress set the mixed fruit and water in front of Astrid and me.

"Zachary?" Astrid's voice pierced through my crowded thoughts.

"Huh?" I glanced up from the paper.

Her brows arched. "Do you need anything else?"

I shook my head and peered down at the fruit. "Nope! This looks perfect!"

I went back to half reading the paper. I didn't want to switch the conversation to Amos quite yet. Eugene was by no means a huge city, but it was large enough to get lost in. The thoughts of him not being here or Jonas mistaking Eugene, Oregon for a Eugene in another state crossed my mind. And what if we did find him? Would he be receptive … or violent? Would he be grateful or possibly hateful? As much as I wanted to believe that he would be like Jonas, I couldn't dismiss the potential for things going poorly.

Hoarding the negative thoughts, I finished my bowl of fruit and my water, then hunted for bicycles in the classifieds.

"Refills?" the young waitress asked while carrying a clear pitcher of ice water toward us.

Astrid held her glass up. "Please."

"Do you know of anywhere to get bikes around here?" I asked, reaching for my own glass to pass to her.

"Bike Works," she said without hesitation, topping off Astrid's water. "That's where I got my bike from. It was used, but the owner rebuilds them before he sells them."

Astrid shrugged. "Let's check it out!"

We trailed along the sidewalk to the vast hills, the buildings behind us shrinking.

"She said to turn here." Astrid pointed at a street sign, then referenced a napkin where she had written down the directions.

We swung around a corner to a strip of buildings that were divided into different neutral colors and claddings.

"There it is!" I picked up speed, passing a public trashcan and crossing the empty street.

"Yep!" she said as she caught up. "Bike Works." The sign resembled a chalkboard with a gray, wooden frame. The business name had been stenciled in the center.

We hopped past a paperback maple tree and neared a brown stucco building with windows stretching across the entire storefront.

I held the oversized black door open for Astrid before following her in. The shop felt more like a garage than a store with an acid-stained cement floor. Six tables stood in the center, three on each side of the front entrance that created a walkway toward the back, where accessories hung on the wall beside another door.

A man in his thirties wearing a white T-shirt that contrasted his dark skin stood behind a table with an upside-down bike on it. "Those are some new faces." His gentle yet booming voice whittled a smile. "How can I help you?" he asked while wiping grease from his hands onto a thick red cloth.

"Well, we actually got into town yesterday." I turned toward a rack of bikes stacked along the wall. "We're looking for used bikes. You were recommended by Amanda over at GJ's."

Astrid nodded and set her bag on the closest table before taking off for a stand of luggage racks for bikes.

"Amanda!" He grinned. "That girl rides her bike into the ground. She spends more time changing tires and tightening her chain than most spend pedaling." He stepped forward and held his hand out. "My name is Johnnie Snowell, by the way."

"Johnnie." I arched my brows and shook his hand. "My name is Zachary, and this is my girlfriend, Astrid. We just moved here yesterday from the southeast."

He let go of my hand and nodded at her. "What kind of riding do you do?"

"We got a place on the other side of the river. We need something that can get us back and forth, to and from town; it's about a ten-minute drive by car. We don't plan to be here long, though, so we don't want to spend too much money." I crossed my arms. "The last time we bought bikes, it was at a pawnshop … but looking back, I don't think they were built for distance riding."

He paused for a moment. "I think you should go with fixed speeds. There aren't many hills around here that require high gears unless you leave the city, and they require less maintenance." He scratched his chin. "Did the bikes you bought at the pawnshop have wide tires, or were they thinner like these?" He pinched the rubber on the flipped bike beside him.

"They were definitely thicker. Not super thick, but not nearly that thin."

"Yeah. That makes sense. The thicker the tire, the more resistance you have against the pavement. It makes it harder to ride long distances. The only reasons you'd want a thicker tire is for off-road riding or comfort."

"We've already learned something!" Astrid said and slapped her knee.

Johnnie smiled at her. "I have one that will fit you. It's a guy's frame, but most of them are nowadays."

She gave him a thumbs-up.

"As for you"—he turned to me—"you're taller, so we'll have to get creative. I have an old three speed that just came in, but the gears on it are bad, so we could strip them."

"Okay, great! How much would it cost to buy the bikes and have mine converted?"

"Hers is ready to go. I'll give that to you for eighty dollars." He shuffled past the second column of tables toward the rack of bikes on the far wall. "Yours I'll do for ninety-five dollars including the parts. You can do the work yourself to save money if you want to." He lifted a yellow bike from the top rack and leaned it against a table behind Astrid, who was fixated on a hanger of saddle bags. "Everything here is built with quality parts, so they'll definitely last you. I only replace parts that need to be replaced though—so keep that in mind."

I nodded, noticing how easy it was for him to pick up the small yellow frame. "Sounds good."

"Yours is in the back." He slipped through the doorframe behind us before quickly returning with another frame cradled in his arms, the chain sagging below its pedals.

I took the load from him and leaned it against Astrid's bike.

"All of the instructions and tools you'll need are in this," he said, walking toward me with a five-gallon bucket in his hand.

While Johnnie helped Astrid adjust the seat, I deciphered the instructions that showed me how to convert my bike to a gearless ride. I turned the black frame upside down and compared it to the diagrams, identifying each piece of the gear system before deducing what could be wrong with it and taking it apart. The sprockets were bent, the wires frayed, and the chain rusted. It was amazing that the drive train of the bike could be so damaged while the frame only wore rust on the nuts and bolts that held the steering fork and handlebars in place.

"I'm going to hold the handlebars," Johnnie said, straddling Astrid's front tire with his knees. "Now, put your heel on the pedal. Your leg shouldn't be bent when the pedal is at the bottom of its cycle."

"Like this?" she asked as I sorted through the bucket for a screwdriver.

"Perfect! Is it comfortable?"

She dropped her feet to the ground. "Very! Can I try it out in the street?"

"Of course!" He let go of the handlebars and ambled to the door to hold it open for her while she bounced on the balls of her feet, pushing the bike through the shop and out the door.

The latch clicked shut behind them, and I continued stripping the metal pieces. Just as the instructions had suggested, the mechanics were structured like onions. Each piece was its own separate layer, and it proved easiest to deconstruct one layer at a time.

Astrid and Johnnie returned before I could fit the new parts on. "Hey Johnnie." I spun the bike's wobbly wheels. "I don't know if these tires are going to work."

"Hmm." He let the door close behind him once Astrid stepped inside with her bike. "I have an idea," he said, then disappeared once again into the back room.

"Bikes look a lot more complicated when you take them apart, huh?" Astrid discerned, approaching my table and propping her bike against the one beside mine while I flossed my weld points with a rag.

"These are off my bike," Johnnie said, emerging with two black wheels wrapped with low-profile tires in his hands. Astrid climbed onto the table beside her bike, crossed her legs, and started picking at her shoes. "I ordered them a while back but didn't like the way they looked. I'll let you have these for an extra $175. They already have Kevlar tires. The same setup would cost you nearly $300 new," he said matter-of-factly.

"The wheels cost more than the bikes." Astrid snickered.

"Yeah, well, unfortunately I don't have any used wheels or tires." Johnnie dropped the wheels to his side and peered off at an installation of wheels pinned to the wall like Olympic Rings. "Everything in stock is going to cost about the same, just not as nice."

"Okay," I said as my legs bobbed.

"I'll throw in a black chain to match. It'll look awesome with your black frame." He set the new pair beside my bike and returned to the back.

Boom-click-click-pop. Boom-click-click-pop. Astrid started beatboxing, humming a random melody behind the percussion section of her lips and tongue.

"What song is that?" I asked, keeping tempo with a wrench against my hand.

She paused her track. "It's by 'I just made it up because I'm bored.'" Then she picked up where she had left off.

"What can we do to her bike to give it more style?" I yelled to the back.

"Couldn't hear you," Johnnie hollered. "Be right there."

She stopped the beat again. "Look, I know that your bike needed a lot of work, which is why you have to change things, but mine is fine." Astrid propped herself up on her elbows. "Let's not waste money on things we don't need right now. I feel bad enough using your money."

"You deserve something nice for yours too!" I hung my head, playing with the ends of the wrench.

"Zachary, you bought me a bike. You do too much for me. Plus, I like the look of my little yella fella!" she said, patting its frame.

Johnnie returned with a box that held a coiled black chain. "What did you say again?" he asked from the doorway.

"Nothing, sorry. I figured it out."

I switched the chain out and tightened the new one between the sprockets before locking the quick release on the front wheel and flipping the bike upright on the ground.

"I can't believe how much lighter it is!" I tugged upward on the saddle with my fingers, lifting the back tire off the ground and dropping it again.

Johnnie met me in front of the counter. "Those old tires and gears were heavy!"

Astrid got up from the table as I swung my leg over the seat, and we adjusted the height. I hopped off, then walked the bike through the front door that she held open for me. Swiveling my foot on the pedal until it felt secure, I pushed all my weight into it and coasted. It was effortless but stiff. Much easier than the bulky bikes we'd ridden in Oklahoma. I leaned into the turn, circling a handicap street stamp on the other side of the strip and rode toward the shop. Astrid gave a thumbs-up when I squeezed the brakes a few feet in front of her.

"You love it?" She bit her lip and crossed one leg over the other, balancing with the toe of her shoe.

"I love it." I squinted past the glare of the bright sky and swung my leg over the seat. "Let's go pay and get outta here!"

When we re-entered the shop, I rested my bike against the side wall, its handlebars even with the thick white paint that coated rough drywall.

"Would you like to purchase the membership?" Johnnie asked as we ambled to the checkout counter.

"I don't know if we'll be here long enough to use it," I said. "But thank you for everything. Actually … " I bit my lip, thinking back to our stolen bikes. "We need bike locks too. Do you have any?"

"It was no problem. And sure," he said with a nod.

"Wait!" I added, taking notice of the computer beside him. "Would you mind it if we used your computer to look something up before we left?"

"Not at all," he answered, typing the cost of our bikes into a register that sat beside the monitor.

"What do we need to look up?" Astrid spun her hair between her fingers and tucked it between her top lip and nose like a mustache.

"Amos." I paused. "We might as well do it here rather than ride all the way back to the library, don't you think?" I said as we rounded the counter.

Astrid loosened her lip, the strand of hair falling to her cheek. "I guess."

"I've already tried social networks and found nothing."

"When did you do that?" She crossed her arms.

"With my phone before the van was stolen."

"Oh." Her arms fell, and she shook her head.

"Whoa, whoa, whoa. Wait a second. What are you looking for?" Johnnie stepped away from the counter and scratched his head.

"Long story," I said, reaching into my back pocket. "But first, what is our total?" I pulled my debit card from the front slot.

"Uh." He continued to punch into the keypad. "It's $355." He smacked the last key and looked up.

"What about taxes?" I asked, handing over my card.

He grinned. "There's no sales tax here." He took my card and swiped it.

"What? Really?" Astrid perked up.

"Really!" Johnnie winked and handed me my card back. "So what is it that you need the computer for?"

Chapter 26

AMOS JOHN SCHROCK, EUGENE, OR headed the top of a search engine with pages of history listed below it. The first entry matched the address on the envelope from Jonas.

"The Horse and The Carrot," I mumbled, pointing at the link for Johnnie to click on. "This news article says that he started the business in 1961 from his home in Eugene Oregon. 'Schrock used his farming background to touch lives all over Oregon, providing horse therapy services and teaching agriculture from his own backyard.'"

Johnnie scrolled down, tapping his finger on the counter.

"'Schrock is noted for his extensive work in the community and donations to local schools and charities.'" At the bottom of the page, a business phone number was listed.

I twirled a pen between my fingers. "Should we call it?" I asked Astrid, scribbling the digits onto a pad of sticky notes that sat between the monitor and register.

"I think so. It's probably better to be rejected by phone than in person …" She stood on the sides of her shoes and balanced against the counter. "It looks like he's a good guy, but we still don't know him. There's nothing wrong with keeping safe."

"I agree," Johnnie added beside us, crossing his arms.

I peeled the paper from the pad and fidgeted with its corners. "You're probably right."

"Probably." She lifted her head, unwilling to let good sarcasm slip by. "Hey, uh, Johnnie?" She faced him with her hands clasped in front of her chest.

"Let me guess." He pressed his fingers into his brows. "You guys don't have a phone?"

"Yu*p*," she answered, emphasizing the *P*. "So, what do ya say?"

He dropped his gaze and paused. "First off, I think y'all are crazy. Traveling to the other side of the country with no transportation or a way to communicate." He clapped his hands together, bobbing them with his words. "Second, I think this is for a really good cause, and for some reason, I trust you more for it. So, yes, you can use my phone."

Astrid and I laughed hysterically.

"He doesn't know the half of it," I heaved.

"Also, I don't usually say 'y'all,'" he added, "but since you're from the southeast, I wanted to take full advantage of the opportunity."

At that, we doubled over in laughter until Johnnie gave in. He reached below the register and grabbed the phone hidden beside the printer. As he stood, the sticky note with Amos's number caught his eye, and the room grew quiet.

"So what now?" he asked. "You call this guy and tell him you have a letter from his long-lost brother?"

"I guess," I said, kneading the dented paper.

Astrid snatched the slip from my fingers. "You ready?" She cleared her throat.

"Sure." I held my hand out for the phone.

"You don't have to dial the area code," Johnnie said as he handed it over, pressing the talk button with his thumb.

I pushed the speakerphone button, and Astrid read the number aloud. I dialed before pulling the letter from my back pocket, every ring longer than the one prior. I rubbed the worn ink on the envelope where Jonas had written his brother's name and waited.

A weathered voice answered in long gasps. "Hello?"

"Is this Amos John Schrock?" I asked.

"It is," the voice wheezed.

"My name is Zachary Byrd. I'm a friend of your brother, Jonas." My grin widened, and I turned toward Astrid, who gave me a weak smile, then covered her mouth and nose with her hands.

"That can't be." Amos paused. "My brother died in the war." His volume escalated over the thick congestion in his chest.

"No, Amos. He lives in Oklahoma. He's been writing you letters; he actually gave me one to give to you." I waved the letter in the air.

"I got his letters," the man retorted. "Never opened them."

A few moments of silence passed. "Why not?"

"I figured they were found after the war or came from the military."

I paused, shaking my head and scratching my neck, frustrated at how complicated his assumptions had made the situation.

Dismissing the gaps in his thinking, I pushed the subject further. "Jonas told me about the war and leaving everyone behind at the farm." I held my breath, stepping onto the sales floor. "Do you mind if I bring this letter to you?"

"I suppose not …" His words slowed to a crawl.

"Excellent."

Astrid sat on one of the bike assembly tables, biting her nails, while Johnnie remained bent over the counter.

"See you soon," I added.

"Okay …" Amos coughed. "Do you have the address?"

"1524 Ba—"

"Yeah, that's it."

The line went dead, but the moment was still alive. Before I handed the phone to Johnnie, he shuffled over to the computer, looking up directions to Amos's house. Astrid remained silent.

"It's a little over five miles," he said, kneeling to turn on the printer. "It shouldn't take you more than twenty-five minutes."

"Awesome. Thanks, Johnnie!" I smiled, propping my hands on my hips. "Do you mind printing out directions to Bethel's as well?" I asked, circling back around the counter and writing down the address.

"Sure. No problem." He grabbed the note with Amos's address and typed it into the computer.

I caught Astrid slumping over out of the corner of my eye, her head bobbing with her restless leg. "You don't have to come if you don't want to." I circled around the counter and rubbed her arm.

"I know." She crossed one leg over the other as the printer shot out directions behind me. "It's fine. I'll go."

"Are you sure?"

"Yeah." She stood and grabbed the papers from Johnnie. "You ready?"

We pulled into Amos's gravel driveway as the sun poured onto its gray shingles. Everything around us was quiet and still. The house resembled an old western stable with red exterior wood paneling and an A-frame roof, much like the barn that we'd taken grates from back at the homeless camp, but nicer. We got off our bikes and pushed them alongside the white fence that enclosed several acres of grass, gnawed to the dirt in spots by the appetites of the horses that roamed it.

An off-white metal garage door echoed when we propped our bikes against it at the end of the driveway.

"You ready?" Astrid stepped in front of me, patting the stray hairs down on my beard.

I exhaled loudly, holding my stance long enough for her to finish grooming me. "Yeah, you?"

When she was done, we ambled to the door. Two knocks later, creaks from the back of the house crept closer.

The door swung open. A frail man with clear tubes wrapping around the sides of his face down to a small tank stood in the doorway, leaning on a cane.

"Amos?" I asked, recalling a familiar wheezing on the phone.

"Come in." He dropped his gaze while his hunched body circled back around to the hall, pulling his oxygen tank behind him. When I closed the door, everything went black. Following the shine of his white hair, we rounded a corner where a dull light at the end of the hall beckoned us. We trailed behind, passing pictures of horses and pastures that hung crooked from nails as we neared the light.

At the end of the hall, cracked yellow drywall opened to a warm room of faded striped wallpaper and brick lit by a table lamp and a muted television—unfurnished with any signs of family.

"Take a seat." He gestured to a couch that had been pushed against the far wall as he let out a groan, holding the oxygen cord to the side and lowering himself into the recliner beside the couch. "So, you say you know my brother and that he's still alive?" He choked out a laugh, then a deep cough took over.

"Yes, sir," I said as Astrid and I both eased ourselves down on the front edge of the couch cushions. "He asked me to bring you this letter …" I reached into my pocket and pulled out the crinkled envelope.

He extended a trembling hand and clenched the paper between his knuckles before bringing it to his chest and retrieving the folded paper from the envelope. I followed his eyes until his pupils grew and took shelter behind tears. The more he read, the more his hands shook. "He is still alive," he said aloud.

I turned to avoid his gaze, picking at my fingernails. How is order implemented in a situation like that?

Astrid read my pale complexion and stiff jaw. "Amos," she said in a soft voice, "we spent the night with your brother and his wife. You have nieces and a nephew who all have kids now, and Jonas wants you to meet them. They want to be part of your life."

Her words were delicate and direct.

"Does he know about—" He coughed, then paused to collect enough breath to finish his sentence. "Does he know about Momma and our sisters?" His voice crackled as he wiped his face with a handkerchief. "Does he know that"—he wheezed again—"after he left, the entire family fell apart?"

"I don't know." I dropped my head to hide the moisture pooling in my eyes, hinging my fingers behind my neck before blinking and looking upward. "You should talk to him."

Amos folded the letter and fit it back into the envelope, setting it on an end table beside him. He crossed his arms with his gaze glued to the frying pan infomercial on television.

Astrid slid her heels back and wedged them between the threaded gray fabric of the couch and the floor, propping her head on her palm and resting her fingers on her mouth. Seconds passed, and then he nodded.

She patted my shoulder and pointed to a phone that sat beside the letter on the end table.

"I'm going to call him. Is that okay?" I asked, reaching over the armrest of the couch for the phone.

He nodded, keeping his focus on the pockets of hot air that gathered in front of his bloodshot eyes.

"Okay."

I dialed the number that Jonas had given us for their store. The phone only rang twice before Mary answered. "Antique Attic. How can I help you?" she said in a polite tone.

"Mary, how are you?" I replied, smiling to forge a chipper tone. "This is Zachary."

"Zachary!" she exclaimed. "It's so good to hear from you! How are you? How is Astrid? Where are you?"

"We're both fine and in Oregon! How are you?"

"We're doing great!" she said, lowering her voice. "We haven't received your insurance check yet, by the way."

"Oh, yeah, I forgot to tell you, but we worked that out already. It's being wired to me directly." I tapped the back of the phone, shifting my gaze around the room for something to focus on. "I hate to cut this short, but is Jonas available?"

"Oh, of course," she said. "He's right here." The phone thudded and sizzled as she rubbed the receiver against what I assumed to be the palm of her hand.

I brought the phone to my shoulder and whispered to Astrid. "Mary had to get him."

Amos stared blankly at someone spinning a wheel on a television game show.

"Hello?" Jonas answered. "Zachary?"

"Jonas." I quickly raised the phone back to my ear, exhaling as I spoke. "I'm here with Amos. Would you like to speak with him?"

The line fell silent. I pictured Jonas's frozen face plastered with a grin, overlooking the store from behind the register.

"Jonas?" I said again.

"Yes." He coughed. "Sorry, let me go to the back room. Give me a minute."

The phone thudded again, this time followed by the distant sound of Jonas's and Mary's voices.

"He's getting the other phone," I whispered again to Astrid, hoping Amos was ready to talk.

"Zachary?" Jonas said when he picked up the other line.

I brought my free arm to my side and shifted on my feet. "Yes?"

"Mary! You can hang up that other line," he called to her, remaining silent until the other line clicked. "All right," he said in a calmer voice, "is he still there?"

"Yes." I swallowed. He was there physically at least. "One second."

Moments later, Astrid stepped in again. "Amos," she said, "Jonas is on the phone." She took the receiver from me and held it out to him.

He gripped it snugly against his ear, his painful breathing feeding the handset.

"Amos, is that you?" Jonas's voice distorted through the earpiece.

"Yes." Amos's chin trembled, puddles lapping the brims of his eyelids.

Astrid guided me toward the front door. "They need to work this out on their own."

As I stepped backward, Amos's tears streamed down his cheeks. After hesitating, I turned and followed the dark foyer to the door.

Astrid did the same, turning the knob behind her after we'd stepped outside so the latch wouldn't make any noise. I listened intently to my surroundings: the distant traffic, the birds, the swishing of our shoes flattening the grass, and my nails scratching against my head. My mind made up the details of their conversation.

Love. Terror. Shame. Disillusionment.

We mounted our bikes and rode back to the street. Air circled my face, and the revving engines of sporadic cars passing grew louder.

The truth. The truth. The truth.

My mind looped as we reached the house, searching for the

liberation in myself that I had seen in Amos when we crossed the bridge over the river. The pain—he'd let it go.

"Dibs on the shower," Astrid joked, pulling into the driveway ahead of me.

"It's yours!" I smiled, staring down at my handlebars while we hopped off and pushed our bikes across the yard.

We locked them to a chain secured around the big tree near the door-converted outdoor table, then diverged.

I knew Bethel wasn't home—her car was gone—but I approached her back door and knocked anyway. Nothing stirred, as expected, so I checked the knob. The brass twisted in my hand, and I cracked the door open.

I stepped in and peddled around the kitchen in search of paper. While Jonas had lived his life in an ashamed gratitude to the ones he had hurt, Amos had spent his time hiding from the truth, performing good deeds to make up for the things he couldn't face. Both had spent most of their lives in silence, dismissing substantial parts of their true identities.

It made them restless.

You are restless.

I drew the line.

When I had written the letter to my mom while at the camp, I hadn't told her everything because I'd been afraid of her judgement. Up until that moment, I had spent my life running because I thought my purpose should make others proud. I expected that of myself, because I felt that others had expected it of me.

But I was proud. I'd found happiness and lost my fear of the future. Perhaps purpose was understanding purpose. I knew what it meant to be alive, as opposed to the countdown I had been living before. I saw the value in things society had tried to hide.

You're restless because your perception of purpose doesn't align with your actual happiness.

The thoughts flowed quickly, and the more I acknowledged them, the lighter I felt. My hands stumbled over a white cordless handset on an end table cornered between the couch and love seat in the living room. Frantically, I dialed my mom's number and let it ring until the machine answered.

"Mom, it's me: Zachary." I paced to the back of the living room and down the hallway.

"Zachary!" She picked up, the machine beeping in the background. "Where have you been? I got your letter and tried to write you back, but it was returned."

"Yeah, about that letter," I began. "There's more you should know." I paused for a moment, soaking in the surreal nature of being comfortable enough with myself to be honest about who I was. "What happened was horrible … but it opened my eyes."

The unmistakable grunt of a chair from our old dining room table held the line. "To what?" she asked.

"To …" I squared up to the kitchen island and peered out the window to the backyard, Astrid tiptoeing in a blue towel over the deck from the boathouse to the houseboat. "To myself."

"Sweetie, you were never lost." She exhaled as Astrid kneeled in the houseboat to pick up a white T-shirt she had just dropped. "You have an education. A home. A family that loves you."

"I had more than I could ask for. More than I probably deserved … but I didn't have a sense of self." I shifted around the island to the sink.

"If your dad was around, this would—"

"Mom, this has nothing to do with my childhood." I bit my lip and stared at the popcorn ceiling. "I can actually remember how beautiful our family was before he passed. I wish I had been more grateful for it."

We both stopped, letting the words sink in.

"Then what is this about?"

"I don't want to feel ashamed for who I am anymore. I don't even think I knew it was shame until now—until the accident—and then I learned what real shame actually was."

Her voice wavered in the background. "It wasn't your fault."

"And I'm still trying to accept that." I raised my voice.

You can't accept your innocence if you can't accept what happened.

I softened my tone. "How is he?"

"He opened his eyes. Your Aunt Fay said that he has been responsive. She knows someone in the family."

My heart beat harder and harder until my breaths grew short.

"Why don't you come home, and we'll work this all out?" she pined.

"I don't have anything to work out." I closed my eyes and let everything go, opening them to find the boathouse peeking through the kitchen window. "I am home."

"What do you mean?" she asked as if I were speaking in tongues.

Astrid slid the door open to the boathouse and tossed her shoes into the yard, leaving the curtains free to blow in the wind.

"I'm going to be okay. I met someone here." My cheeks rose. "Her name is Astrid."

"Really?" She coughed and lightened her tone. "How did you two meet?"

"At a concert ..." I paused. "In Atlanta, actually. We stayed in the van together until it was stolen, then shared a tent at a homeless camp, hopped a train to Vegas, and slept on a bus to get to Eugene, Oregon. She blindly followed me to deliver a letter to a long-lost brother of someone that we met along the way."

"Don't be funny, Zachary. Where are you really?"

"I'm in love."

"Zachary." Her voice softened to a whisper. "Zachary, I'm so happy and proud."

I stepped closer to the kitchen window. "Thanks, Mom. Thanks for always being there for me, even when I couldn't see it."

"I just want you to be happy. That's all I ever wanted for you."

"I know that now," I said, a euphoria blossoming in the back of my mind. My future with Astrid was clear when it wasn't a secret. "Mom, I need to go. I'll keep in touch though." I slid the phone down my face as she said her goodbyes, and I pressed the end button.

After setting the phone on the counter, I trailed out the back door, passing our bikes and the outdoor table to the boathouse. I parted the curtain and stood in the doorway. Astrid balanced at the foot of the bed, pulling her underwear up under her towel with her back to me.

"I love you," I said with new meaning.

"I love you too." She titled her face, revealing a smile.

I slid the door closed behind me and stepped toward her.

Her hands froze halfway down her chest, where she had been pulling up her bra.

She didn't need to know it was the first time I meant it unconditionally. She just needed to be shown. I took another step forward and gripped my fingers between the strands of her wet hair. She dropped her towel as I turned her head, pulling her lips into mine.

Chapter 27

The first month in Eugene felt like the first month of my life. It was like I didn't exist until coming clean with myself, and since then, my worries had been more like tiny movements pushing me toward something greater than myself.

"Can you go ahead and set the table?" Bethel requested, bending over an open stove in her polka-dotted apron as she pulled her oven mitt snug on her hand.

"Sure," I said, entering the kitchen through the screen door and letting it close behind me. "We already did the place mats and silverware. What dishes do you want to use?" I flattened my knuckles on the counter, my mouth watering at the sight of the cauliflower and tofu lasagna with butternut squash sauce she slid from the oven. I'd never had it before, but she had talked it up that entire week.

"What place mats did you use?" she asked, breaking my trance and setting the pan on the stovetop. "Wait, wait! Don't tell me. I like to be surprised!" She squinted at the sideboard, where mats were evenly piled.

"Okay." I laughed, shifting toward the cabinet that held the plates.

"And the china, duh!" She flipped her hair. "This is a damn celebration! One month anniversaries only happen once!"

We both giggled, and I grabbed the china along with silver serving dishes and crystal glasses. I stacked everything on a shiny metal tray and sidled to the door.

Pushing the screen open with my back, I sidestepped down the stairs and into the yard until Astrid's smile stopped me. "Watch out for the hose." She set a pitcher in the center of a teal barn door that had been converted into a table by Bethel's dad shortly before he passed.

Astrid pointed at the columns of water arcing from the sprinkler onto the yellowed grass that had withered away in the summer heat.

"Thanks!" I said, stepping over the green rubber pipe that snaked its way to the house, then setting everything onto the table.

"How long until we can eat?" She stuck out her bottom lip and raised the back of her hand to her forehead. "I'm sooooooo hungry!"

I spread dishes and silverware out across the sheet of glass that surfaced the table, everything reflecting the changing colors of the leaves that hung from tall trees above it. "She was pulling it out of the—"

"Dinner is served!" Bethel emerged from the back door with her standard English accent, balancing the lasagna across her arms while gripping candlesticks in each of her hands. She traipsed to the table and leaned her hips against it as she laid the dish on the table, followed by the candlesticks. "Everyone may be seated for our moment of silence," she said, lighting both wicks with a single match that she procured from behind her ear like a bobby pin, striking it against a strip on the side of the table.

It was hard to fight my grin when Bethel had so sarcastically used her proper English accent in her request. But she took the moment of silence seriously; it was her substitute for prayer. Thirty seconds where we could reflect, pray, or whatever we felt inside our own skin. We never talked about what we did in that time either. It was kind of therapeutic.

"So, do you plan on staying for a while?" Bethel broke the silence, peeling the tinfoil on the steamy lasagna back far enough to carve into the saucy pasta. "You seem to be fitting in nicely!" She held a slice out for Astrid on the spatula.

Astrid lifted her plate, locking eyes with me as Bethel filled her dish.

"Before you two go off making any big plans to leave or

anything, there is a teaching position open at my school in the history department."

I snapped my attention to her.

She shrugged her shoulders and brows simultaneously. "It's for seventh and eighth graders. It would look good on your résumé, even if you only do it for a year." She set down the spatula and picked up her wine, burying her smile in the glass she kept half full.

"That sounds like a great opportunity"—I tapped my empty plate with my pointer finger—"but Astrid and I haven't even discussed staying yet." I really did like the thought of a teaching job, but I didn't want to corner Astrid.

Astrid took a bite of her lasagna and wiped her mouth with a napkin. "I like it here." She chewed before taking a sip of her wine. "I think you should do it."

"Really?" I leaned against the table and beamed.

"Lasagna?" Bethel asked, pulling another slice from the steamy pan.

"Oh yes. Please!" I picked up my plate and met her in the middle.

"The opening is fresh. The person you'd be replacing quit today to go work at a museum in Portland. They'll have subs in the room until the spot is filled." She cut a piece for herself and centered it on her plate, then covered the pan up and set the spatula on the table beside it. "I talked to the principle and got you an interview for tomorrow afternoon." She ducked her head, her cheeks glowing a light shade of red.

"That is so soon!" I laughed. "I literally only have two changes of clothes though. Neither is fit for an interview." I shook my head, reclining in my chair.

"Take it easy. I still have some of my dad's stuff here. You're about the same size he was. I'm sure we can find something for tomorrow, and if that doesn't work out, the thrift stores here are amazing."

I dug into my food, then took a sip of water before answering. "Thank you."

"You. Are. Welcome." Bethel smiled and took another bite.

Birds whistled and crickets chirped over our silence for the rest of the meal.

"Bethel," Astrid said, letting her fork clatter to her plate. "Do you think I can get a ride from you in the morning? I need to get my pictures developed."

"Of course! Are they digital? We might be able to do that here."

"No. They're from an old film camera." Astrid smudged the imprint of her lips on her glass. "I'd take my bike, but I don't want the prints to get scratched up on the ride home."

"Yeah," Bethel said, stacking a few dishes and stripping the tinfoil from the pan. "Do you know where you want to have them developed?" She folded the foil and placed it beneath the candle, the melting wax oozing onto it.

Astrid threw her hands up and chuckled. "No, I figured you would."

"Actually, my friend Todd has a dark room. I think he's your best bet of getting film developed anymore; everything has gone digital."

Astrid shook her head. "I know!" She chortled and folded her hands under her chin. "Digital is cool because it saves paper and all that, but I love film. It's my guilty pleasure!"

Bethel laughed and winked. "We all have our guilty pleasures." She tilted her head, then gasped, straightening in her chair. "Wait a second. I have an idea! How about you and Zachary drop me off in the morning, then use my car. That way Zachary doesn't get sweaty before his interview riding his bike."

"Actually, I'd rather not go to your friend's house without you—at least not the first time. Can we go when you get off?" Astrid asked.

"Yeah," I cut in, wiping my hands with my napkin. Feeling uncomfortable for her to go to a random guy's house alone, myself. "That could work out better. I can take my bike with me in your car to the school, then ride it to the bike shop afterward. I was going to help Johnnie with his new stock anyway." Though that was a lie—he'd mentioned doing stock himself, but I hadn't offered to help.

"Great," Bethel said, standing and collecting dishes from the table. "After everything is washed up, we need to find something for you to wear." She tilted her head while eyeing my shabby clothes.

After cleanup, Bethel led us to her parents' old bedroom that she had closed off after they'd died. The bed sat centered in the room against the back wall with an accordion-style closet and a much smaller green wardrobe to the left of it. "What color suit do you look best in?" Bethel asked, opening the closet.

"I don't know," I answered, shaking my head. Suits weren't my thing. Apart from renting a tux for a friend's wedding and borrowing blazers for funerals, I had never worn one.

"Gray," Astrid interjected.

I looked at her with a raised brow.

"What? Men in gray suits are hot." She bit her lip and smiled.

We all laughed, and Bethel nodded. "Gray it is!" She pulled a jacket, slacks, and a white button-up shirt from the armoire.

"Shoes, shoes, shoes," she mumbled under her breath, bouncing her fingers across the tongues of each pair lined up in neat rows on the right side of the closet. "What size are you?"

"Ten, ten and a half?" I said, struggling to remember the last time I had bought shoes.

"Great!" Bethel talked over me, reaching headfirst into the pit of clothes. "These are a size too big but are practically new!" She grabbed a shined pair of brown Allen Edmond laced dress shoes. "My father didn't like to waste money … but he did believe that his Sunday's best should be an honest *best*."

She laid the clothes out on the bed, selecting a plain blue tie from a hook to finish it off. "What do you think?"

I stepped around Astrid toward the bed and centered myself in front of the suit with the pants hanging over the edge. The three of us stood shoulder to shoulder. I looked up at their beaming faces one at a time for affirmation. "It looks amazing!"

"Great!" Bethel said while Astrid pumped her fist as if she had just won something.

I packed all the hangers onto three fingers and hung them over my shoulder before heading back to the houseboat. Astrid snuck in a hug for Bethel with an unusual exhibition of affection when she went to pick up the shoes.

"Thank you so much!" she said into her ear.

A pang of jealousy hit, mainly because of what had happened between Astrid and Lisa, but I knew I had to let the past go; otherwise, I'd risk destroying everything over what was potentially nothing.

Potential is a powerful word when it's a reoccurring thought, and thought is a powerful tool when contemplating potential.

I put the negative thoughts to rest after Astrid turned and kissed me. "I love you."

Distrust leads to discontent and disconnect. People are bound to let you down when you expect them to.

"I love you too," I said with a smile. "I suppose we should get ready for bed. Tomorrow somehow turned in to a big day."

Bethel led us to the back door in the kitchen and gave me a few tips on how to ensure a good interview. Some things were common sense, such as good posture and speaking clearly, while others I hadn't thought of: confident and witty replies without hesitation, keeping my hands on my lap, not sitting until everyone else was seated, mimicking the principle's body language, smiling often, shaking hands before and after the meeting, and rinsing my mouth out with mouthwash ten minutes prior the meeting. She had interviewing down to a science, and her recommendations made the process a lot less nerve-racking.

"You'll do fine!" She wrapped her arms around my neck.

"Thank you." I hugged her with my only free arm. "For everything!"

"No, no, no. Stop!" Bethel let go. "I can't handle sensitive situations." She laughed, wiping a stray tear from the corner of her eye with her thumb and backed into the kitchen, awkwardly closing the door in front of her.

"She's so crazy."

We both laughed, then ambled to the houseboat as Astrid's body playfully swayed from side to side, her shoulder bumping into my arm.

Chapter 28

"Get up!" I said, leaning over Astrid and kissing her cheek.

She rolled onto her side and groaned, flashing the bottom half of the record tattoo on her ribs. "Just take your shower," she whined, her arm flailing in the air. "Wake me up when you're done."

"But I wanted my day to *begin* with a happy *ending*," I said, pulling her toward me.

"You are so stupid," she said. "That doesn't make any sense."

We laughed until I folded into her, smooshing my nose and lips against her cheek to give her one last long, loud kiss.

"I hate you," she finished as I crawled off the bed.

"That's not what you said last night!" I threw a towel around my waist, parted the curtain, and sprinted out the door down the deck to the boathouse for my shower. I slinked inside, accidentally slamming the door closed behind me before hopping over to the shower and twisting the knob to the faucet.

I stood outside the shower in my towel testing the cool water with my hand when she appeared outside the sliding glass door to the boathouse in shorts and a white tank top. "Let me in," she said, rattling the locked door in her bare feet.

"What? I can't hear you!" I mouthed, standing between the round kitchen table and the sliding glass door.

"Come on," she begged, "please!"

I laughed and tugged the door open. Astrid pushed herself against me, her chest covered only by a tank top. I stepped back, my towel shaking from my hips. She gripped me in her palm, biting my neck and guiding me into the now steaming shower. Drenched, she ran her fingers through her hair and dropped to her knees.

"Oh my—Astrid." I gulped, bracing myself against the slick fiberglass wall with my shoulders, my fingers tangled in her hair. She kissed my thighs, her shirt now transparent.

I picked her up and propped her body between my waist and the shower wall, then peeled off her tank top, balling the wet fabric and throwing it out of the stall. The tan lines on her chest glowed, but nothing could compare to the shine in her eyes. I set her back on her feet and slid her jean shorts off, kissing where her underwear should have been. She moaned as I propped her right leg over my shoulder. My tongue caught shower water that cascaded down her stomach. I palmed her breasts, her gasping vibrating beneath my fingers.

She dropped her leg and pulled me up by my hair. My nose danced up her neck until I nibbled her ear, panting. She kept her head still and bit my lip while she angled her hips and arched her back. Her teeth loosened their grip. I grabbed her hips and forced her her against me. She jerked me out with a tight grip, bent over a little more, and then guided me inside of her, slowly working in and out. I dug my nails into her hips and heaved into her as hard as I could. I swiveled my slipping feet and pounded into her again. She screamed and clawed at my stomach. I pulled her shoulders to my ribs, pinning her hand between my hips and the crook of her back, while her frame quivered against mine.

My mind numbed, and my body demanded more. I grabbed her by her hair. She widened her legs, rubbing her fingers between them when I rammed into her again. With one last hard thrust, I pulled out. She kneeled in front of me, shoving me into her mouth, and met my gaze. I grabbed her hair and pushed her neck against the wall with my hips. She worked me in and out of her throat, her hands begging me to finish. My eyelids tightened and my head fell back.

"I'm about to—Astrid." My toes curled against the textured shower floor.

She bobbed her head and then pulled away, dropping against the shower wall.

I stepped out of the way of the streaming shower so it could rinse what was left of me off her.

"Holy fuck." She gasped.

I propped myself against the wall as the shower water beat against my back. "What?"

"That was … passionate." She dropped her head before finding the strength to stand.

"Passionate seems like a good word," I said, grabbing the soap from the rack that hung from the spout and lathering it on a bath sponge that sat beside it. "Better than the words I would have used." I grinned, trailing the sponge across her stomach and sliding my hand to her back.

"What words would have you used?" She turned to rinse the bubbles from her stomach while I scrubbed her shoulders.

"Uh … an exorcism." I cleared my throat and laughed.

"That's a good way of putting it." She spun with a smile and grabbed the sponge. "Just don't put any of those demons in me." She cleaned between my thighs and grinned.

I wore a change of clothes under my suit and packed my shoes into my backpack before unlocking my bike from the tree and stuffing it behind the back seat of Bethel's car. When we entered through the door to the kitchen, Bethel had just begun spreading the food on the kitchen island.

"Good morning, y'all." She guffawed like a mad woman at the southern phrase.

"Yes, it is," Astrid said under her breath and pinched my butt.

"What?" Bethel froze, then set a plate of veggie-sausages onto the table.

"She said good morning," I cut in while heat creeped up the back of my neck.

Astrid grinned and took her backpack off. "Bethel, do you mind if I use your clothes for going into town today? My clean clothes are still a little damp from washing them in the sink."

Bethel put her hands on her hips. "I told you that you could use my washer and dryer!" she pivoted around the corner of the island. "Look at you! You're both w—" Her eyes grew behind her glasses. "I'll go get you something." She scraped the last blueberry pancake from the pan on the stovetop before dropping it onto a large plate and scampering down the hallway. "Be right back!"

"Awkward," Astrid whispered, kissing me on her tiptoes.

"So, what are you going to do during the interview, Astrid?" Bethel shouted down the hall.

"I think I'll help Johnnie get started with stock." Astrid straightened, shaking her shirt to dry it as Bethel cornered the hall into the kitchen. "Do you mind if I leave my film in your car?"

"Not at all." Bethel dropped the clothes onto an empty chair at the end of the table. "Eat up! We have to go!"

I admired Astrid's decency, asking Bethel for permission even when she didn't really need to.

Bethel plucked the top pancake with her hand, steam floating off it. "Hot-hot-hot-hot!" She dropped it onto her plate and shook her hand, taking her seat at the table.

"I think I'll change before I eat," Astrid said, inching away from her chair. "I don't want to get everything all wet."

I grabbed the plate of pancakes from the counter and sat down at the table with them, drizzling on syrup.

Astrid snatched the clothes and ran into the hall.

"What time should I have the car back?" I asked.

Bethel covered her mouth as she finished chewing her food. "I'm generally done with everything by three."

"And what time did you say my interview was?"

"Ten." She sipped and swallowed her tea.

I sat back in my chair and scrunched my face. "Ten? I thought you said it was in the afternoon?"

"Did I?" she recollected. "I'm sorry! I mean, ten isn't really morning."

"No worries. That actually works out better. I can take Astrid to Johnnie's and hang out there for a bit." I cut into my pancake.

"Okay, that's great. Sorry again." Bethel scooted her chair away from the table and stood. "Just leave your dishes." She eyed the clock above the sink. "We're running a little late."

"Are we really?" I hopped out of my chair with more than half of my pancake still left on the plate. I reached into the drawer beside me, grabbing a sandwich bag and dropping Astrid's share of breakfast into it.

"Eh." She picked up her bag from the floor beside the kitchen counter and swung it over her shoulder. "So long as I'm there before the bell rings. Let's go."

"I'm so short!" Astrid yelled, her heels pounding down the hall until she appeared in a pair of shorts that made her legs look like twigs and a T-shirt that hung almost to her knees.

"Or I'm just really big." Bethel chuckled.

Astrid shook her head and rolled the waistline of her shorts. "You have a more developed figure than me. I'm jealous."

"Girl, don't be." Bethel batted her hand. "I'm jealous of you and your size zero pants."

I dug my face into my palm and shook my head. "We're going to be late." I strode to the front door and held it open.

I saved time by dropping Bethel off at the front door. The school itself was separated from the street by a row of trees and a sidewalk; in the distance sat a haze of mountains with swirling mists suspended in the heavy morning air around their bodies. It was the first time I had ever seen the school she worked at—the one I'd hopefully be working at soon.

"All right. Don't forget: ten o'clock." Bethel paused with a hand on the door. "Actually, be here at nine forty-five." She scrambled for her bag on the floor, then took off toward the school. "Good luck!" she shouted, waving from the double-hung doors as the bell rang.

"Hurry! You're going to be late," Astrid called to her, climbing over the center console into the front seat.

By the time Bethel had entered the building, Astrid had clicked her seatbelt. "I saw a plaque for Bethel's parents sitting on her dresser when I was changing into her clothes. The date was for this month. We should do something special for her."

"Yeah, definitely," I said, distracted by the view. "We owe her that."

Astrid followed my gaze. We sat and stared at the mountain line that filled the negative space of the horizon. I shifted in my seat, loosening my tie. The more I thought about the open position, the more it mattered to me. I had studied history for four years but never really planned how I'd use it. I honestly hadn't thought about what I was going to do with my life since the wreck, but there I was, facing an opportunity as if I had planned it all along.

"That is beautiful, isn't it?" I posed.

She was too captivated to answer at first. A few seconds passed, and she brushed the hair from the side of her face that had hidden her glassy eyes.

Every negative possibility flashed through my mind. "Astrid, what's wrong?"

"I didn't think I could be this happy," she admitted while her eyelids overflowed.

I bit my lip and grabbed her hand. She curled her wrist, hugging my forearm with our hands on her lap. The stress-free nothingness—happiness—was all she'd ever wanted, and this job opportunity meant there was potential for us to stay and bottle that feeling, carrying it with us like a picture in a locket around our necks. Humility scrolled down her face with each tear as they fell to her trembling chin.

I rolled into a gas station halfway between the school and Johnnie's shop, slowing until the tank aligned with the pump.

I shifted into neutral and pulled the emergency break, then turned off the engine. "Do you want anything?"

"No," Astrid said, lifting her naked feet up onto her seat, her shoes crossed on the floorboard. "Thanks though." She hunched her arms on her knees and rested her chin on them.

"Okay." I unbuckled my seatbelt and reached for the door handle.

"Zachary?"

I paused with my hand around it, my gaze transfixed on the steering wheel.

"Do you think this will actually work out when the shine wears off?" Her voice didn't fluctuate, and she didn't move.

"What do you mean?" I turned my head toward her, then shifted my gaze to the radio after she avoided eye contact.

"I don't know if I was made for this."

"What about it are you not made for?"

I remained motionless in the silence that followed, staring at the faded stickers that labeled the features across the black, hard plastic dash.

"I don't know." She wiped her face with her palm and dropped it to her shoulder. "I'm afraid this will eventually end. It's stupid." She lowered her legs to the floor and picked at her nails. "Is there such a thing as too happy?" She laughed, wiping her face once more, this time with the back of her hand.

"Stop overthinking things." I leaned over the center console and brought her forehead to my lips. "That's my job." I grinned and winked.

She smiled. I swung out of the car and circled around the rear bumper to the gas pump. After sliding my card into the machine and punching in my pin, I fitted the nozzle into the tank and leaned against the car while it gulped the gas a gallon at a time.

Was it all real? Were things working out?

Yes.

Had it only begun? Can anyone be completely sure of anything?

Hardly.

The fuel pump clicked and stopped counting. As I turned, Astrid climbed out of the car with her backpack on and lifted the hatch.

"What are you doing?" I asked, screwing the cap back on the tank.

She let go of the handle above her head and pulled my bike out. "I need some me time. Do you mind if I use this?" she asked, gripping the handlebars.

"Well, I guess not." I pivoted on my heel, the hard sole of my too-big shoes crunching the rocks. "We're kind of in the middle of nowhere though. Where are you going?"

"Johnnie's," she said, tipping the bike so she could swing her short leg over the tall frame.

"I don't mind driving you. I—"

"It's fine." She pushed herself up onto the saddle, balancing against the car and straightening her backpack. "Good luck at your interview."

I inhaled sharply, my mind racing with the million ways I wanted to respond. "Okay, thanks," I said as everything came into focus. Every reason I had—everything in me that needed her to stay—was a reason she felt the need to leave.

I twisted in place when she took off from the parking lot and merged onto the empty street.

I opened the car door and sat in the driver's seat, closing it behind me.

"Fuck!" I slammed the steering wheel with my palms. "FUCK-FUCK-FUCK!"

My mind raced again, breaking my body into a sweat.

My thoughts blurred while I glared out the windshield at two birds perched on the stop sign, Astrid's pancakes sitting on the dash.

"Fuck." I flung the door open, scattering the birds into a frenzy as I made my way inside convenience store and let myself in.

"Do you have mouthwash?" I asked the clerk, passing by the bars bolted to the inside of the door.

A girl with black hair gelled to the side of her head nodded. "Yeah. Below the condoms there on the right." She leaned over the counter in an unbuttoned polo, showing off her loose bra.

"Thanks." I passed between the first two racks, reasoning past the fact that the mouthwash and condoms needed to be in the same section. I kneeled to study my travel-sized options. Cool mint in a teal bottle—refreshing—and fluoride in a green bottle—not so impactful. I grabbed the teal bottle and made my way back to the counter, the girl keying in the register with her knuckle since her long bedazzled acrylic nails prevented her from using her fingertips.

"That'll be $1.49," she said while I set the small plastic bottle on the counter beside a cardboard stand of lighters and reached into my pocket to pull out my wallet.

"Debit, please," I said, squaring my hips between my palms that rested on the edge of the counter.

"We have a five-dollar minimum."

I hung my head. "Are you serious?"

"Yes." She responded without so much as a nod or an apologetic smile.

I ran my tongue over my teeth to keep the words in and lifted my head.

"You can buy something else to make up the difference."

My face remained stiff. My mind, however, was anything but still. It generally took a lot to wind me up, but this was the wrong morning. I was strung tightly in a game of tug-of-war between the interview and Astrid's lack of faith.

"Can't we make an exception?" I slid the bottle a little closer to her. "I really doubt that cutting me a break is going to bankrupt the business."

"We have an ATM behind you if you'd rather use that." She nodded at the back wall.

I spun around, facing an ATM framed like a refrigerator in a wall of random knickknacks, then I turned to her, biting my lip. Doing my best not to overreact, I marched to the ATM and shoved my card in.

"A three-dollar fee will be added to your withdrawal, do you accept?" the machine spat out.

I propped my hand on the top corner of the ATM, dropped my head between my arms, and counted down from ten.

"Okay, I give in," I said and dropped my arms, trudging back to the counter. "What's something I can get for $3.50? I'm not paying the machine three dollars."

"There's gum across from the mouthwash." She keyed in the new amount. "That would be two cents short though. But I guess we can let that slide."

"Oh, you're a saint." I smirked and handed her my card before returning to the aisle with the mouthwash. "Which golden pack of gum over here is worth $3.50?"

"The one shaped like a cup." She perked up and tilted her head, offering a half-witted smile.

I grabbed a green pack of gum that matched the flavor of my mouthwash, stormed up to the counter, and signed my receipt.

"Anything else I can help you with?" she asked.

"No." I strained to grin. "You've been great." I pointed my thumb at a beat-up door next to the snack aisle. "Are these the bathrooms over here?"

"Yeah, but they aren't for customers." She slid my card.

I stepped away from the counter and surveyed the empty store. "I doubt anyone will know," I said, gathering my things, including my card, and headed to the dirty white door.

"Sir!" she prompted as if words would stop me. "It's locked."

I rested my hand on the handle and closed my eyes.

"Sir, I need to ask you to leave," she said in a raised voice.

I exhaled and twisted the knob. The door opened. "Thank you!" I took a step in and turned the lock.

I set the plastic bag of gum and mouthwash on the back of the toilet, then gripped the edges of the white pedestal sink beside it as I focused on the rusted drain below my face.

Change the direction of your mind, and your life will follow.

I fought the urge to fly … or dive? Over. Under. The lines blurred.

I snatched the bag from the toilet tank and ripped the plastic off the lid of the mouthwash before throwing back a shot. Swishing it between my teeth, I splashed my face with water.

The pep-thoughts didn't help. I spit it out and tightened the lid on the bottle, then dried my face with a brown paper towel that ripped under my fingers against my cheeks.

I balled the shredded bits between my hands, slammed them into the trashcan, and with the plastic bag strangled in my grip, I unlocked the door and stormed out.

"Yes, sir. He just walked out of the bathroom," the clerk said into a cordless phone behind the counter. "He's leaving now." She leered.

Not giving in to her lifeless existence, I waltzed out the front door and headed for the car.

Thirteen minutes left.

Chapter 29

Nearing the door to the school's office, beads of sweat dotted my forehead. "Physical. Safety. Love and belonging. Esteem. Self-actualization." I spoke under my wavering breath, then bent over and took a sip from a fountain outside the door, the water's cool temperature amplified by the mouthwash that still coated my tongue and my cheeks. I stood and wiped my mouth before straightening my tie and taking a deep breath.

Focus. Focus. Focus.

I twisted the stainless-steel handle and pushed the door open.

"May I help you, sir?" a young lady with a sharp nose asked, caramel blonde curls bouncing above her shoulders as she talked.

"Yes, ma'am." I sauntered up to the counter and folded my arms beside the clipboards stacked in front of her. "I'm here for an interview."

"Oh, you must be Bethel's friend! She's told us all so much about you and your girlfriend. You're the first one to interview for the position!"

"My name is Zachary"—I held my hand out and cleared my throat—"and thank you, ma'am."

"I'm Kelley. It's a pleasure to finally meet you, Zachary." She offered a large smile and a loose handshake that lasted longer than it should have. "I'm sure you'll do fine!" She slipped her fingers from my palm, blushing while she reached for a clipboard. "Why don't you have a seat, and I'll page Mrs. Elauter." She gestured to the plush blue chairs behind me.

"Sounds great." I smiled and sat in the one closest to the window, my legs bobbing beneath me.

I propped my elbows on the armrests while studying the walls until a poster of a man in a top hat caught my eye.

"Attitude is a small thing that makes a big difference." Winston Churchill posed above his famous quote, his stiff lower lip jutting out beneath his large, rounded nose.

Some called him the greatest Brit to ever live; others would laugh at the fact that his attitude was something to be emulated. I tried to focus on the relevance of the figure, but his words kept speaking over my deduction of his character.

Moments later, the quote set me off.

Attitude. It will complete or defeat you. Prioritize your reactions from moment to moment, situation to situation, face to face. Don't let a momentary lapse destroy your potential.

Potential. Potential. Potential.

Let it remain infinite.

I crossed my arms, shaking my head at the thought of what Astrid had said before she'd left: Was there such a thing as too happy?

Hell, don't let any type of lapse destroy you. Life goes on.

The door opened, and a short lady with thick-framed glasses appeared.

"Mr. Byrd! How are you?" She held her hand out and approached, her black heels leaving indentations in the carpet behind her.

"I'm well, thanks." I stood and met her in the middle of the floor, taking her hand. "How are you?"

She dropped her arms to the side of her gray dress and shifted her weight from one foot to the other. "I'm great. We've heard a lot about you. I cannot wait to hear about this trip of yours Bethel mentioned."

In that moment, my heart sank. I hadn't thought about how I was going to turn my story into something professionally attractive.

"Well, I can't wait to tell you about it," I said, forging a grin.

The anxiety of treading down the hall had been inebriating. From that point on, all I remember is sitting in her office and hearing, "You're hired."

"Excuse me?" I said, breaking out of my trance.

"All we need to do is a drug and background test, then you can get started." Mrs. Elauter opened a folder on her desk and scrawled her notes on a blue and white form. "Mr. Brown left behind his lesson plan, so you can follow it for the rest of the year and make your own after that. We don't want the kids to get off track."

My face lit up at the thought of putting Astrid at ease. "Thank you so much!"

"No, thank you! This saves the school from dealing with angry parents and a handful of subs. You'll be hired as a long-term sub, and once you pass your certification exams, we'll hire you on full-time. Just fill out an application and background consent with Kelley. She'll be in contact to let you know when your drug test will be."

I shot up from my chair and pivoted behind it. "Sounds good! Thank you for this opportunity!" I darted through the door and softly latched it as I exited.

The confirmation of a future teetered like a pendulum in my mind, knocking anything else that wasn't part of that vision to the side. I followed blue and white tiled floors around the corner to the front entrance and exited into the parking lot, where I had parked Bethel's car out of view on the side of the of the school. After stripping down to the thin pair of shorts and T-shirt I had worn beneath the suit, I hung Bethel's dad's clothes in the back seat of her car and locked it up, leaving her keys behind the gas flap.

The doors of the school cracked open, and Bethel swung around the corner toward the car. "I am so proud of you!" she yelled as I leaned against her back bumper, putting on my shoes. "Get over here and give me a hug!"

She didn't break stride until her arms wrapped around mine, pinning them to my sides. I could only wrap my forearms around her, and even those were partially incapacitated. "Thank you so much. I don't know how to repay you," I said after the moment settled.

"You earned it, Byrd. You don't owe me anything." She released her grip, resting her hand on my shoulder.

I didn't fight with her. She was simply too generous, and there was a heaviness in my heart that would never let me forget it. But something even heavier tugged at it, thrusting it into my wrenching stomach.

Don't overthink it.

I didn't leave until Bethel was back inside, knowing she'd want to drive me if she found out I didn't have my bike. It took ten minutes to get to Johnnie's from the school by car, so the walk was bound to take a while. I slung my backpack around my shoulder and put one foot in front of another.

After following the sidewalk for a couple of miles toward the mountains and past small businesses and neighborhoods, my mind shifted from the fear and anxiety of not having control to how I could show Astrid everything would be okay.

You don't have that kind of power. Just be there as yourself, not a hero.

I wondered if she still needed her space. Maybe I needed some too.

I glanced up from the gray concrete that I had been following to a fork in the road. Left would take me to the bike shop, and right would … well, right was the unknown. Somewhere for me to view at things from afar.

I split ways with everything I knew and ventured off. Soon, grass replaced the sidewalk. The road dipped with a hill and then rose with another, tree branches extending to the edges of the street, almost close enough to touch.

My shadow grew when I approached the top of the second hill, wheat fields taking the place of trees that bordered the street. I stepped onto the shoulder as a car zipped by and spotted a human-sized trail at the end of the field like the one Pete had disappeared into the day I'd met him.

I hopped a ditch and picked up a fallen branch no longer than my arm.

How long can your heart be uncertain when your life has been making big decisions for you? How long will it be before life makes the bigger decisions for you?

The questions jabbed at me while I picked the twigs and leaves from the branch, shaving it to a stick. Then I whipped it through the empty space in front of me.

Take control. Stop blaming yourself.

Take control. Someone has to.

I kicked up dust, the wheat field dipping at my feet, where a steep hill greeted me.

My life was more promising in that moment than it had ever been. I had to let go of my past if I was going to have a future.

The memory of my dad building a porch swing in our shed flashed through my mind. My mother and my grandmother had been on a short vacation together in Florida at the time. I'd glanced at my dad from the yard every now and again while my friend Jim and I played soccer. Later that day, my grandmother's car rolled into our dirt driveway, stopping where we played in the yard. My mother flung the passenger door open and shot across the yard at the sight of the swing.

"You know how to keep a woman happy!" she'd said.

My grandma crossed the yard with her camera in hand. "Do you know how hard it was to keep this a secret all weekend?" She laughed, beautiful in age with a smile creased on her cheeks. She sauntered onto the porch after my mom. "Everyone sit on the swing, and I'll get your picture."

My parents sat, and I crammed between them as my mom hoisted my sister onto her lap.

Stop focusing on Astrid and start supporting her.

I threw the stick over the hill into the thick of the crops and made my way back to the street.

Chapter 30

The sun had fallen toward the horizon by the time I made it to Johnnie's shop.

"Hello?" I called from the door as I broke through the opening.

"Zachary?" Johnnie hollered from the back. "Still doing inventory."

I paced between the rows of tables to the open doorway behind the counter.

"Where's Astrid?" I asked, eyeing the racks that had taken a new form with all the organizing they had done.

"Bethel picked her up earlier." He wiped his hands on his shirt. "What's her situation?"

"Who's? Bethel's?" I chuckled.

"Yeah, is she single?"

"Yeah! She's cute, right?" I spotted my bike leaning against his work bench. "You should talk to her."

"She's not baby crazy or anything, is she?" he asked while I stepped over a box of handlebars and made my way to the bench.

"Seriously?" I hid my face in my shoulder, the urge to laugh scrunched between my brows.

"Yeah, is she?"

"No!" I lost it, my shoulders still bobbing between chuckles as I picked my bike up and pointed it toward the front door. "Just talk to her."

"It's a valid question!" he said, then paused. "Where are you going?" He stretched his arms over his head, the tips of his fingers grazing a florescent lamp that hung parallel to the tall ceiling.

I studied his face for any clues as to what Astrid may have said. "To surprise Astrid. Did she seem okay today?" I asked, balancing my bike against my hip and twisting my palms around the tight grips.

He dropped his arm to his side. "She was quiet, but we were working, so I think she was just focusing. She's a hard worker," he said, pressing on my front tire. "How often do you check the pressure in these?"

"Rarely." I sighed and pushed my bike onto the sales floor.

"You need to maintain your ride! Take care of it, and it will take care of you!" he called out behind me.

"Got it!" I threw him a thumbs-up as I pushed the door open with my elbow.

I weaved in and out of the neatly organized aisles of the discount store, into the gaudy out-of-season holiday ornaments. After grabbing two strands of lights, I ambled over to the home décor section for clothes pins, adhesive hooks, and tea candles, then grabbed a double pack of cream cakes with birthday candles on my way to the self-checkout lane.

Once I slid my card through the reader and used the bagging station to fit everything into my backpack, I eased the cakes into the front pocket. Then I headed out the door, mounted my bike, and cut across to the end of the block, where a stoplight killed my momentum, a handful of cars silhouetting the sinking sun ahead of me.

This is the next phase; you can't be the same person that you were.

The street cleared, and the cool air of the oncoming night brushed against my knuckles.

I stood on one pedal with all my weight until the bike lurched forward. Lights blinded the corner of my eye. Then a horn blared. My mind blanked as my head pivoted. A small car with oval headlights charged at me. I made a sharp turn toward the curb, and the driver laid on his horn again. I wasn't quick enough. The car swerved, but it was already too close. The side of it slammed into my body. My ankle twisted off the pedal, my hands ripping from the handlebars. My arms stiffened in front of me while my bike ran headfirst into a nearby post office box. I dove into the pavement, ripping the skin from my palms. The tires of the car squealed, and I rolled repeatedly, landing breathless on my stomach.

Then the driver's door opened. "The light was red!" a man yelled from the street.

I opened my eyes and lifted my head. He crossed over to the passenger's side, checking for damage. Streetlights blurred in and out of focus. I dropped my head to my arm, then flopped onto my back and panted. The thudding of the man's boots grew distant until his car rumbled to life and he sped off, the bass of his loud exhaust rattling my chest.

I opened my eyes again. Everything was still blurry. My head ached. My body throbbed through the numbness of shock.

My gasps found their rhythm after a minute of fighting the urge to vomit. I unfolded my arms at my side, then grabbed my bag and rolled toward the street to a trashcan bolted to the sidewalk. I wound my fingers through the opening of the cage that anchored it to the street, then heaved myself closer to the grated metal canister, my bones popping between struggling muscles.

I grunted and stood, leaning against the blue metal frame for support—the webs of my fingers stretched against the struts. Barely able to balance, I stumbled backward as I shifted my weight onto a bus stop post, grabbing my bag by a strap and dragging it behind me.

"Fuck!" I yelled over my backpack's zippers scratching across pavement as I dragged it behind me, hanging my head when the light pole dug into my shoulder.

Symmetry. Fault and consequence don't care if you meant to do something.

I suppressed my bellowing and straightened against the post, transferring the weight off my right ankle. My bike hung off the sidewalk, halfway in the street. Unable to put pressure on my ankle, I limped over to the mailbox that I'd hit.

With one hand on the flat tray in front of the inbox slip, I lifted the bike's handlebars. The paint was a little scratched and the saddle torn, but everything else seemed fine. I yanked my bike the rest of the way onto the sidewalk, then eased my injured ankle over the frame while I balanced it between my legs. Carefully, I slid my arms through the straps of my bag and crowded my lungs with the cooling air before turning around and coasting to the corner of the sidewalk.

The streets were quiet. My head bobbed on my shoulders.

Symmetry.

I quivered onto the pedals, pushing off with my good ankle and then lifted my weight onto the saddle as the injured one throbbed in my shoe. My body shook too much for me to pick up speed along the white lines and parallel parking spots.

With bent knees and leaves crunching beneath my wheels, I broke out of the city with my life and met the bridge. I stood, sliding into the momentum. Panting, my doubts came back into focus when our boathouse by the river appeared over the guardrail.

Do the right thing. Don't push her away.

I ducked and let gravity take over on the decline of the bridge, only pushing hard enough to keep up with the crank of my bike. Momentum carried me to our street, squeezing the brakes before my tires touched the dirt driveway.

As expected, Astrid and Bethel weren't home yet. I used my bike like a walker to keep the weight off my ankle as I made it through the yard to the boathouse and dropped it onto the grass just before the deck. Pink and orange hues reflected off the water behind a yellow floodlight that dimly lit the outside of the boathouse from the short overhang of the roof. I limped over to it and slid open the unlocked glass door to our room, gently setting my bag onto the bed, and hobbled to the center of the floor. I winced with each step, doing my best not to let my scrapes and cuts brush against anything.

The numbers 6:30 PM glared at me from the digital clock on the nightstand. It had already been a few hours since Bethel picked Astrid up at the shop.

Hang the pins.

Gripping the front zipper with my knuckles, I pulled it open and yanked out the cakes that oozed in the packaging. Of course they'd been crushed. Why wouldn't they be? What made me think that the world would allow me to deliver a grand gesture without a fight? I threw the cakes aside, along with the birthday candles I had planned to light, then broke into my bag to collect the lights, hooks, and clothespins.

I adhered the hooks two feet apart just below the ceiling around the perimeter of the room, then plugged the lights strands into the outlet near the door and draped them over the first hook before winding them around the next, following that pattern until they circled around me. Then I clipped on the wooden pins, two between each pair of hooks, and randomly assorted the tea candles around the room.

After grabbing a change of clothes from the dresser, I stumbled to the door. I ventured outside and stood in the wide space, feeling a flow of warm blood reach my abrasions until they burned. The driveway sat empty. Rushing, I hurried to the boathouse, turned on the shower, and jumped into stinging-cold water—scrubbing the dry blood and rocks from my skin with a washcloth wrapped around a bar of soap.

My ankle hovered an inch above the tub floor, the scar where I'd dropped the grate on it visible. Soon steam permeated the air as hot water kicked in and flushed through my lesions. I twisted the faucet knob further, the air growing too heavy to breathe. Water scalded my abrasions, cooking the torn skin around them to a darker shade of red.

As the scars populate, the pain becomes irrelevant.

I turned the knob again, the pain weakening my muscles until I could barely stand—then I rested my weight onto the injured ankle.

But for now, let the pain cleanse you.

The water continued to dig through my open skin before the torture hardened my pity into anger and numbed my mind.

I turned off the shower and bent my knee, taking the pressure off my ankle. My head dropped to my forearm that I'd propped on the white tiled wall, my lungs still gasping for air as my body tingled in the residual heat. I wished I could stand there forever. Stopped time, even.

I grabbed a cheap towel off the wall mount around the corner and wiped its coarse fabric over my tender body before unfolding my clothes and putting them on one limb at a time. After dressing, I faced the window over the kitchen sink that contrasted the rest of the room—framing a barren, dark driveway.

Back in the boathouse, I stuffed all the trash into my bag to put into Bethel's recycling bin later, including the smashed cakes. Then I dropped my bag onto the floor beside the bed before lighting the candles around the room.

There was nothing left for me to do. Nothing to keep me busy. Nothing to keep me distracted. Nothing. Like anything else, nothingness shone in a new light. For the time being, it paralyzed me, whereas nothingness usually gave me a world of potential to fight for.

I turned off the overhead light and lay down to the stentorian voices in the attic of my body. Fostering the devil, my inner child lashed out with jealousy through the paper-thin walls of my apprehension. Who was I? What did it mean to have something outside of myself that completed me? Should I have paid more attention to being steadfast on my own?

The windows grew dark when my thoughts quieted, aside from the reflections of light that hung around the room.

Bothered by the brief absence of my thoughts, I made myself focus. In need of a constant, I searched for something to cling to inside myself. There was nothing. The void collided with loneliness and the thought that temporary circumstances would leave me empty.

Had I always been this way?

Yes.

Whatever happens, happens. I detached myself, remembering that I was capable of letting go when I had to.

The glass door slid open, and I flinched.

"What's this?" Astrid poked her head in. "Are you okay?" She slid into the room, gawking at the candles.

"I'm fine." I hopped off the bed, limping on my right ankle.

"Why is it so hot?" She reached for the light switch by the door.

"I must have fallen asleep," I lied. "I wanted to sur—"

The bright bulb scorched my eyes.

"Oh my god. What happened to you?" She dropped a flat brown paper bag onto the bed and rushed over to me.

"I'm fine," I said, shielding my face with my hand. "Just a small bike crash."

"This doesn't look small, Zachary!" She pulled my arm free. "Have you cleaned the cuts?"

"I took a shower."

"I'm going to get something to wrap it up with from Bethel's." She let go of me and ran through the open door.

The pattering of her feet racing across the yard faded as the kitchen screen door creaked open. "Bethel!" She yelled before slamming the door behind her.

I stumbled to the edge of the bed, where she had dropped the paper bag, then opened it, glossy prints from our trip slipping from an envelope into my skinned palm.

I grinned and shook my head as I hung the first photo of Jonas with his tongue out from the day Astrid had bought the camera.

The countless memories slowed my pace until my thumb caressed pictures I couldn't account for: groups of people sitting on steps, some standing, and others cross-legged on the sidewalk. In another, Lisa flashed a smirk, riding between two train cars as Pete and I had done. The list went on and on as I continued to hang the prints until I appeared again in the picture, ending at the houseboat.

"You didn't have to do that," Astrid said under her breath from the doorway, peroxide and ointment in one hand, and gauze, tape, and bandages in the other.

I grinned while hanging the last picture above her head. "I wanted to." I let go of the pin and eased my hands back down to my side. "These are really good!"

"Thanks," she replied with a feeble voice, then shuffled to the foot of the bed and sat on her legs, laying medical supplies out beside her. "Let me fix you up." She patted the quilt in front of her.

I placed the paper bag beside her supplies and sat in front of her with my legs hanging over the edge.

"Where did you find those people playing instruments?" I asked, pointing at the picture hanging from the ceiling.

She poured peroxide on my arm and held a cloth underneath so the infected liquid didn't drip. "I met them not far from the coffee shop after you and I split." She wiped my arm and ripped the paper from the gauze. "Most of them knew Lisa," she finished, squirting antiseptic onto the gauze and taping it to my arm. "That's how she found me."

"Ah." I dropped my head.

"Zachary." She moved on to the next scrape. "I'm sorry for this morning."

I didn't respond, not wanting to make it obvious that I'd been dwelling on it all day.

"It isn't your fault," she continued, wiping the torn skin from around my forearm. "I hope you didn't take it personally. I just needed space, I guess."

"It's all right." I tensed as she poured another dose of cold liquid. "But I wish you wouldn't just shut me off."

"When I shut you off, you should know I need space." She giggled.

"Yeah, well, it's not that easy." I lifted my head and poked my finger through my beard to scratch my chin.

She lifted my shirt, forcing me to raise my arms so she could remove it and inspect the rest of my torso. "Why's that?"

I flattened my hair. "Because I hate to see you upset. I just want to fix whatever is bothering you."

"Do you have anywhere else that is messed up?" she asked, tilting me forward to examine my back.

"Just the scrapes on my face and hands, and then some on my legs."

"Your face isn't that bad … and there isn't much I can do about your hands." She dropped onto her knees in front of me. "Zachary, you won't be able to always fix me when I'm broken." She crumpled the trash into a ball and tossed it onto the nightstand. "All better," she said, standing and ambling to the light switch by the door. "But you always being here makes it easier."

I pulled back the sheets and hoisted myself onto the pillow. After flipping the lights off, she hid with me, hip to hip, under the covers.

"This looks amazing by the way." She turned her head and kissed me on the cheek. "Thank you."

Pictures circled our heads like a solar system over a child's bed. We were left to dream not of heights that we may one day reach, but of the heights we'd fallen from to find each other.

Chapter 31

Astrid slid a box across the floor to me, and I placed it on the shelf as the phone behind the front desk of the bike shop rang.

"Will you get that, Zachary?" Johnnie asked, passing me a pile of colored bandanas on his way to the back room.

"Sure!" I said, already headed in that direction.

I lifted the outdated, cordless handset off the hook and leaned against the desk. "Bike Works. This is Zachary." I picked at the dented black plastic on the back of the headset.

"Zachary? This is Bethel!" she said in a frantic, high-pitched voice.

"Hey … what's going on?" My body went rigid, and I gripped the phone tighter.

"I'm going to the store," Astrid whispered across the counter. "Do you want anything?"

I shook my head as Bethel's muffled voice came through the earpiece.

"Kelley's looking for you. She said she made an appointment for you today for your drug test. What number did you give her?"

The front door chimed while Astrid hopped out onto the sidewalk.

"Crap! I gave her my old number. It was prepaid but got stolen with the van." I ran my fingers through my hair. "I'll get another one. Do you know when and where the appointment is?"

"Yes. She gave me the information in case I heard from you." She paused for a second and muffled the receiver, her voice mumbling to someone else in the room with her before putting the phone back to her ear. "You should still call her. Tell her that you've been busy getting everything situated before you started the job or something." Bethel spoke sternly under her breath, urging me to lie … "It's at Corp-Testers. I'll text the address and phone number to Johnnie. Your appointment is in an hour. Do you think you can make it?"

My mind sifted through the details, then paused. When had she gotten Johnnie's number?

"Zachary?" Bethel tuned me back in. "Can you make it?"

"I don't know." I boomeranged around the counter. "I have to go home and get changed. I'll probably need your car again."

"You won't have time to make it to the house and then to the drug test." She sighed. "Just—just borrow clothes from Johnnie. He lives near the shop … I think."

"Johnnie," I yelled to the inventory room with the phone to my chest, "do you mind if I use your shower and borrow some clothes? I have to take a drug test for work."

"No problem," he said, poking his head through the doorframe.

I pressed the phone to my ear. "Okay, thanks for your help, Bethel. I'm going to head to his place now. Just send the address."

"All right, will do!"

"Talk—"

The line went dead in my ear.

I placed the phone back on its hook. "Thanks, Johnnie," I said, peeping through the inventory doorway at him while he dug through a red portable toolbox.

"No problem! Are you riding all the way there on your bike?" He unscrewed a rear wheel from a used bike beside him as I strode past him to the work bench.

"Yeah. Is your place far?"

"Which testing place are you going to?

I scrunched my eyebrows. "I didn't know there was more than one. Bethel said she sent the address to your phone. It's called Corp-Testers, I think?"

Johnnie's face turned a light shade of red when he reached into his pocket. "It was on silent. But yeah, this place is kind of far." He put his phone to sleep and slid it into his pocket. "You should just drive my truck."

"You have a truck?"

"Yeah. It's at my house. I live close by, so I rarely drive it to work." He returned to the loosened wheel. "Can you pick up bubble wrap from the hardware store while you're out? They have it in large quantities. Tell them it's for me, and they'll know what size to get."

"Sure." I leaned on the bench. "That's no problem. Would you mind if Astrid and I used your truck to pick up new clothes?"

"That's fine. Where is she?" He dug through the toolbox and picked up a wrench.

"She went to the store."

"You can pick her up here on your way to the test. My truck is parked around the back of the house." Johnnie had a rigid type-A personality and therefore always had a plan. Though, in his attempts to turn down his need for control, he had become overly passive.

I simply nodded as he tossed the keys onto the bench in front of me.

His house was less than three hundred yards from the shop. A high-pitched roof with an attic window lay hidden behind the trees in his yard. I hobbled down the driveway and followed it to the rear of the house, my ankle still sore but loosening up with each step. Overgrown bushes and patches of hard grass and dirt had created an opening to the backyard, where I found a truck hiding beneath a carport.

I rounded the corner to the back deck, where a pot with nothing but soil sat next to the door, then unlocked the worn deadbolt with the key Johnnie had lent me and let myself in to freshen up and get changed.

Within minutes, I was sauntering back through the dimly lit hall to the deck. I made my way down the steps, sifting through Johnnie's keyring until I found the key to the truck. It was an older two-door model much smaller than most modern trucks. I twisted the round silver lock that had sunk into the faded red paint of the driver's side door and climbed in. The engine turned slowly the first couple of attempts as lights on the dash flickered. After another try, it fired up. I rolled down the windows and squirmed in the seat. My hands straddled the steering wheel, then it hit me.

This was really happening. It was really here.

My eyes searched for pinholes of light in the tall, tangled trees that surrounded his house.

Get to it, then.

I had seventeen minutes to get to my drug test.

Seventeen minutes.

I tugged the automatic transmission shifter into reverse, backed out into the street, then shifted gears and cut through a side street. Soon I arrived at the bike shop.

When I got there, Astrid stood waiting for me at the front door of the shop.

"Let's go!" I motioned her over through the open window.

"Johnnie put the address in his phone's GPS," she said, sprinting to the passenger's side door and hopping in next to me. "He said just to follow it." She stared at the device with widened eyes.

"How far away does it say we are?" I asked, adjusting my line of sight while she propped it up against the gauge cluster.

"Twelve minutes."

I peeked at the clock, then at the phone again. "Cool." I pulled into drive and merged onto the two-lane road. "So, what did you get me at the store?" I asked with a cocked head, baring half a smile.

"You said that you didn't—" She squinted and stopped short. "Why do you insist on upsetting me?" she asked, leaning on the center console and propping her head up.

"It's really all I have anymore." I dropped my hands to the bottom of the steering wheel to view the gauges as the truck let off a faint squeal. "But really. Did you get gum or anything?"

She gave me a blank stare. "Why are you dressing up for a drug test?" She kicked her shoes off and crossed her legs beneath her.

I tipped to the side, tugging my wallet out of my back pocket and setting it in the cup holder between us while we crossed an intersection. "I don't want to come across as unprofessional is all."

She cocked her head, peering down at my wallet.

"What?" I stuck my arm out the window. "It was hurting my butt."

"Sir," she said, stiffening her tone, "it is not very professional to talk about your butt."

"Hardy-har," I mocked. "But really, do you have any gum?"

"No."

"What did you get?"

Astrid looked out the open window, her hair dancing around her face in the wind. "Feminine products, if you must know." She tapped the door handle.

"You have a visitor?" I tickled her side below her ribs.

"You're stupid." She giggled, grabbing my hand and placing it in my lap. I kept my head forward but focused on her from the corner of my eye. "It's more like, *we* have a visitor."

She concealed her smile the best she could, but mounds formed in her cheeks.

"Rawr!" I yelled, attacking her again.

"NO!" She laughed, smashing herself against the door.

We arrived with one minute to spare. The building was nothing more than an old, blue, sun-stained storage container in the middle of a dirt parking lot that had been converted into an office—not at all the type of medical testing establishment I'd expected. The sign was nice though, which was the only thing that comforted me enough to go through with it.

"Are you going to come in or just wait in the truck?" I fanned dust from my face that had seeped in through the windows.

"I'll stay out here. I'm still kind of nasty from riding bikes this morning." She rested her chin on the window sill. "Besides, I'm more comfortable out here in the getaway vehicle." She slouched in her seat and winked.

"Okay. I won't be long." I kissed her on the forehead, which felt a little warm against my lips, then got out and strode toward the steps of the worn-out building.

"Welcome to Corp-Testers," a woman's raspy voice called before the door had completely opened.

"Yes. Hi. I have an appointment for eleven o'clock," I said, stepping inside between two artificial fig trees to a window that framed a big-boned woman at a desk.

"Your name?" she asked as I closed the door, flipping a paper on a clipboard.

"Zachary Byrd."

"Yep. Please fill this in the bathroom behind you." She signed the clipboard and handed me a clear cup with a white lid, then pointed at the door closest to me.

I moseyed across the white linoleum to the door marked with a unisex symbol at the top. As I entered the confined space, my shoes scratched over a thin layer of dirt. I turned to close the door when a chill of courage churned in my stomach. I filled the cup until it was warm in my hand, and then with a jiggle of my leg, zipped my pants and exited back into the lobby.

"Set it on the counter with your driver's license, please," she said before I could cross the floor again, not even glancing up—her eyes remained fixated on the clipboard. "Have you done drugs in the past six months?"

"No ma'am," I answered, placing the cup on the counter in front of me and pulling out my wallet.

"Have you ever had to receive medical attention due to drug or alcohol use?"

I rummaged through my cards and set my ID beside the cup. "No ma'am."

"Have you ever experienced memory loss after using drugs or alcohol?"

Her list went on and on. I could have worn a loin cloth and clown shoes with a needle sticking out of my arm, and she wouldn't have cared so long as I answered the questions and had a legal ID. She simply checked off the boxes like she had been told to do.

Does life have a box of its own? You know plenty of people who live like it does.

"Are we done here?" I asked, tapping my shoe after the thirty seconds of silence that followed her last question.

"Yes, sir. We'll be in touch with the school. Have a great day." Her face remained blank as she kept scribbling on the sheet of questions.

"Okay," I said, accidentally scraping the scabs on my palm against the corner of the counter. "Have a great day!" I clenched my fist to tame the pain and grabbed the knob with my other hand to egress.

Spots formed in front of my eyes with the flood of light outside, hiding the world from view while I blinked to fill the flash of white canvas with color. Astrid's feet hung out of her window.

"Whatcha doin', girl?" I hollered like a giddy farm boy in an old western, treading down the bowed staircase and across the dirt parking lot.

She leaned her pretty little head dressed in sunglasses out the window. "I'm writin' stuff." She waved a pad of paper in the air. "Did you pass your test?"

"I don't know," I said, crossing to the driver's side. "You didn't slip any drugs into my food, did you? Because if you did"—I opened the door and climbed in—"we need to switch out that piss."

She chortled. "Well, you don't want to use mine!" she said and continued writing.

"What are you working on?"

"Do you think Johnnie would hire me full-time?" she asked, evading my question.

"I'm sure he would," I answered, pushing against the steering wheel until my back flattened against the seat. "But I think you should try to sell your pictures!"

She smiled and grabbed my hand. "I could do both," she said, giving it a squeeze. "I want to start saving again though. I don't like mooching off you all the time."

"I don't mind." I wrapped my fingers around the nape of her neck and rubbed her cheek with my thumb.

"Well, you should," she said.

I dropped my hand as she let go of the other and closed the half-sized notebook before snugging her yellow number two pencil into the spiral.

"Besides, I'll end up hating myself if I don't find something to keep me occupied while you're at work."

I thought about how miserable I'd be if I were her with nothing to do all day and nodded. "It looks like our vacation is ending!" I shook my fist at the sky.

"Or maybe it's just starting." She smiled and stretched over the console to give me a peck on the cheek.

"Lunch?" I asked with a calm, cool smirk, pulling the truck into drive.

She flung her arm out of the window as we veered onto the street. "Let's."

Chapter 32

Astrid sat on the tailgate beside me in the grocery store's parking lot and stabbed her knife into the peanut butter, then choked up on the blade before pulling out a huge clump and dabbing it onto her bread.

"What?" she asked when I glared. "I really like peanut butter, okay?" She shamelessly spread it across her bread and wiped the knife off on the crust for good measure.

"Is there enough left for me?" I bit my lip, leaning over the jar that she balanced between her bent knees, her bare feet dangling in the cool air.

"SHHH!" She laughed, then dug her knife into the peanut butter, claiming another chunk. "Is that enough?" She held out the clump with the knife jutting out like a lollipop stick and scraped it on a fresh piece of bread before I could answer.

"SO … MUCH … PEA-NUT … BUTTER!" I strained to lift the bread from her hand as she stabbed the knife back into the jar. "CAN'T … LIFT … "

"YOU'RE STUPID!" She talked just above the sound of my failing strength. "Here, let me help." She jumped off the bed with her bread hoisted near her face, kneeling on the blacktop beneath my hand, which shook under the weight. "I can help," she said again, studying the scene.

"Hurry!" I grunted. "Can't hold on much longer!"

"I got it!" She lifted my hand with nothing more than a finger, then hopped up beside me.

"Oh." I cleared my throat. "Do you need the jelly?"

"Don't feel bad. I am the strongest person in the world. And yes, please." The tailgate pressed into her thighs as she laid my piece of peanut butter bread beside hers on a paper bag. "Wait." She held a hand up.

"What?" I paused with the jelly still in my grip.

She lowered her hand and held it out with her palm up. "Pass me the scalpel, nurse."

"Is that knife or the spoo—"

"Hurry! We don't have much time!"

I took a wild guess and grabbed the handle of the knife in the peanut butter jar. Tugging the blade as hard as I could, I sent the jar of peanut butter across the bed of the truck.

"Nurse!" Astrid didn't break character, her hands shaking while a minivan rolled by behind her.

"Sorry ... it was stuck." I pouted, handing her the knife coated with peanut butter remnants.

She spread the leftovers onto my piece of bread in a panic. "Petroleum jelly," she ordered, sticking her hand out again.

"What are you building over there, Dr. Frankenstein?" I said under my breath like a scorned child, holding out the jelly and spoon.

She spun the lid and scooped the jelly onto two new pieces of bread, then smashed them on top of the peanut-butter–slathered slices.

"Oh my god, that was so extensive." I grabbed my sandwich off her paper bag, and then placed my own sack on my lap so I wouldn't mess up the clothes I'd borrowed from Johnnie.

She sat beside me and ate her sandwich as any normal peanut butter and jelly surgeon would.

"I must say"—I licked the peanut butter from the roof of my mouth—"it is much better with more peanut butter. Good job."

"I do what I can." She took a bite of her work and smacked her lips. "So, what else are we going to do today?"

I peered off into the distance and swallowed. "I asked Johnnie if we could use his truck to get clothes." When she didn't respond, I set my sandwich onto my bag and wiped my hands against one another.

"He said he didn't mind but asked that, in exchange, we pick up bubble wrap for him."

She still didn't speak.

"I know you don't want me to—"

"Let's do it." She shoved the rest of her sandwich into her mouth, barely able to close her lips as she hopped off the tailgate and climbed in the truck, sticking her arm out of the open window. "Bud only begau—" she held a finger up and swallowed. "But only because it's getting cold, and I will be paying you back for everything you buy me!"

I stored the remaining crust in my teeth, rolled the bag up, stuck it in my pocket, and lifted the tailgate before meeting her in the cab.

I took a bite from my sandwich, pulling it from my mouth. "Can't we just enjoy a meal?"

"Take a right out of the parking lot!" She pointed toward the road.

I started the truck. "How do you know where were going?"

"The phone, duh!"

I mimicked her words without using vowels and cocked my head from side to side.

"Stop it and drive!" she said, slapping my arm.

I grimaced and rubbed it. "Fine ... geez." I shifted into drive and veered across the parking lot.

"Did you know Bethel and Johnnie have been talking?" I slapped the steering wheel.

"What?!" She gasped and dropped the phone before pivoting in her seat. "How do you know?"

"This morning. When Bethel called me about the test," I started. "Well, when I was figuring out how I was going to get to the boathouse to change and still make it to the test on time, I mean. She suggested I go to Johnnie's because it wasn't too far from the shop, and that I should just use his clothes."

"No way!" Her eyes widened as she balanced her elbows on the console. "What did you say to him?"

"Nothing. What was I supposed to say? I ignored it." I flung my hand in the air. "But you should have seen Johnnie's face when I told him she had suggested I go to his house."

A soft female voice from the phone cut in with directions. "Turn left at Eastwood Drive."

"This thing doesn't give much of a warning." I pushed the blinker lever down and slowed to make the turn while Astrid adjusted the visor to shield her eyes from the sun.

"OH MY GOSH!" She screeched as something fell to her lap in my peripherals.

"What is it?" I asked, doing a double take.

"Bethel's school ID!" She picked up the card, tethered to a blue lanyard. "We have his phone. Why don't we look through their texts?" She shook the glaring LED screen in my face.

"We can't just look through his personal stuff!" I shook my head with both hands on the wheel.

"We aren't saints, Zachary." She jerked the phone away and opened the messaging app. "UUUGGGHHH!" she groaned seconds later, dropping it onto her lap. "He deleted everything!"

"HA!"

"Your destination is four hundred feet ahead on the right," the phone instructed.

Astrid tucked the lanyard back into the visor as we maneuvered into an empty spot not far from the door of a corrugated metal building. We got out and strode through a thick brick entrance, where a clearly disposable society had discarded clothes either because of eating too much last winter or the changing trends.

"Look at this." She walked over to a rack of men's button up shirts. "What size are you?"

"It varies. Large to extra large," I said, sliding hangers to the side as I looked for something that caught my eye.

"What about this one?" She held up a white-banded dress shirt that still had the tag on it.

I rubbed the collar between my pointer finger and thumb. "Isn't that a little last century?"

"What?" She turned the shirt around so it was facing her. "You have no idea how much it would turn me on to see you in this and a nice vest with your sleeves rolled up."

"Sold." I snatched it from her and draped it over the arm I'd reserved for the *buy* pile. We found a few more button-ups. No more banded collars, but we did find a nice vest to go with the one we had, and even slacks.

After that, we split up to find casual clothes for the oncoming colder weather. Most of the outfits in those sections were either too large, too small, or too flashy for me. There were a couple pairs of jeans and a shirt that I liked, but knew I'd have to go elsewhere to get enough to last the harsher months. I gave up and walked to the women's section to see if she was having better luck.

"Dresses won't keep you warm!" I said, spotting her from an outside aisle.

"But they're my favorite!" She stomped her foot. "And they will with enough sweaters and leggings." She nodded at a rack of jeans, then huffed and crossed the aisle to more dresses.

"Whatever you say," I said, cutting through the racks toward her. "But don't be asking me for my jacket when you're cold." I grabbed her load and folded it over my free arm.

She hung the flowing green fabric that she was looking at back on the rack. "You wouldn't leave me to freeze!" she said, grinning.

"What about new sneaks?" I thumbed over the racks until I spotted shoes loosely exhibited on shelves.

"I'm fine," she said. "These still have some miles left on them." She leaned on the outside edges of faded pattern of her black floral shoes that were now separating at the toe.

"Mmm." I grunted, then studied my own pair of Era's that creased when I bent my toes, rubber jutting from the sides. "All right, I guess."

She slid a hand under the pile of clothes I'd been holding for her. "You ready?"

"I don't mind carrying them," I said, so she dropped her arms while I led the way to the register.

"I promise, I'll pay you back," she said, stepping in front of me.

"Thank you for lending me the money for the time being though." She balanced on her tiptoes and planted a kiss on my cheek.

"Really, don't worry about it. I like taking care of you." I shook my head and set everything on the counter in front of a young teen who sat behind the register in a teal shirt and aviator-shaped glasses.

"Well, I feel bad." Astrid tugged on her thumb and rocked from side to side.

I unfolded anything that may have doubled over when I laid it down while the cashier remained distracted on her cell phone.

"Don't. Seriously. I enjoy doing this for you," I said, kissing Astrid on the top of her head.

"You have to be running out of money though." She crossed her arms. "We can't keep spending. Even with it getting cold out, I'm having second thoughts about buying this now."

My face lit up, and I spun on my heel. "I forgot to tell you though," I said, clapping a hand to my forehead, "the insurance money came in. They gave me $2,300 for the van!"

"That'll be $163.57," the cashier said, setting her phone aside.

"See," I told Astrid, reaching for my wallet. "I expected to spend more than that on my clothes alone. Thanks to you and your thrifting skills, I just saved a ton of money!" I opened my wallet and pulled out my card. "Do you take debit?" I asked.

"Sure do." She pushed a card reader my way that had a self-contained keypad. "Just slide the card, enter your PIN, and hit the green button."

At the hardware store, employees rushed from aisle to aisle, but the front register remained empty. While we waited for someone to help us, Astrid and I perused the store for tools and project ideas. In the last aisle, I came across a row of portable space heaters, each with different features.

"Do you think we should get one before it gets too cold?" I asked, projecting my voice to the opposite end of the aisle, where she stood examining an oversized flashlight. She returned it to the shelf and joined me to scope out our options.

"Do you think we'll need it?" she asked.

I bent to a lower shelf and tilted a box toward me to read the specs. "I guess we can get by with what we have until it gets cooler," I said and let go of the box.

"I just hate spending money, especially when you're the only one who has any right to it." She clawed at her wrist.

"Don't worry about it. I have a new job, and you said you'd talk to Johnnie about working at the bike shop. In the meantime, we have to get by, and I don't mind making that happen. I feel like spending a little of my savings to get started is the smallest thing we've dealt with since we met," I joked, my eyes bulging.

She chewed her nails, then dropped her fingers to her chin. "I guess you're right. I'll ask Johnnie about work when we get back."

"Okay," I said with a weak smile. I was proud of her, but that didn't ease the guilt I'd unintentionally cast upon her. I supposed I should have been happier that she didn't want a free ride. Even at the bottom of a barrel, she'd swim in the last few inches of water. If it were anyone else, they would have barely kept their head above the current as the exhausting undertow syphoned the hole beneath them.

But in my confidence in making things right, I had grown selfish. I wanted control; I had provided a solution to bypass whatever austerity we may have faced due to poverty or a lack of options. I was draining what water that old barrel had left, instead of plugging it and filling it up.

Poverty? Really? It's funny how the thought of a small amount of money and something to prove will change an attitude.

"Oh!" I said, distracted by a man with a mullet in a red vest who passed our aisle. "Sir, do you work here?" I asked.

"Yes." The man's steps stopped abruptly, and he appeared at the end of the aisle. "How may I help you?" he asked, leaning against the capper.

I scratched my head. "Johnnie Snowell from Bike Works asked us to pick up some bubble wrap."

"We can do that!" The man rounded the corner, and I followed him to the front of the store while Astrid hung back. He stopped at the main desk and flipped through a notebook of alphabetized bar codes until he found what he was looking for, then scanned it. "Johnnie usually gets the 24-inch rolls, but all we have left are 12-inch ones and 48-inch ones. Will one of those work?"

"How long before you have the roll that he usually gets?" I asked.

"Just a second. " The man punched the numbers into the computer.

Astrid appeared at the end of the next aisle, where she held a flower-shaped wind spinner against her chest.

"Astrid!" I called. She tilted her head before spinning to face me. "Do you want one of those?"

"They're only a few dollars." She dug into her pocket and pulled out change and a wad of singles. "I can buy it myself." She poked at the palm of her hand, counting coins under her breath.

"The 24-inch roll won't be here until the end of the week, sir," the employee said from behind the counter.

"Hmm." I scratched my chin. "Just give me the 12-inch roll, and he can pick up the bigger one when he needs it."

The man scanned the notebook again and pecked at the keyboard again. "Would you like to add that to his account? If so, I'll need to call him to verify."

"No." I grabbed my wallet from my back pocket and unfolded it. "I got it." I handed him my card.

As the man swiped it, Astrid dawdled up to the register with her glossy wind spinner, running her finger along the yellow petals resting on top of a long green metal stem.

"You find one you like?" I asked her, retrieving my card from the clerk.

"Yeah." She admired its sharp leaves. "Does it smell real?" she asked, shoving it underneath my nose.

"Oh yeah! That takes me back to when we used to run through the plastic flower fields as children," I said with a chuckle.

"Would you like to get that as well?" the man with the mullet asked.

"Oh, no," Astrid beat me to the punch, laying her wadded-up

dollar bills and coins on the counter. "I've got it." She brought the flower up to her own nose, covering her smile with its yellow spinner. "It's something I can mark our home with." She stretched up on her tiptoes and kissed me on the cheek.

Before heading back to the bike shop, we stopped by the boathouse. The clothing bags on Astrid's lap nearly swallowed her on the way; only her arms and hands poked through, spinning the head of her plastic flower.

"Where are you going to put that?" I asked when we pulled in to the driveway.

She turned to me, then gazed at the flower as the boathouse rocked gently on the wake of a passing boat ahead of us. "In the yard in front of the boathouse. I was thinking beside the door." She shifted below the bags, stacking them between us for me to grab so she could get out. "What do you think?"

"That's a cool spot!" I agreed, opening the door and looping the handles of the bags around my wrists. "We really do need to work on our home decor, huh?" I laughed, staggering out of the truck.

"I can help with those." She slid her short legs out of the truck, meeting me in front of the hood.

"Don't worry about it." I smiled. "Go plant your flower!"

We traipsed past Bethel's house and the outdoor table, then forewent the tree that we'd chained our bikes to.

She stopped before we got to the deck and pressed the hard metal stem into the ground. "There," she said, wiping her hands against one another. "That should do it."

Chapter 33

There was a lot to bring home on my second day of teaching, so I left my bike behind and caught a cab since Bethel had a meeting after school. When I got back, I rushed from the driveway to the boathouse so I could change and get back to the bike shop. I tugged the door open and hopped from the deck onto the barge to find Astrid already on the comforter. "How did you get home so fast? I thought you were going to talk to Johnnie about working with him this afternoon?" I unbuckled my belt and whipped it from my waistline.

She hopped off the bed, then wrapped her arms around me and gave me a kiss. "The conversation with Johnnie didn't take nearly as long as I had expected. He hired me on the spot!" She stepped back, hinging her fingers in my empty belt loops. "He said he was coming to tonight's dinner too."

"Congratulations! I knew he would; he's a smart man!"

She dropped her chin to hid her smile. "Thanks. How did your second day go?"

"It went really well. These kids are a lot smarter than I anticipated. I think I'm going to like it!"

"Good." She grinned and kissed me again.

"Did you figure out what we're going to cook?"

"Yes!" She faced the bed, where her things lay scattered across the sheets. "I copied this recipe with a star beside it from one of her cookbooks in the kitchen," she said, reaching into her backpack to pull out the ingredient list. "I stopped by the store on my way home. Everything is in Bethel's fridge."

I tossed my own bag onto the bed. "What is it?"

"Grilled garlic parmesan zucchini," she recited, following the words with her finger. "And premade chocolate chip banana oat cake for desert. Oh! Also, a fruit salad."

"That sounds so good!" I licked my lips. "What time is she supposed to get home, again?"

She glanced at the digital clock on the nightstand. "Four-thirty. We have about thirty minutes."

She folded up the recipe list, and we took off across the yard for Bethel's house, entering through the back door.

"How good are you at cooking?" she asked, flattening the recipe list onto the island's granite countertop.

"I got by in college, but I'd say that's all I did—get by. I'm not very good at it."

"Oh." She dropped to her knees and pulled a pan out from under the oven before turning the knob to preheat it. "Well, I was just looking at the recipe." She nodded toward the list. "It may or may not be a little above my skill level. I've never cooked anything like this."

"Neither have I!" I straddled my arms on either side of the yellow paper, reading the steps.

A knock sounded at the front door.

"Do you think that's Johnnie already?" She glanced up from the counter, her arm halfway inside a grocery bag.

"Did he say he was coming this early?" I circled the kitchen island and made my way to the living room, where I peered into the peephole on the front door.

I swung the door open and stepped aside. "Johnnie!"

"Where should I put my bike?" He nodded at the handlebars, which jutted out past a blooming Azalea bush.

"Uh." I put a hand on my hip and scratched my head. "We chain ours to a tree in the backyard." I stepped outside, closing the door behind me.

"You really shouldn't leave your bikes outside." He grabbed his by the handlebars and directed it into the side yard. "Don't you have somewhere you can put them inside?"

"Not really." I pointed at our miniature boathouse and houseboat combo as we turned the corner.

"Is that where you live?" he asked, tripping over himself when we approached the tree.

"Yeah." I smiled.

He pushed his bike passed the table, then stared again at the boathouse. "Mmm."

I stopped in my tracks and raised an eyebrow. "What?"

"It's just a lot smaller than I expected," he said, laughing.

"Do you know how to cook?" I asked while he leaned his bike against mine.

His eyes bulged, and he bit his lip. "I love to cook!"

I grinned, and we headed back into the house.

"Looks like we got us a chef," I announced, ushering Johnnie into the kitchen.

"Really?" Astrid did a double take as she sprinkled parsley into a bowl of melted butter and garlic.

Johnnie traced his finger down the recipe on the counter. "Does she have a grill?" He picked up a nearby zucchini. After washing it off in the sink, he sliced it on the butcher block sitting next to Astrid.

"No." I shifted around the island to the stove. "This is gas though."

He stopped slicing for a second. "That could work." He dropped the zucchini, set down the knife, and wiped his hands on his shirt.

"I'll set the table!" Astrid grabbed Bethel's chinaware from a cabinet over the sink and stacked the dishes on the counter before counting the plates and taking them outside.

Johnnie shuffled past the sink to the corner of the kitchen and opened the toaster oven, then took out the wire rack and laid it over the back burner of the stove.

"What's that for? The stove already has grates," I said, scratching my beard as he picked up the deep square pan that Astrid had fished out from beneath the oven.

"Since she doesn't have a grill," he said, igniting the stove beneath the wire rack, "I'm improvising. Is there anything else that needs to be cooked?" His hand hovered over the heat radiating beneath the rack.

I referenced her shopping list that lay beside the sink. "I don't think so. We're making a fruit salad, and the dessert is premade."

A spring groaned when Astrid opened the screen door to the kitchen.

"You didn't plan on cooking anything in the oven, did you?" I asked her.

"The zucchini," she said, reaching into a cabinet to pull down the glasses.

"Awesome," Johnnie said, twisting the knob to the off position. "I'm going to cook them on the stove instead."

She nodded and set the glasses out on the island, then filled them with silverware and napkins. "Zachary," she said, wedging the glasses between her forearm and ribs. "Can you start on the fruit salad?"

"Sure." I dug through the cabinets for a bowl big enough to mix everything in.

"The zucchini will only take ten minutes," Johnnie said with his back to us as he eased the strips, seasoned with bread crumbs, garlic, and pepper, onto the rack, sprinkling shredded cheese over them. "What else needs to be done?"

"The oil lamps need to be lit to keep the bugs away, and that's about it," Astrid replied while fetching placemats from the pantry.

Johnnie slipped on oven mitts and dropped the pan over the rack to complete his makeshift grill. "Can do."

The two of them went outside as I sliced apples using the same knife and cutting block that Johnnie had used for the zucchini. I removed the bag of grapes from the grocery sack and picked them from their stems, dropping them into a bowl with chunks of pineapple. As I peeled a banana, gravel crunched in the driveway. I ducked to see through the living room window. It was Bethel's car.

"Shit. Shit. Shit," I said under my breath, then set down the knife and sprinted to the back door. "It's Bethel!" I hollered through the screen.

"Crap!" Johnnie lit the last lamp and darted into the kitchen. I held the door open while Astrid straightened the silverware at the head of the table before following him back inside.

"Stall her!" I shooed her with my hands to the front of the house and eased the door closed while she snuck around front to greet Bethel.

"These are done." Johnnie picked up the pan with his mitts to reveal strips of zucchini smothered with melted cheese.

"I'm about done here too," I said, slicing the last banana and adding it to the bowl.

He flipped the pan he had been using as a lid, setting in on the stove and shoveling the strips from the rack into it with a spatula.

"Here, let me help you get that," Astrid said to Bethel outside, their voices muffled.

Bethel's short words filtered in through the single-pane windows. "Can I just set my stuff down?"

"I'm going to run this to the table." Johnnie grabbed the pan of zucchini with his mitts and backed out of the kitchen through the screen door. He eased it closed with his foot as I rinsed the knife in the sink.

"Bad day?" Astrid asked, her voice bouncing between the trees and the side of the house.

"I love those kids, but their parents aren't so pleasant. I missed ukulele lessons today for a parent teacher conference." Bethel sighed.

I mixed the fruit with one hand while scooping the bowl up with the other and trotting outside to the table.

"Zachary!" Astrid called out in a charming voice as soon as I set the bowl on the table. "Can you come help us?"

I jogged around the side of the house. "You call for me, Astrid?"

"Yeah, Bethel needs help getting her things from the car. Also, she doesn't think I'm a nice person," she said, straightening her brows. "She asked me why I was being weird and going out of my way for her."

Bethel's jaw dropped. "That's not what I—"

"I could have told you that!" I said, kissing Astrid on the lips while I relieved Bethel of her load.

"Let's get everything out of the car later; you guys need to come see this sunset!" I said, moseying around the side of the house with Bethel's books stacked on my forearms.

"I get that parents have their own way of raising their kids," she continued, her arms flailing. "But if a kid does act up, and I punish them by cutting their break time or giving them silent lunch in the detention room, the parents should support me. Not reprimand me for picking up their slack." She stopped in her tracks at the corner of the house, propping her hands on her hips. "Aw, look at that sunset! This is one of my favorite things about this house."

Astrid and I glared at each other.

"You can't really appreciate it unless you go to the center of the yard where the boathouse isn't blocking it," Astrid said while walking ahead, motioning for Bethel to follow.

Bethel must have really loved that sunset though, because she didn't miss a moment of it. Standing only ten yards from the table, she didn't even notice Johnnie, the food, or the oil lamps. "This is so pretty. I should raise your rent for such a view." She laughed at herself. "But not really."

Astrid rolled her eyes at me.

I shrugged. She had to go inside eventually, right?

"So anyway." Bethel picked up where she left off.

I guess not.

"This kid's parents call in a conference. Obviously, Mrs. Elauter is used to parents overreacting, so—"

"SURPRISE!" Johnnie cut her off, tossing his hands in the air.

Bethel spun around, her hands catching the hair that flew into her face. "Oh my! This is gorgeous!" She brought her hands to her cheeks. "What is it for?"

"Well," Astrid plodded ahead of me, her lose-fitting dress hanging to her thighs, "I saw the plaque in your parents' bedroom. We just wanted to do something nice for you since we figured today would be difficult for you."

I set the books in an empty chair.

Bethel dropped her hands and smiled. "My parents didn't die on this day. That plaque had their anniversary on it. They celebrated thirty years not long before they died, so I had that plaque made for them!" She scooted toward the table. "But I really appreciate the support. It means a lot. What better way to pay respects than to celebrate their anniversary!" She wrapped her arms around both Astrid and me.

Afterward, she made it to the table, where Johnnie stood still stunned by the facts, his hands in his pockets and a sheepish grin on his face. Astrid and I couldn't hear what she'd whispered in his ear when she hugged him, but he froze and his eyes grew beneath his thin brows, his face glowing against his dark cheeks. Their hug lasted for a solid ten seconds until Bethel stopped holding him and kissed him on his cheek. He bowed out of her embrace and cleared his throat, avoiding eye contact.

"Did you see that?" Astrid whispered and slapped my arm.

Bethel stepped back from Johnnie and curtseyed. "I'm going to go powder my nose, and then we can eat," she said in her proper accent. "Also, if you can't tell, Johnathon and I are going steady!"

Astrid and I golf clapped as if we didn't already know, and Bethel bowed again before scurrying through the back door into the kitchen. Johnnie's red cheeks permeated his brown skin and lit up through the cracks of his fingers that he used to cover his smile. Astrid and I took our seats.

When Bethel returned, Johnnie pulled a chair out for her at the head of the table beneath the large oak tree that our bikes were chained to.

"Why, thank you, Mr. Snowell," she told him in her fancy accent while pointing her nose to the sky and raising her limp hand for him. He took it and led her to her seat, even though it made him blush again.

Astrid kicked my leg under the table. "Are you taking notes?"

"Ouch!" I said, patting my pockets. "I forgot my pencil."

"You'd better find one!" She crossed her legs and folded her arms across her chest, her new clothes emphasizing her cleavage.

Bethel leaned over the zucchini and took in a big whiff. "What are we having?"

"It's grilled garlic parmesan zucchini." Astrid grabbed the spatula and slid a strip from the pan, easing it onto Bethel's plate. "We also have fruit salad." She coaxed the spatula under another strip of zucchini pasted to the pan with cheese. "Would you like another piece?"

"Please." Bethel nodded before smiling at Johnnie.

Astrid gave her another slice, and Johnnie passed her the bowl of fruit salad.

We all filled our plates with zucchini and passed the fruit around. When it made its way to me, everyone waited while I finished loading my plate, then we all took our first bites at the same time.

"This is amazing." Bethel spoke into her fork, a string of cheese dangling from the corner of her mouth.

"Oh my god!" Astrid's eyes bulged. "It really is!" She seized another bite with her fork.

I raised my glass as a compliment to the chef, chasing the garlic with a sip of southern-style sweet tea.

"So, Zachary," Bethel said, brandishing a piece of pineapple on her fork, "what did you think about Astrid's pictures?"

"I honestly didn't know what to expect," I said, bowing my head while wiping my mouth with a napkin before peering back up. "But they look amazing! Have you seen them?"

"I did!" Bethel jumped in. "I told her she should sell copies; I've never seen anything like them!"

"What pictures are you talking about? The ones from your trip that you got developed?" Johnnie glanced at Bethel's perfect posture and removed his elbows from the table.

"They were taken during the trip, but they weren't *of* the trip." Astrid took a breath to slow her exhilarated pride. "At least not all of them. There are a few from when we were on the train and then other random ones from other things we did, but most of them are of objects interacting with the sun."

"Do you want to see them, Johnnie?" I asked, grabbing Astrid's hand.

"Yes! Of course!" he responded without hesitation.

"I'll get them!" She let go of my hand and used the table to hoist herself into a standing position.

"When did you get that flower wind spinner? I love it!" Bethel asked me as Astrid moseyed across the yard in a loose fitting red dress and navy leggings we had bought at the thrift store until she silhouetted in front of the yellow light that cascaded through the large glass doors of the boathouse.

"Yesterday," I said while Astrid pulled the pictures from the clips beyond the open glass door. "Astrid bought it to 'mark our home with.'" I grinned.

"Maybe it will bloom into more one day!" Bethel smiled as I faced her and Johnnie, then took a swig of tea.

"Maybe," I said, patting the hair down on my arm that stood to applaud the thought.

When Astrid emerged moments later, she lowered herself into the chair, then passed the photos above the bowl of fruit to Johnnie.

"We should do an art show at the bike shop," he said while thumbing through the travel-sized gallery. "We could blow them up and display them on the tables."

Astrid picked up a picture of the pond where we'd fed the catfish. "I couldn't ask you to close your shop for an art show. Besides, I don't think they're actually good enough to sell."

"No, seriously. It would probably help my business—get new faces in the door. People would come for the gallery, but they'd also get to see what the shop is all about," he said, inspecting a picture up close. "We can promote it together."

"Are you sure?" Astrid looked at Johnnie and then at me, wringing her hands.

"I think it's a great idea." I put my hand on her shoulder and gazed at the picture of the catfish pond still in her hand.

"I agree," Bethel added.

"When would you want to do it?" Astrid asked as her voice crept an octave higher.

"Let's do it in a couple of weeks—at the beginning of next month," Johnnie suggested. "That will give us time to promote it. He cut into the chocolate chip banana oat cake and put a piece on Bethel's plate. "I can't stop thinking about this art show idea now. I have old metal wire at my house that we could hang the prints from the ceiling with."

Astrid scooted her plate toward him for a slice of the dessert. "That would be really cool! But prints like that are kind of expensive."

"We wouldn't be able to do all of them." He pulled his knife from between the cake and her plate. "We'll print your favorites."

"And we can put everything that is not blown up into little picture books. They can all go in order," Astrid said, licking her thumb. "Like, have the things that happened between two larger prints in a book between them. Does that make sense? We can call the little photo books 'details.'"

"I can't wait to see people's reactions," I butted in. "It'll be like a small journey they take as they walk through the show.

Astrid forced a half-chewed piece of cake down her throat and licked her teeth. "How cool would it be if we left a notebook at the last station for people to comment on the work? How the journey made them feel."

I limbered back in my chair. "That would be awesome. To see how what we lived is perceived through others."

She picked up another picture from the center of the table; this time, it was of the view from the train overlooking the desert.

"Cheers!" she said, stabbing a grape with a fork and holding it out.

I bobbed through my bowl for a pineapple and knocked it against her grape. "Cheers!"

Chapter 34

Almost two weeks of work had passed for us at our new jobs, and we loved every second of it. Astrid had also worked hard on promoting her art show, though it seemed that the Bike Shop's popularity had already gained a lengthy guest list. The title was simple: The Art Show at Bike Works. To the point and easy to remember.

"I have something for you!" I said, stretching my neck through a narrow opening in the houseboat door—the rest of me half-dressed for work while I stood in the light gray air of the morning.

Astrid yanked the covers tightly around her shoulder and rolled over until her back was to the door. "What is it?"

"Come look!" I pulled my head out of the room and sprinted across the yard before ducking behind Bethel's car.

Bethel bent over and peered through the windows toward the boathouse. "I don't think she knows where you went." She laughed, pointing at Astrid, who stood craning her neck in search of where I'd sprinted off to.

I stepped around the car into clear view and waved her over. "Astrid!"

She snapped her head in my direction. "I had to put on my sweater!" She yelled next to the outdoor table, straightening the elastic waist of her red pajama pants. "It's a lot colder than I'm used to this time of year." She neared the car, then made her way to where Bethel and I were standing.

"Okay," I started, barely able to speak through my jaw-locking smile. "We know you've been working hard on the art show and that you're saving up to buy your own prints."

"Yeah … " She covered her smile with her palm.

I lifted the hatch. "Well, I'm super proud of you. And I love you so much," I continued, blocking an enormous boxy object covered with a thin white sheet. "So I got you something!"

When I sidestepped out of her way, she stared at the sheet and raised an eyebrow before flitting her gaze between Bethel and me. She cautiously ducked under the hatch and removed the sheet to reveal a landscape picture of her with her head on my shoulder, asleep on the bus.

"What's this?" She gasped, tears coating her eyes. "It wasn't in my film."

"I had the lady in front of us take it and send it to me." My eyes welled up. "I didn't think she'd actually send it."

She took another step closer, leaning her thighs against the bumper of Bethel's car and balancing over the large glossy print. "You're picking my nose." She let out a quick chuckle, a single tear falling to her chin.

I laughed and threw my arms into the air. "I am!"

"It's perfect." She fell into my chest, squeezing my ribcage.

"Wait!" I patted her back, then opened my arms. "There's more!"

"I can't handle anymore!" She giggled to fight the tears that were soaking into my shirt, then stepped back.

Bethel lifted the corrugated board from the top of the pile to reveal a picture of the boathouse.

I rubbed her shoulders, unable to keep my hands to myself. "There in the bottom left"—I pointed at the flower—"is the wind spinner you bought. I took that picture with Bethel's phone."

"You really need to stop!" She sobbed again.

"One last thing!" Bethel said, bouncing on her heels, blubbering just as hard, if not harder.

I leaned over and removed the print from the top of the pile. "I also had prints made of all the pictures you marked to be hung over the stations."

She sniffled. "How did you pay for all of this?"

"I used my first paycheck and Bethel waived a month's rent." I returned my print to the trunk, and Bethel did the same.

She threw her arms around Astrid's neck. "I'm really not a good business owner. I get too close and give everything away."

"Thank you both! That is too nice!" Astrid said as they broke apart.

I grabbed the handle on the open hatch as they cleared the way for me to close it.

"I love you." I turned back to Astrid and wrapped my arms around her again.

Moments into a hug that could have lasted forever, Bethel cleared her throat and shuffled her feet. "I'd hate to break this up, but we've got to get to the school."

Astrid let go of my neck and sniffled, pulling the sleeves of her sweater over her fists. "My stomach is upset. Do you mind letting Johnnie know that I'm sick?" She peered up at Bethel.

You should have bought that heater.

I intertwined my fingers.

"Here." Bethel dug through her purse. "Take my phone in case of an emergency. You can text him."

"Cool. Thanks," she said with flushed cheeks and stepped onto her toes to kiss me on my neck, then whispered into my ear. "You are beautiful."

My second-period class cleared out, fertilizing my anxiety for Astrid. I settled in to grade papers, filling the deadened monotony of my planning period. I couldn't get past the first three words before my thoughts distracted me. I reclined in my chair, rocking against the stiff spring that propped my back up. I couldn't focus on anything else. I stood and strode to the window. Burrowed in the corner of a brick plaza across the street sat a small convenience store. The words *prepaid phones* flashed in neon red. I needed to talk to her.

The next thing I knew, my feet had carried me out of the school and over to the covered sidewalk, cutting through a shallow ditch until I reached the lights that drew me like a moth to a flame.

Buzz! An electric sensor went off when I opened the door.

"Excuse me, sir," I said to an older man who sat reading the news behind a blue linoleum counter, "where are your prepaid phones?"

The man ran a shaky hand through his gray hair, and he set down his paper before taking a closer look. "By the door." He nodded at the metal rack near the window. "Most people get the red one."

I turned and sifted through the rack until I found the right one. Pulling it from the peg, I read through the details: unlimited talk and text, three gigabytes of data.

"That one's $59.99," the man said.

Caught off guard, I spun and approached the counter. "No sales tax is a beautiful thing." I laughed, digging for my card and handing it to him.

The expressionless man slid it through the card reader and held it out, but I was too preoccupied opening the hard plastic. "Do you have any scissors I can use?" I lifted my head as he set the card down between us.

"I have a box cutter." He reached into a cup filled with pens and pulled out a hidden blade.

"That'll work." I grabbed the handle and sliced the thick packaging, then handed the blade over. "Thanks!" I retrieved my card and trekked outside to an overstuffed trashcan. Ten minutes later, the phone was set up, and I dialed Bethel's cell number. It must have rung at least nine times until the voicemail picked up. I hung up and dropped my hands to my waist before closing my eyes. The vision of Astrid shaking in the middle of the desert after we had jumped off the train flickered in my mind.

I opened my eyes and dialed again.

"Hello?" a wary voice answered.

"Astrid, it's me, Zachary. You sound better!" I said, ambling back toward the school.

"Thanks. Yeah." She paused for a second. "I am feeling a little better. Whose phone are you on?"

I crossed the shallow ditch and hopped onto the sidewalk. "I broke down and finally bought one. It's just a prepaid."

"A job. A phone. Are you trying to domesticate us?" she asked in a raised pitch.

"What?" I stuck my hand into my pocket and laughed. "No! Of course not!"

"Well, thanks for checking on me. And thanks again for the prints! I can't stop thinking about them." Something squeaked in the background on her end.

"Where are you?" I asked.

"I'm looking for a new place for us." She cleared her throat. "It's getting colder, and even with a better heater, it's way too drafty in the boathouse."

I squeezed my eyes shut and shook my head. "I was honestly thinking the same thing. Are you just riding around looking for rent signs?" I chuckled.

"No!" she interjected. "I've been looking through the classifieds online with Bethel's phone."

I stopped in my tracks. "Oh? Find anything good?"

"I'm actually at the first place now," she said in a gentle voice. "I like it though. But I need to look around more."

"Okay! Well, I trust your judgement." My face reddened while I folded all my reservations and requests under my tongue.

"Thanks!" Her voice grew distant. "Well, let me jump off here."

"All right. I love you."

"Love you too." The line went dead.

I flipped the phone in my grip and fixated on a dark stain in the center of a handicap parking spot in front of the school.

Chapter 35

People lined up outside of the bike shop as we finished decorating for the art show. Astrid had made a playlist from the record that her father had played during dinner when she was growing up, adding similar songs to her calming memories. Its smooth voices filled the bike shop, the cheap digital copies crackling and popping as if a needle were carving them from vinyl.

"What do you think about the wreath that Bethel and I got yesterday on our ladies' day out?" She smirked, lifting a tray of vegetables from a portable table that we had set up behind all the stations.

"I like it!" I said, straightening the corners of the tablecloth underneath before facing her. "But not nearly as much as I like that white dress you have on."

Astrid ran her fingers between the top two buttons of the banded neck shirt she had convinced me to buy at the thrift store. Her sharp, slick nails curled until the creases of my wrinkled collar. "Well, I couldn't have you one-upping me on my big night. You with your rolled-up sleeves and gray slacks," she said, then purred.

"You'd outdo me in a burlap sack!" I grinned, fixing the uneven seams around my shoulders.

"Oh yeah?" Her breaths grew short as her arms dangled by her sides. "You have no idea how much I am craving a carrot."

"Really?" I stepped closer and wrapped my hand around the crook of her back with a sly grin.

She held a carrot between our faces and took a huge bite from it.

"Oh yeah!" She moaned, crunching it between her teeth. "That's the spot."

"You know what!" I let go of her and stepped back, pointing at the door. "I hope Johnnie takes your wreath down."

She laughed.

"And then … " I grabbed the clipboard off the portable table and flipped a page. "And then, I hope you stub your toe!"

She picked up another carrot, this time dipping it in the ranch dressing in the middle. "That's so mean! Why would you ever wish something like that on me?"

The echo of the back door opening bounced off the walls of the inventory room. "Hello?" Bethel shouted, her voice growing closer. "I've got the notebook!"

"We're up here!" I replied, sitting on the edge of the table.

Bethel traipsed past us to the last station and pulled a notebook with a pen tied to its spiral from her oversized purse. "Where's Johnnie?" she asked, setting the notebook down and straightening it until it's edge was even with the end of the table.

Astrid finished her carrot stick and joined Bethel. "He went to shower and get changed," she said, picking up the black pen. "This is very DIY. I love it!" She hugged Bethel. "Thank you for your help!"

"It's no problem and totally worth it!" Bethel said as they let go. "I mean, have you seen the line outside?"

"We can only see the beginning of it from here." I pushed myself off the table and took a few steps toward the front door, where people blocked all the windows surrounding it. "Is it long?"

"I'd say there are at least forty people out there," Bethel said, polishing a small black plaque with the bike shop's business name on it before setting it on the first station.

Astrid blushed and dropped her gaze to the notebook.

"You okay?" I wandered over to her and rubbed the back of her arm.

She nodded and clutched her stomach. "I'm just nervous. But I'll be fine," she said with a deep breath.

"Wait a second." I froze. "How will people know what to use the notebook for?"

"I was going to stand near the end of the show and tell people." Astrid lifted her head.

I threw my hands up. "You can't stand here all night. I'll make a sign!"

I fled to the inventory room to find something to make it with as Johnnie popped in through the rear exit.

"Hey, man, do you have anything I can make a large sign with?" I asked Johnnie.

"Uh." He set his water bottle and a stack of plastic bags on his work bench. "I have an old white sheet that I use as a dust cover." He stooped and pulled out the folded fabric, placing it beside his water bottle. "And there should be some black paint over there." He wrapped the handles of his plastic bags around his wrists, nodding to an inventory rack that held various cleaning items, a bucket, a can of black paint, and even a trim brush while he passed me and stepped onto the sales floor.

"That should work!" I gathered the materials, whipped the sheet out onto the floor, and centered myself on it like a whale in a lake.

Create a new reality. Create a new reality.

My mind looped until the words materialized in bold strokes in front of me.

"Johnnie!" I called out over my shoulder, still kneeling over the sheet. "Can you help me hang this real quick?" I set the paint and brush aside before grabbing one corner.

"Sure." He hustled through the inventory doorway and grabbed the opposite corner. A few beads of paint ran down the letters when we lifted it. "Where should we put it?"

"Let's hang it from the ceiling tiles above the checkout counter."

I followed him through the door to the sales floor.

"What do you think?" I called out to Astrid, nearing the sales counter.

She stopped fidgeting with the contents of the plastic bags on the food table and spun around. "That. Is. Perfect." She took off toward us, Bethel not far behind her.

"Here, take this corner," Johnnie said, holding the sheet out for Astrid to grab before climbing onto the counter.

"Can you hold this for a second?" I gave my corner to Bethel, who stood wide-eyed at the process.

"Oh!" She giggled. "Sure." She slid across from Astrid and held my corner as I climbed up on the counter, standing between the computer monitor and the edge.

"Let us know when it's straight," Johnnie said while we both leaned down to take hold of the sheet again.

"Sure!" they echoed before jogging around to the front of the counter.

We pushed on the ceiling tiles just enough to wrap the corners around the bent strips of metal that held the tiles up.

"Johnnie, can you lift your side up about an inch?" Bethel instructed.

Astrid tilted her head and rubbed her fingers across her collar bones. "That will pull the letters into the ceiling."

"Oh yeah …"

"Zachary, drop your end about an inch," Astrid requested while demonstrating with her hands.

I moved it the slightest bit with my fingers, keeping it pressed against the beam.

"Perfect!" She clapped.

We tied what was left of the sheet around the metal strips and let go of the tiles to secure the fabric. I stooped and pivoted my hand on the counter, then jumped down. Johnnie followed suit and met me in front of the sheet to admire our work.

"Create your new reality," Bethel read. "Write about your journey in the notebook." She stood admiring it. "This is a great place to hang it too, because when you walk in, you go left and make a U-turn around the tables, ending here at the counter, where you get the instructions on the sheet."

"That's the idea." I laughed at her over explanation.

"What else needs to be done before we open up?" Johnnie asked, gawking at the sheet.

Astrid surveyed the room and tugged on her fingers. "Nothing. I think we're ready."

"May I do the honors?" I nodded at the locked door.

Astrid strode to the front of the shop and took a deep breath as she strode the face of the room one last time, stopping in her black flats at the portrait of us on the bus. "You may." She smiled.

I followed and gave her a kiss on the forehead before heading to the door. "I'm proud of you."

"Thanks," she said while dropping her head to hide her glowing cheeks.

At the door, the crowd murmured on the other side of the glass. "Everyone ready?" I gripped the thick deadbolt with my fingers, twisted it, and let the night in. "The show starts over here," I said, pointing a younger couple to the first station.

I shoved a stopper under the door and circled around the tables until I reached Astrid.

"I cannot believe this is happening!" she said, swaying.

"Me either." I draped my arm around her shoulder, hugging her with one arm as a group of people approached the first table, their faces lighting up. "You did a really good job!"

For an hour and a half, Astrid had taken the time to answer questions. I hung back with Bethel at the refreshment table while Johnnie kept a watchful eye on the shop.

"You guys should walk through the show now that the line has died down." Bethel nudged me with her elbow.

"You think so? You don't need help?" I glanced up at Astrid, who flashed me a quick grin before someone else stole her attention.

"I think I can handle serving vegetables and punch." Bethel smiled and poured another drink, then set it on the table. "Besides, we're almost out." She picked up the last jug of punch and twisted the top off.

I nudged the next empty cup toward her. "Yeah. That would actually be nice. Thanks!"

"Go!" Bethel demanded, pointing at Astrid and shooing me away. "Go, go, go!"

I ambled over to Astrid, then cupped her hand in mine and whispered into her ear. "Want to relive this one more time?"

Astrid clutched my fingers and grinned. We pushed through the crowd to the door and squeezed into the freezing night air.

"Do you think it's possible to make this feeling last forever?" she asked as we huddled close together at the end of the line.

I shoved my hands into my pockets and teetered on my heels, tensing my muscles to fight a chill. "What feeling is that?"

"I don't know." She swung a little with me as the line staggered forward but caught herself. "I guess it would be happiness."

I flattened my feet on the pavement, pulled a hand out, and grabbed hers. "I do." I admitted, rubbing her palm with my thumbs. "I think everyone has their demons ... and there's a difference between instant gratification and sustainability."

Her head dropped.

"But since we've been here and have worked through all the kinks"—I lifted her chin with my finger and grinned—"I'm certain that none of this is instant gratification."

"If it ends, does it mean we were wrong?" She peered up at me with her big blue eyes.

My cheeks fell. "Do you see it ending?"

She shook her head. "No. Just anxious, I suppose. We don't have as much control as we'd like to think, you know?"

I laughed. "I think we've proven that we can work through whatever this world has to throw at us."

When the line inched forward and we reached the first station, the couple already occupying it leaned against the table to study the details before stepping back to see the full picture.

"The artist is Astrid Mavis," a girl in her early twenties read aloud.

"I can't believe people still use film," a guy beside her commented, flipping through the photo book. "I wonder where she went to school."

I lightly poked Astrid in the ribs and held a thumb up.

She covered my thumb with her hand. "Stop!" She laughed.

"Sorry! I just get excited!" I snickered.

Like everyone else, we both wrote in the notebook at the end, dated our entries, and tore our thoughts from the spiral. People stood everywhere: inside, outside, even revisiting the exhibit, all holding the small white piece of paper in their hands that detailed how the show made them feel and what kind of story they connected with it.

I strutted to the center of the room and called for everyone's attention, turning in place. "I would like to thank you all for coming out to The Art Show at Bike Works," I started as a few people whistled and others clapped. "I walked through the show, just as you did, and wrote down what I took from it at the end. The difference is, the artist who created this presentation for you tonight allowed me to actually live the journey with her." I paused and looked around the room at the evenly lit faces that grew quiet in an instant, the same beauty I'd seen in Astrid's pictures. "At first, I didn't know how to handle her."

I waited for the chuckles to clear the room.

"Now, I don't think I could handle life without her. Astrid Mavis, everyone!" I said while gesturing toward her.

The room erupted with applause and cheers, and I couldn't help but join in.

She tilted her head and beamed at me. "Thank you all for coming," she echoed, meeting me in the center of the room. "I want everyone to know that I had my doubts about Zachary too." She glanced at me, getting another laugh from the audience. "But I think I'll keep him." She grabbed my hand. "Zachary and I went through this show together and listened to what a lot of you had to say. We also wrote down what we took from the show at the end."

"What does yours say?" I cut in as several people whooped and others gasped.

Astrid took in the enamored faces around her, then turned her attention to me. "Defeated by joy!" She held the paper in the air and dropped her head with a smile while the crowd cheered. "What does yours say?" she glanced up and yelled over the lingering murmurs.

I held the paper above my head like she had done and met her gaze. "I'm happy it's not over."

Chapter 36

"A minimum of two pages and in MLA format," I said over the kids' sliding chairs and mumbles as the bell rang. "It's late if it's not in my inbox by Friday morning before class!"

"Mr. Byrd," Kelley's voice rattled through the intercom's speaker across the room.

I tilted my head, and my eardrums popped. "Yes?" I asked, opening the top drawer of my desk and grabbing a delicate black box, gripping its smooth, felt skin in my palm as if I were warming up a baseball.

"Bethel asked me to send you home with some work that her students turned in," she said while I pinched the lid open to reveal a thin stoneless gold band shining like a diamond on top of a floor of coal. "Do you mind coming to the office to pick them up?"

She deserves better.

"Be right there!"

I snapped the lid closed and pushed it into my tight pocket, leaving my room open and gliding down the hall to the office.

When I opened the office door, Kelley had a stack of papers wrapped in a loose rubber band waiting for me.

"Was Bethel sick over the weekend?" she asked, leaning over her desk with the fabric of her coral-colored button-up shirt draping far enough from her neck that her white lacey bra peeked out from beneath it.

I focused on the poster of Winston Churchill. "Astrid has been a little sick lately. Could have something to do with that."

Her brow furrowed. "Oh yeah. Astrid." She straightened and tilted her head.

"We missed you at the art show on Saturday!" I said, reaching for the first stack of papers.

"My son was having a sleepover. My house was full of kids." Her eyes grew and she let out a long breath. "Being a single parent is a full-time job."

I patted my pocket as my phone buzzed against my thigh, then arched my eyebrows. "That sounds like a long weekend!"

"It was." She flattened her knuckles on the desk and bit her lip.

"Well, thanks for the papers. Have a good day!" I said, grabbing the last bundle and stacking everything into one arm.

"You too!" She hurried around the counter. "Here, let me get the door for you." She turned the knob and pushed the door open with her back.

"Thanks." I grinned, careful not to brush against her while I squeezed through the narrow opening she'd allowed.

"No problem." She rubbed her neck and retreated into the office as I pulled my phone out of my pocket.

A text from Bethel appeared on the screen: "Astrid and I found a cool house that we think you'll really like!" Even in texts, her grammar and spelling were perfect. "I'll pick you up after school. Meet me at the teachers' parking lot in thirty minutes."

"Okay." I sent the first portion of my message. "Did Astrid ever go in to work?"

I continued the trek back to my classroom, phone in hand, and turned the corner.

Buzz! Buzz! My palm tingled from the vibration when I passed through the empty doorway.

"Yes. We're both feeling better now."

I sat on the edge of the desk, laying the papers beside me and typed, "All right." I stared at the screen for a second, then erased the message. "See you soon!" I typed before pressing send.

When I got to the parking lot, Bethel was waiting outside in Johnnie's truck, her expression hidden by large sunglasses that covered the top of her cheeks, protecting her eyes from the sun that had finally revealed itself.

I opened the passenger's side door. "Where's your car?" I dropped her papers onto the floor in front of my seat and climbed in.

"I needed this to pick up something for the house." She shifted into reverse as I closed my door and buckled my seatbelt.

I crossed my ankles. "What do you think you were sick with?"

"I think I drank too much this weekend." She laughed. "But I don't know what's wrong with Astrid. She can't seem to shake it, so I took her to the urgent care center."

"What?" My head jerked toward her. "Where is she?"

"She started feeling better by this afternoon and rode in to work for the last part of the day. She wanted to show the house to you, but Johnnie needed her help with something."

"What did the doctor say?"

"Well, she felt better by the time we got there, and when they mentioned the cost, she decided to not go."

I shook my head and stared out the window.

"I think she's honestly fine though." She scratched the back of her hand that hung from the steering wheel. "It's probably from the boathouse. I was thinking about this earlier. It's a house on the water, so who knows how much mold and stuff there might be!"

"I guess." I shifted, then slumped in my chair. "So how did you find this new place?"

"Online." She flipped the blinker and looked both ways before pulling out of the parking lot. "It's like a little cottage but closer to town than my place."

"That's cool." I drummed my fingers on my legs. "An easier commute would be nice."

We took the usual way home: through the city, over the bridge, and right into patches of trees … but veered off the road into a tiny front yard.

"What's going on?" I turned around and peered out the rear window.

"What do you think?" She nodded at a bungalow-shaped house to my right and shifted into park.

"Wait." I did a double take. "Is this it?" I grinned.

Too excited to speak, she nodded again and hopped out of the truck.

"This is amazing!" I said as I opened the door and climbed out.

The yard stretched out to the river, which wore the gold complexion of late afternoon. The house had white siding and stood on about three quarters of an acre of land. Perfectly squared large windows, symmetrically spaced, hung on each side of a red door dressed in a black door knocker and knob.

We crossed the yard to the porch, where an pitched roof jutted out over the wide entrance, protecting us as a light drizzle splattered the windows beside us. Thick towering trees lined the yard, sporadically placed behind the house with their canopies overlooking the roof like the trees at Bethel's.

"It doesn't have a driveway," she said, digging through her pocket, "but we didn't think you'd care." She offered a half-cocked smile, condensation freezing in a fog, blurring the details of her face.

"I see that." I grinned, wiping ice from the window and cupping my hands against the glass to see in, squinting to make out the details.

"Let's go inside!" she said while grinding the key into the lock.

"You have a key?" I straightened and followed her in.

Dark hardwood floors paralleled high ceilings that opened into a living room. I stepped inside and wiped my shoes off on a teal oval rug, then cut across to the kitchen.

Age-polished appliances sat in a *U* shape around an open space. There was just enough room for a breakfast table beneath the long, horizontal window that hung against the back wall. Deeper into the kitchen, the view through the window revealed a narrow deck leading into backyard.

Bethel crossed in front of me and opened the stove door. "The appliances are old, but again, we assumed you wouldn't mind." She cleared her throat and stepped back. "I think it gives it character."

I put my hands on my hips and spun slowly on my heel. "Well, it's the little things like this that make this place affordable. Because you know this view isn't cheap." I paused for a second, then pushed the lever on the sink before shutting it off. "Unless you live in someone's art studio on a barge in their backyard!" I laughed, rubbing the spots on the stained faucet.

After that, we backtracked through the living room into the connecting hallway, where three doors in a deep, reddish stain contrasted the white drywall. My fingers traced a beaded line where wallpaper had once adhered to the bottom quarter of the wall as I followed her into what would be the bedroom for Astrid and me. Wood paneling bowed from the walls in several places. I scratched my nails across the faux-grain past two accordion-style closets that stood side by side on the wall closest to the door until a window view overlooking the river appeared again.

"What do you think?" Bethel asked. "This is the only room with wood paneling."

"It's perfect!" I slicked my hair back.

"Good!" She clapped her hands. "Let me show you the bathroom."

We walked to the end of the hall, where a single bathroom capped the walkway. White linoleum curled beneath the gapped baseboard.

"Again," she said, sticking her head between my shoulder and the doorframe, "it isn't perfect, but you can make it nice."

I sauntered in and lifted the toilet seat that swiveled on its hinges.

"The toilet is clean though!" I joked. "I'm sold. Has Astrid been here yet, or did she just see it online?"

"She's been here, and she loves it!" She closed the bathroom door as we both stepped into the hall. "Actually, I haven't been completely honest with you. Why don't you open the third door?" She clasped her hands in front of her mouth, her body sweeping from side to side.

"What's in there?" I asked, grabbing the knob with my neck craned.

"Open it!" She bit her lip while I faced the door and pushed on it.

An empty crib sat in the room with two frames on the wall above it.

"Did the last tenants leave this?" I asked, stepping through the doorway.

"Astrid?" Bethel called out from the hall before popping her head into the room with me. "Is she not in there?"

"No." I slid my hand into my pocket and squeezed the little black box. "Is she supposed to be?" I laughed, barely able to contain my excitement as I eased past the door.

"Yeah." She frowned and joined me in the center of the room, placing her hands on her hips. "She must have gone outside or something. I'll go get her!"

Bethel left the room, the floorboards creaking when she ambled down the hall. "Astrid?" she shouted from the kitchen while she opened the back door. "Astrid!"

I inched closer to the crib, pulling my hand out of my pocket with the box still in my grip. Inside the bold black frames were the notes from the art show: "Defeated by joy," and "I'm glad it's not over." A smile tugged at my lips.

Then I dropped my gaze to the bed of the crib, where the plastic flower-shaped wind spinner rested.

It will mark our first home.

The hair stood up on my arms and the back of my neck, my eyes glazing over. She was pregnant, and she'd let me know in the most beautiful way she could.

"Astrid!" Bethel's voice rang throughout the house.

My shoulders dropped as I snatched the black box from my pocket and set it in the crib, tugging on a piece of paper that jutted out from beneath the spinner.

"I'm sorry. I can't do this." Astrid's handwriting was unmistakable.

My hands shook, and I peered up at the frames.

Defeated by joy.

TANNER LUTHERAN

Though his stories are fictional, Lutheran tends to use pivotal real-life experiences as cornerstones in his work.

In this particular piece, Detached, he writes as if the roles were reversed and he is no longer the victim of an accidental tragedy from his childhood, but rather the culprit.

Lutheran grew up on the coast of North Carolina, where he became passionate about writing at a young age in his seventh-grade creative writing class.

Look for music, videos, and other media related to Lutheran and this series at:

www.TannerLutheran.com